FALTER,
KINGDOM

The Unnamed Press
P.O. Box 411272
Los Angeles, CA 90041

Published in North America by The Unnamed Press.

1 3 5 7 9 10 8 6 4 2

ISBN: 978-1-939419-75-0

Library of Congress Control Number: 2016947150

This book is distributed by Publishers Group West

Cover and interior art by Alycea Tinoyan
Design and typesetting by Jaya Nicely

FALTER
KINGDOM

A NOVEL

MICHAEL J. SEIDLINGER

The Unnamed Press
Los Angeles, CA

"You get the invitation, man?"
"No, but you'd think I'd get one. It's my exorcism."

PROLOGUE

Everyone I know is already talking in the past tense, going on and on about how this is all going to end soon. I hear it in the halls before class. I hear it when we should be trading homework. I hear it in the invites I get to graduation parties. I hear it from Becca whenever we do anything.

"You can't forget, Hunter. This is way serious."

Like I'm really going to forget.

It's all I can think about anymore.

I'm told everywhere I turn that these years *were* the best years of my life. Our reign as seniors *coming to an end*, and here we are. But the way everyone's saying it, it sounds like this is the best it'll ever get.

It can't be that serious.

But the more I think about it, the more it seems to make sense. Maybe I'm underselling it.

Give it enough thought and I can basically warm up to any idea. Even if I don't really feel like it's serious, thinking about it a lot will make it stick. It will make it *real* serious.

School is almost over.

In the fall, I won't be walking up the narrow steps to Meadows; I'll be walking up the narrow steps that lead to the student union building at State. Think about that. Really try to let it sink in.

Yeah, I guess it's pretty final, huh?

"I can't believe we're graduating. Like a month from now."

I'm chatting with Becca. We're always talking online.

She's my girlfriend so it shouldn't be weird. But sometimes it is. Well, not weird. It's just kind of annoying. I like to sign out for a few minutes, just to cut out, and then sign back in. Becca thinks my house has shitty Internet. It's an excuse that's held and, man, I want it to hold on tight.

But we've been going since almost the beginning of high school. Nothing's changed since she asked me out toward the middle of freshman year. It's been good. And it's been a while, yeah. She's gotten used to me and, really, I've gotten used to her. Even the things I can't stand.

Same as anything else:

If I think about it enough, I get used to it.

"You never did ask me to prom..."

"It's like a few weeks away right?"

I watch the little icon flicker once, twice. It means Becca typed something but deleted it and started again. It also means she didn't like what I said and now I'm going to have to be the one who fixes things.

"You're still going to ask right?" She adds an emoji, a teary-eyed cat.

I look at the paused unboxing video, wanting so much to just watch the rest of it. Kind of ruins the enjoyment factor when I'm interrupted.

I look at myself in the mirror hanging above my bed. It takes a second for me to realize that the person I'm seeing in the mirror is me. With time and aging, I can almost grow a full five o'clock shadow. Know what that means?

That means a full beard. That means whatever it means.

Becca won't let me grow a beard, just like she won't let me grow my hair out. I thought about letting it grow long, earlier this year. I'm a senior, I should kind of look older than I am, you know? Give my plain brown hair/brown eyes look a little face-lift.

But yeah, I keep my hair short and face shaved. Becca's preference.

I look away from my reflection, plain looks and all, and push that thought aside. Get to fixating on that stuff just makes it harder to deal with life.

Life is constant.

It won't let me just kick back and watch unboxing videos online.

I send her an emoji, a winking dog wearing a suit.

She replies, "?" and then "WTF."

I guess it doesn't make much sense. I thought it looked like I was holding back a secret. Like saying, *Never know when I'll pop the question.* "Pop the question." Sounds like we're getting married.

That's another thought to push aside.

I type, "Surprise. It'll be a surprise."

Becca types, "It better," winking smiley where the period should be.

I stare at what she just typed, fingers light on the keys.

The winking smiley. Can't stand the winking smiley. Becca uses it a lot.

I go back to the tab with the unboxing video. I stare at the paused frame. I look at the time on my phone.

Three A.M. It's the weekend. Tomorrow's—well, technically to-day's—Sunday. Don't have school, but that wouldn't change much.

I'm not much of a sleeper. I'll stay up as late as I can when I want to. I stay up even later on the nights when I need to get the most rest.

Go figure.

But that's my cue to exit. It's my go-to excuse, "Got to go."

"Yeah, it's kind of late." And then she types, "Can't believe it's really happening. We're graduating."

I tell her, "Yeah. So crazy. Night."

"Love you," she types, with the heart emoji added.

I do the same, from practice. I don't even need to think about it. It's typed, right there on-screen.

Then I sign out and go back to the video clip.

My night begins when there's no one else who I need to talk to. Don't have to keep up appearances; it's just the glow of the computer screen and me. It's just this room and me. Being here is sort of a sanctuary, late at night.

I like watching the unboxing videos the most. But other videos—especially video game walk-throughs and retro stuff—work just as well. Most popular videos on the site are music videos and other trending pop culture stuff. But I skip even the recommended viewing clips. I just like the simple stuff.

Kind of wish I got ahold of some beer earlier. Mix these videos, beer, and the quiet of a darkened room and that's about as close as I can get to feeling calm.

IV   MICHAEL J. SEIDLINGER

But yeah, there's something medicinal about unboxing videos. The best are the ones where they take their time, cutting through the cellophane all carefully, meanwhile treating even the inserts and thin brochures that come with the camera, or phone, or game system, as equal as the fragile new device.

This is one of those videos. I've watched it before.

Watching the guy pull the phone out from its factory-sealed bag, I can almost forget about graduation. I can almost forget about all the insanity that's getting around at school.

But there are some things I can't quite push from my mind.

Like, okay, I could really talk, and I mean *really talk*, about the stuff I find so fascinating, the stuff I won't even talk about here. I can do that, but whenever I do it's kind of like seeing people's eyes glaze over.

I'm not even saying anything insane, at least I don't think I am, but it happens. I talk a different kind of talk and suddenly no one's listening.

That's society. That's life.

That's what I think about at three A.M., when sober and streaming videos instead of sleeping.

It's best to just keep to things that work, things that everyone can relate to and talk about. With so many views on this unboxing video, I think it's pretty smart to say that I'm not the only one watching unboxing videos. I'm not the only one vegging out on streamed videos.

We're all doing it. Some of us just aren't getting the most out of it.

Everyone's enamored (I love that word), but no one's making the most of what these videos can do. No one's really connecting with the existential (another word I love) power of these videos. It's not just the opening of a brand-new phone or game system; it's a glimpse of the future. It's like every single thing that's being opened is the first in what'll be one long life of ownership and possession. And, man, there's something so compelling about being there for that first look. Okay, *now* I sound like I'm insane.

My eyes half open, I bring the laptop with me to bed, under the covers, and I can almost forget about graduation. Out of the corner of my eye, I see the kind of stuff I've been trying to ignore all day. I see the kind of stuff that started this morning.

This time it's the bedroom door opening by itself.

It started with one of my mom's vases found shattered to pieces in the hall. Mom thought it was me, stumbling half asleep at night, who broke it. I'm not that clumsy. Still, she installed night-lights in the hallway like they would help.

The door cracks open, maybe three inches, just enough to see one of the night-lights: no one at the door.

The door closes as gently as it opened, the sound of the door clicking back into place.

The whole thing lasts maybe ten minutes. But yeah, some things I can't just push aside. Some things make it harder to veg out on videos.

Stuff's been happening all day. It's all so exhausting to think about.

What's causing it, well, yeah, about that...

I'll get to it. Just let me watch one more video.

IT WAS AN HOUR OR SO BEFORE SCHOOL LET UP FOR THE
weekend, but Brad, Blaire, Steve, and I were late for final period
so we were like, *Fuck it,* and walked the trail that led from Meadows
through to the southern tip of the city and beyond. Walk far enough
and you'll see all the buildings let up and some sense of a forest
pulling in, taking over.

The spring weather in full effect, I felt pretty good. Getting out of
final period made this work for me so damn well.

The fact that Brad always has a cooler full of beer in the trunk of
his car didn't hurt either. I usually wait until someone cracks one
open before cracking into my first, but that day, it was different.

"You guys hear?"

Brad was driving me crazy, spreading gossip like an attention
whore, a walking tabloid.

Brad brought along some dude I don't really know named Steve,
and they were going on and on about the latest on Nikki.

Nikki Dillon. She's the "hot" girl—has been since sophomore year.

Nikki Dillon—the one who seemed to have a new guy every week.
Not because she slept around; the world knows it's more like she

just lets guys audition to play that role. Doubt anyone ever gets in her pants, which makes the whole world only want to know more, everyone talking about the latest.

Like clockwork, I'd hear about it just like I was hearing about it now.

Brad with the "Yo, so I heard from Kev who heard from James who heard from Greg," and then it goes on like that, a stepped-on piece of gossip that I shouldn't care about.

But it's Nikki.

Everyone is at least somewhat interested in hearing about the latest on Nikki. And Blaire is no different. Blaire's been a bud of mine since sixth grade. She and I might have given it a shot if: 1) I hadn't met Becca, and 2) Blaire lost that thing I can't stand. She has this way about her that makes it so that we never get along. Let me make better sense of it.

I mean, Blaire's great. She does my homework and I do hers for the subjects where we falter, the stuff I'll never need and the stuff she'll pledge, later in life, to be against (she thinks extracurricular activities are a waste of time).

Blaire just, I don't know, seems to see through the front I put up. And by "front" I mean I'm usually not really listening to people.

It's okay.

It's true... I'm really not.

I kind of do this thing where I listen, but I'm also paying more attention to how the conversation works. There's a sense to every conversation, even the ones that are nonsense. There's a rise and fall to everything said, and there's momentum that I pay attention to all the time, watching where it'll go next. And on that day, hearing Brad tell us about Nikki's latest guy, I listened but I also sipped from a can of beer. And beyond that, I walked the trail, my gaze to the ground, listening to how Brad and Steve traded gossip that couldn't be true with this sort of mutual enthusiasm that I almost felt jealous about not having.

But I had the beer so I had a perfectly good excuse.

Blaire looked at me, that judging look.

I offered a can. "Want one?"

"Um, yeah, okay."

I knew what she was thinking. "What?"

Blaire shook her head. "Nothing."

Here we go again. Either I kept asking or she'd just tell me.

I took another gulp.

She didn't even open her can.

Blaire sighed. "I'm just saying, when are you going to tell her?"

Why now? But then why did I even need to ask? I already had the answer: because it's Blaire. She brings up whatever she wants whenever she wants. It's probably why she's stuck around. Persistence makes for someone who isn't easy to ignore. It's complicated.

"I figure it's almost graduation," I told her.

"That's disgusting." Blaire made a face. "Ugh."

"She's going up north and I'm staying here going to State. It'll work itself out naturally."

Blaire rolled her eyes. "I don't get you, Hunter. I really don't."

There probably wouldn't be a whole lot to get if we really got along. But Blaire has always been sort of my opposite. If she were in my shoes, she would have ended things with Becca weeks after going steady.

Where am I? I'm years in, putting in time.

But, you know.

Maybe you don't.

That's kind of why I'm going on about what happened on this day.

Yeah, well, we walked the trail to the point where it ends and it's all just trees and, even at high noon, you get, at best, an inch of light before it's all shadows. This is where we all used to go to get scared. All the grade school kids hung around this forested zone back when shadows were all we needed to get our thrills. But little do the kids know that if you keep walking south, you'll end up in a clearing that really shouldn't be there. You don't really see it coming until you clear the last patch of trees. It's a muddy pasture pockmarked with rocks and beer cans and other garbage. Footprints in the mud all over the place.

I couldn't tell you how often this place becomes the scene of a killer party. We're talking some of the best I can remember. I can't really remember any one party in particular, but yeah, it's usually half the school, bonfires and plenty of what we need to get mellow.

During those parties, everyone can almost be the same person.

But the clearing wasn't where we were going that day. We had somewhere else far more secluded in mind.

You keep walking south, pushing past a water tower and that one abandoned car without wheels or axles, totally shot to shit, full of bullet holes—eventually you'll get there.

This is the place.

Falter Kingdom.

I'll try to explain it. It's kind of a simple picture, nothing really wrong with it. You might see it and think, "So? Just another place where high school kids chill and smoke." But the first clue is how it should be a sewer tunnel but it's too big to be one. The concrete opening is the size of a car tunnel, and looking in you see nothing but darkness.

That darkness, it doesn't let up.

Someone painted a crown around the opening of the tunnel. You can see the black paint, the spikes of the crown, from really far away. It has something to do with the lore, what people say about it.

I've been here a number of times but I've never taken part.

The thing about Falter Kingdom is that it's not just any tunnel. The tunnel is full of darkness and it goes on and on and on, without end. People say that initially it was supposed to be part of the city subway system, but the mass transit authority discovered that, a couple miles in, there was a weak point, a sort of fissure. The fissure released all sorts of frequencies and energies and stuff. That's what you get when people turn spirituality into hard science.

People used to play around with the thought that there was another plane of existence, probably because ours was too much of a bummer to be the only one. Everyone knew ghosts existed; they'd speak to you if you dared to listen. But demons want what people want, whatever that means.

Nearly half of the employees working on the tunnel attracted demons. Like anywhere else, the demon chooses you and you've got no choice. It latches on to you and you don't have a whole lot of options.

Back then, it was really expensive to get rid of them. You couldn't just call up a priest and get exorcized. You had to fill out a ton of paperwork, go to a number of experts and stuff. By the time they could get rid of it, there was basically only the demon left, the person gone, fully possessed.

So that's how the legend goes. The legend of Falter Kingdom.

A bunch of us go here just to feel the change in atmosphere. A lot of Meadows students go here to prove a point.

But see, when we arrived here that day, we just wanted to be alone.

I wanted to get drunk. I was willing to listen to Brad if it meant getting a head start on the weekend. I didn't think I would have to run the gauntlet.

But I'll get to that.

We arrived at Falter Kingdom and the first thing that happened was our cell phones all lost signal. Again, that's part of the fun of the place.

Blaire hadn't been before and Brad was being a dick about that.

"Know what that means, bro?" He nudged me in the arm.

I finished my second beer, took the unopened can from Blaire, and said, "You know she won't go through with it."

That kid, Steve, stood at the opening looking in.

Brad shouted at him, "Careful or you'll be dragged in!"

Blaire snickered, "You're a walking cliché."

Brad signaled to me and I tossed him a beer. "Yeah?" He cracked open the beer and took a gulp. "You know what they say about being judgmental?"

This went on—back and forth—for longer than it should have. I listened and I observed the conversation from where I sat, on a flat rock, drinking the beer probably way too fast.

Blaire wouldn't let up.

Brad was too oblivious to care about anything Blaire could say.

Eventually the conversation made its way back to me. Brad saying something like, "Why the fuck do you keep this chick around?"

But that really wasn't a question. Brad's good at acting like an asshole because he *is* an asshole. I can't stand the guy. But he's there. He's around. We were freshmen when we met. I think it was biology. Yeah, that was the one. We both sucked at the subject. We were failing and quickly facing summer school. We got assigned to some peer group for people who suck at science. We had to be tutored by substitute teachers, meaning we had to take the class twice in one day. It was horrible. Brad being around made it a little less horrible but only because he knew how to get the answers. He knew people.

He still knows people. I don't think anyone really likes the guy but they see value in how he can slack his way through anything.

Brad gets his way. Brad always has beer.

I guess we're friends because I've gotten used to him being around.

Sort of like most people, I get used to them and, in time, it's all the same.

This is as close to getting along as I'll probably ever know.

But yeah, Brad can be a real asshole and I was the one to break up the argument. It was easy—all I had to do was tell Brad to shut up and catch up.

"I'm on my third." I dangled the can. "Which one are you on?"

That was enough to end it, but nothing would change the fact that Blaire wouldn't end up having much fun. Not that she would have. This is what Blaire always does. She spent most of the afternoon sitting on some far rock working on homework assignments for next week. I let her do her thing. We all did.

She was doing my homework too.

Steve, Brad, and I stood at the opening of the tunnel.

Brad went on about all the girls he wanted to try to get with before graduation, like it would be that easy. "I've known the girl since, like, second grade. No way she'll turn down a strapping young lad like me."

Steve sipped from his beer. "Strapping young lad?"

Brad shrugged. "Got it from the band. I looked up the meaning."

Then I said something, because it was a good time to say enough without really having said anything: "You, looking up something?"

Brad laughed. "Yeah, bro, it can't be all porn. Got to sprinkle in stuff to keep trackers off my trail."

That made Steve laugh.

That made me take another drink.

Steve said something about how Samantha—a girl I don't know, but a girl who both Brad and Steve seemed to have been talking about quite a bit—just got into Yale. That impressed Steve, and, for Brad, it seemed to only confirm her status as irresistible.

They talked about how Brad will get all carpe diem and just ask her out. Doesn't matter that she has a boyfriend. Doesn't matter that Samantha wouldn't go for a guy like Brad.

They both talked the same way everyone talked—about how there wasn't much time left.

Either get it done, what you want to do, or you'll never get your due.

Then the conversation turned toward something about our plans before graduation. Steve had his. Brad had his would-be lays. Blaire would have plans too, if she were part of the conversation. I looked back at her, busy highlighting some passage from some book for some essay we both had to finish by some deadline.

Lucky.

At some point she'd come up, Becca.

"You can't waste prom on her, dude. You've already wasted years on her when you could have been seeing other girls."

I did my best to maneuver around the topic. I'm usually good about this, but see, it might have been the alcohol and how it mellows me and I say stuff I shouldn't say or worse. By "worse," I mean being able to say anything at all.

And looking back, I got really drunk that afternoon.

Drunker than I should have. Even Steve got on me about Becca. He talked about how my situation took me off the radar, how nothing good can come from being trapped like that.

I'm not going to go into the exact words, because I can't be sure how it was said, but being in that kind of situation is as bad as it gets. It put me on the spot. It made me *the* conversation rather than part of it.

Blaire found it amusing. I know she did. I didn't look and I didn't hear anything, but being in this situation is what Blaire's been putting me through since we first met. I just wanted them all to shut up, you know? I wanted it all to wash clean, having them there but on mute, so I didn't have to try.

The company I keep... Looking back at that afternoon, it feels like I was stuck on an island with a handful of mortal enemies. It didn't feel at all like a chill time among friends. You get what you put in, I guess.

I chose to stick around Brad. Blaire lingered and I did the same thing.

Yeah, I went with them to Falter Kingdom of my own free will.

But alcohol and competition go hand in hand, and all it took was one mention of the tunnel and Steve shut up. It was obvious that he had never run the gauntlet.

It was a little less obvious that I hadn't either. Every other time I'd hung out at Falter Kingdom, I'd gotten out of having to run. The trick is to wait until it becomes a possibility, the talking about running, and you encourage whoever it is who's being pressured to run, but when he turns it on you, don't freeze. Don't stop and worry. Don't say no. You pretend to think about it. If there's beer, take a sip. By the time any pressure is given, you can ask someone who hasn't run and have him mess up and take on the pressure. So he ends up running and you don't. That's how it works.

End of lesson, or whatever.

But yeah, I was drunk and on a short fuse. Brad was selling Steve on the whole thing, legend and all, and I downed the last of the beer in that can.

Then I said it: "I'll do it."

Instantly the conditions changed.

"Really?" Blaire had joined us, standing at my side.

Brad grinned. "My man!"

Steve didn't say anything. *He* wanted to run it. *He* wanted the respect.

I just wanted the conversation to end. I didn't want to hear any more about Becca.

So they crowded around me as I took my first steps into the tunnel.

"Ten minutes, bud, you got this," Brad said.

Running the gauntlet is more or less exactly how it sounds. You run into the tunnel, into the darkness, for ten whole minutes or until you reach the end. But no one's ever reached the end. So I had to run, sprint really, for ten whole minutes. They synced up and set a timer on each of their phones. On their count—three, two, one—I ran.

It was actually kind of easy, going through with it.

Everything leading up made it feel impossible. I wasn't into running it; I had nothing to really prove, which could be cause for a bigger problem.

But I don't know—

I guess it had a lot to do with being fed up.

With their voices. With their claims. With the fact that they were kind of right: it's almost graduation and nothing's changed.

It's like I needed something to prove to myself. I needed to do something that anyone who knew me would have problems believing if told in the context of some story.

The *actual* running was the hard part. I felt like I couldn't keep to a straight line. I felt like I couldn't run fast enough. The air was thick in the tunnel, kind of a strange musk, the same kind you smell in old basements or places with stale air. The ground muddy and wet, each step had that sinking feeling that you get when you find out you spaced a test or some other important event.

But I ran the whole ten.

It didn't even last that long.

I ran with my eyes wide but they might as well have been closed. The dark was so thick it was like running in place.

Something worth mentioning—you can't really hear anything in the tunnel. You can't hear your own footsteps. I ran until it felt right to stop and turn around. I didn't hear my feet slipping in the mud. I didn't hear my lungs gasping for air. I didn't hear.

If I didn't hear my own breath, there's no way I heard their phones.
It probably doesn't make a lot of sense, does it?

It's hard to explain. Telling it right is usually tougher than you think; it's all about using the right amount of words to get your point across. You say too little and it's just strange; say too much and you're not really making any sense. This is probably one of those situations. It's just that being inside the tunnel felt like... what's that term for when you are frozen in a chamber?

Cryosleep?

It's kind of like that. But there's a better word. Let me look it up.

Oh, right—

It's like being in suspended animation. Stuck in place, but you also know that your body is moving, your thoughts racing, because I could feel the sweat dripping from my forehead.

While inside, I could think about only one thing.

I thought about my body breaking into pieces.

And even now I can't make complete sense of why.

When I made it back to them, you can bet they were surprised.

Brad saw me first. "Shit, bro."

I was drenched in sweat. Dirt caked in layers all over my body.

Steve didn't say anything.

Blaire played *concerned friend*: "Are you insane?"

I asked them if I lasted the full ten, but the words didn't come out until later, after I had lay down against a cool rock. By then Brad and Steve had left. Blaire stayed with me. She was sitting next to me when I woke up. I stirred shortly before the sun completely disappeared.

"Did I make the full ten?"

Blaire stared at me in disbelief. Maybe she really was worried. I'm not sure what she felt that day. But when she told me I had been in there for twenty-five minutes, it clicked into place.

I didn't feel any different but, well, it kind of made sense. I felt peaceful sitting there, letting the information sink in. Like I did something I wanted to do.

We walked back in silence.

I didn't say anything and she didn't say anything.

When we got back to Meadows, our cars were the only ones left in the parking lot. "Where'd Brad and that other guy go?"

Blaire kind of ignored me but also kind of didn't. It was a mumble, one that I maybe imagined. "They went for help."

We left without saying good-bye.

By the time I got home, I felt fine. Not tired at all.

I stayed up with a six-pack that I finished and watched walk-throughs of two different video games. I didn't have trouble sleeping at all that night.

Stuff started happening the following day. Minor things: mostly the broken vase and my bedroom door opening and closing on its own. I misplaced my cell phone twice only to find it where I couldn't have left it. Why would my phone turn up in my dad's pocket when he had been at work all day and I used the phone not ten minutes before it went missing? These aren't really questions, really, just the mind fighting the facts.

And I knew the symptoms.

They say it's best to get rid of a demon quick.

Yeah, I know, I know.

But just thinking about how much effort it would have been to tell my parents... what it would mean for them—their only son, *haunted*—made me feel exhausted. I would never hear the end of it.

So then it just felt better to put off telling them for a little bit.

It won't be much longer.

Soon everyone will know.

MONDAY. WHERE THE HELL DID THE WEEKEND GO? I
didn't get a whole lot of sleep. I mean I actually did—something like
twelve hours last night—but I feel tired. It's probably me. I'm doing
this to myself. I've been fixating on what's been happening lately. I
can't shake the fact that everyone's right: it's almost over. After that
day at Falter, all I can think about is breaking up with Becca. I think
about stuff I should have done a long time ago. Now might be my
last chance. It's now or never.

But, man, I never get used to these mornings.

Note to self: Don't sign up for morning classes next year.

Can't wait to be able to choose when my classes start. I'm going
with the major made for insomniacs. What career paths involve
working late into the night? Gravediggers? Um, doctors, nurses,
mental ward psychos?

Man, I'm tired.

I drive to school the same way I always do: half awake. It's out
of the driveway, then it's a left, right, right, stop at that annoying
intersection with the really long red light that I always get stuck at,
straight past that, two more lefts, and then I'm there.

Meadows. On time for once too.

I park the car in my assigned space and I look at the time on my phone: 7:40 A.M. Know what that means—ten minutes to sleep in my car!

Believe me, this adds up. It helps. Power naps keep me from turning into a zombie. But then again, it's kind of hard to sleep when Brad taps on the glass.

"What, man? Go away." I wave him off.

But he taps on the glass again.

"Fuck," I grumble. "It's open."

He gets in the front passenger seat. He sits down and looks at me.

I look at him. He's a blank stare. "What? It's too early for this stuff, man."

Brad shakes his head. "Bro..."

Of course I know what he's thinking about. I haven't been able to brush it off either. It kind of settles in the back of the mind, making everything I do a little plainer because I'm paying even less attention to the things around me.

"Yeah, I know."

"So wild, dude," Brad boasts, "we had to fucking run and get help."

"Yeah," I say, monotone, driver's seat reclined back, eyes closed.

"But then Steve twisted his ankle like a pussy and we got lost in the fields."

Can't a guy get a few winks?

"And shit, bro, it sucked. Getting lost in that forest is no joke. Being buzzed makes everything look the same."

I yawn. "But you weren't out there as long as I was."

"Yeah, bro, Blaire told me. She said you fell asleep."

"More like blacked out." I rub my eyes. "Did y'all end up copping it?"

"Naw"—Brad snaps his fingers—"texted Jon-Jon and he called it like it is, said, like, if we called the cops they'd be more about trespassing charges."

"Jon-Jon knows what's up." Falter isn't a place anyone's allowed to access. It's one of the places closed off for a reason. But we all know that. It's kind of the point. And Jon-Jon, he always knows. Older than most, he's got the wisdom to make money work for him. He stays at Meadows because it's where the money is. He pulls in as much as he wants selling. He's a good guy, Jon-Jon. Still don't know him well enough to really get a good read on the guy. Then again I don't think anyone does. That's him. That's Jon-Jon. He's a businessman.

"Bro, he's looking for you," Brad says.

I groan. "I've got first period in, like, eight minutes and I still got to pass by my locker."

"I thought first period was free," Brad says.

"That was last semester." I'd kill to get that free period first thing. But no, I'm supposed to be doing awesome at calculus.

"Bummer," Brad says.

"Yeah." I open my eyes, staring at the faded fabric ceiling of my car.

"But, bro, you know what he wants. Fuck, I got to ask too."

"Nothing happened," I tell him.

"You were running that long and you're going to tell me nothing fucking happened?"

I put the seat back up, stretching. "Yup. That's what I'm saying."

"Jesus," Brad says, and sighs, "real bummer."

"World's full of bummers."

We leave the car and walk toward the main building. Meadows is made up of three buildings, two on either side of a big four-story main structure where most of us spend the bulk of our time.

Brad's talking, something about "a bunch of people are going to be blasting it in the fields this Wednesday." It's another party in the middle of nowhere.

I'll probably go. Becca will want to go anyway. Everyone will be there; even if I stayed in, people will notice. The next day at school would be all about how Hunter Warden was a no-show. It's like that here at Meadows.

Everyone knows everyone, especially if you've never met.

I tell him, "Yeah, you know it. Anyway, I'll catch you later."

"Yeah." Brad nods. "Yeah, hit me up at lunch."

He goes his way and I go mine. And there's first period, which isn't worth talking about. I think I might fail the class. I won't, but I would, you see—Blaire's my eyes and ears. She's got the stuff finished and all I have to do is not fuck up the pop quizzes. I fucked up today's pop quiz.

But what are you gonna do, you know?

Calculus. Everyone, even the A students, are over it.

Miss Canaan needs a life. I want to just walk up to her desk and tell her what everyone's been telling me: *It's almost over. You'll never see us again. Why not cut us some slack? Some of us are fun people. If you'd stop stressing the curriculum so much you'd have a better time.*

But that takes balls. Well, more than that, it takes effort.

And I'm low on that lately.

I bump into Blaire before fourth period to exchange homework.

"You look like shit," Blaire tells me.

Yeah, I haven't been able to shake the exhaustion. I yawn it off, make appearances. "Insomnia," I say with a shrug. "What else is new?"

Blaire's hands are all over the homework, checking it like I didn't actually do a good job. I've got this stuff. I'm not an idiot.

English class, that's my forte.

She won't look me in the eye. "You'd tell me, right?"

But I don't hear her until she seems to answer for me—"Yeah, you'd tell me"—and runs off. We don't have any classes together, which is why trading homework works. I know what she's talking about. She was there. But, um, I know she wouldn't tell anyone. At least not until she was sure about it.

During lunch, the student body president, Chris something—I can't remember his name, but really most people just know him as "Chris the Student President" (you know how everyone's labeled something)—he makes a few announcements. It's blah, blah, blah until he finishes with a heads-up stating that yearbook deadlines are in a week.

One fucking week.

It's a wake-up call for most. It is for me. I don't know what to write. This is more than making the most of the rest of the semester; the bio you write is what people remember you by. Every word counts. Some people pay extra to fit in another fifty words over the three-hundred-word blurb limit.

Being memorable.

People talk so much about being remembered and "the one thing you'll be remembered for."

I think about the prompt while standing in line for food. My mom packs me lunch but it's embarrassing. I leave it in the trunk of my car and toss it on the way home. Been doing that since the middle of freshman year.

So it's this junk they serve us, but it works.

The one thing people will remember me for.

I'm not sure I want to settle for just one thing like everyone else. I'm not sure about what I'd write, so I do what I typically do—I put it off for later.

Brad's late to lunch. I end up at our table, sitting with a few others I never really talk to. They're almost finished with their bios.

This guy, Mark, reads his bio aloud. He's really thought it out.

Brad gets there and steals the page from Mark's hands, 'cause he's an asshole and you know he'll never let you down. Brad reads some of it aloud for the entire cafeteria: "Mark Banes excelled at contemporary literature, earning himself an A- average—"

"Come on, Brad, lay off." That's me saying that. I'm the one who usually tries to keep things cool. Do you ever really question the guy who's trying to keep things civil? Yeah, everyone likes that guy, even if they don't really know him. It's how I keep this from getting back to me. And today, I know Brad and a bunch of people are suspicious about what happened in that tunnel.

They have something on me. I'm an interesting topic, you know?

And I just want to make it to fifth period so I can take a nap in my car, get away from all this stuff. Lately, everything's been, I don't know, just too much. It's not just graduation; it's everything. I feel like the pressure is increasing and I'm worried that it might never release.

Kind of melodramatic, yeah.

But I guess it's mostly the fact that I know what's going to happen next.

Brad sits across from me, steals one of my chicken fingers, and starts people-watching. That's how it always starts.

Brad leans in, whispering, "Bro, you see Jess today? Jesus."

Testosterone-fueled annoyance, that's Brad's yearbook bio. He'll be remembered as the dude with so much testosterone he drowned in it, meaning we all ganged up on him and drowned him for being such an asshole.

I don't know why I hang around this guy.

But yeah, I do. I know. I've talked about this already.

"Yo," Brad says.

"Yeah, what is it?" I'm acting like these chicken fingers are awesome, like they taste like more than salt.

"You hit up JJ yet?"

Shit. That's right. I can't leave the guy hanging. He's my source for booze, blunts, and anything else I want. For cheap.

"Not yet, after I finish eating."

"Bro, he'll be pissed."

I'm going, I'm going.

Push the food away and Brad takes it, always hungry.

I always leave via the back entrance of the cafeteria so that I don't have to make eye contact with anyone. But I'm not always that successful, you see.

On the way out, I cross paths with Nikki. She's got this guy, Luke, with her, and he's handing over her purse. As she looks back at the door, I happen to be the one walking out. We exchange glances. That smile, one I've seen before. Strand of red hair brushed with her hand back over her ear. Blue eyes on me. This is where I'd trip and fall if I let it get to me, but I don't. But so what, she smiled at me? So what? She says hello. She says my name. She slows down and waits until I've gone.

So what?

It's not a big deal.

But Brad makes it a big deal.

Goes on and on: "Bro, there's no way you didn't see that...!"

I play it off the way I know how things should be played: "Yeah, I saw."

"You know you have to talk to her now," Brad says.

I'm thinking, "What makes anything mandatory if I don't want to?" Yeah, I want to talk to her, and yeah, I like her—so what? But just because we looked at each other doesn't mean now I'm supposed to let go of my own problems.

What problems?

No, I'm pushing that aside. Not thinking about that.

"Don't be stupid," Brad's saying, as we walk around back, where the theater kids smoke because it's near the auditorium stage.

Jon-Jon and a few others hang here.

You can hear barking from far away. That's Jetson, his corgi. He always brings the dog to school. It'd be a problem if he went to class, but he's got all that covered. Rumor has it he pays off the principal. Halverson gets a cut from sales. It's just a rumor. Gossip.

But that's like all things at Meadows.

Everything's gossip until it's naked truth.

Brad tells Jon-Jon. Of course he tells Jon-Jon. "Dude, Nikki Dillon's got a thing for our bro here!"

Some days I can almost see it happening: I'll start by punching Brad in the gut. He'll wince in pain and I'll wrap—I don't know, sometimes it's rope, other times it's piano wire—around his throat until his neck snaps. I'll say something clever and then walk away. The next day people will know what I did and everyone will be happy. Brad's body is brushed under the floorboards.

Jon-Jon tugs at Jetson's leash. The dog runs up to Brad, hyper and seemingly happy as always. Corgis. Happiness is a corgi.

"Brad," Jon-Jon says without looking up from his phone, "enough."

"Yeah, sorry, man." Brad works on finishing the chicken fingers.

I'm watching him until Jon-Jon asks, "Hunter, how are you feeling today?" Jon-Jon's eyes are almost always glued to the phone in his hands. Guess it's the way he conducts business. But he looks at me like he's concerned. Is he really? You know, I never know what's real or fake with the guy.

"Yeah"—I fake a yawn—"just a little tired."

Jon-Jon leans forward. "That so? How tired are you, on a scale of one to ten, ten being chronic insomnia?"

Uh, I go with an eight, which means I really tell him, "About a five."

Jon-Jon clicks his tongue, looks up at one of the girls, kind of cute, brown hair tied back, red lipstick—no one knows any of Jon-Jon's girls, their names or anything else; I'm pretty sure they don't go here—and the girl hands him a notebook.

Brad with his mouth full: "Is that...?"

It is. It's yesterday's betting pool.

See I kind of started betting on football, baseball, basketball, whatever everyone around me was betting on, because it kept things cool. If I won, I get some cash. If I lost, then whatever. I don't have a stake in any of these teams. I don't even really find it all that interesting. Watching Brad as he flips through the book quickly, for him it's more than just money.

"Hell yes," Brad shouts, "you owe me! Pay up, pay up!"

This is how it goes. Then there's still all the talk about stats, which player to pick, who's got the better team. I just want to make it until fifth period so I can get some sleep.

I lean against the wall while Brad and Jon-Jon talk sports, then about this rapper who's supposed to be in town soon, how Jon-Jon can probably get tickets for cheap, which gets Brad excited. "Get me a few. Perfect bait for landing a date!"

I glance over at Jon-Jon's girls, or assistants, or whatever. I know they find this as dull as I do. Or maybe they don't.

What's the big deal?

I used to feel kind of bad about not being interested in sports or music or that kind of stuff. Culture, I guess. I mean, I still do. I can see how learning about the stats and predicting how ball games will turn out could be really cool. I bet it's satisfying. But before I can really get used to it, they're talking about other things. Never really been into hip-hop or the stuff I hear coming from people's cars. At least at the parties they blast it so it's all bass.

But I guess I never got into it.

I don't really know what I like. Music can be fun to listen to, but sometimes I just like sitting back and listening to podcasts, people chatting about, I don't know, new technology, space, time travel. Weird stuff that doesn't come around often. I guess that's kind of insane.

Jon-Jon didn't bring me here to listen to them talk business.

He asks me, "Too tired for one on me?" He holds up a bottle of vodka.

This guy, there's no way he's getting away with this stuff just by being careful. I say yes and we both take swigs from the bottle, Brad included. We take enough to ease off a little, but right before Brad and I walk back for class, Jon-Jon calls me out: "You ran, huh?"

Back turned, I kind of freeze, feeling the more powerful lull of liquor, how it kind of feels heavier than a beer buzz. Brad nudges me. "Bro..."

I know.

I tell him the truth, the lie I've practiced enough for it to be truth. Trick is to believe it yourself.

"Yeah, man," I say, playing it smooth, "I did."

Jon-Jon stares at me. "Why wasn't I invited?"

Brad chimes in: "Wasn't really planned, like, we got in each other's faces, this guy and Steve... you know Steve? Steve the creep?"

Jon-Jon nods his head once. "I do."

Brad continues: "Well, our boy here got in dweeb's face and then just fucking ran Falter like it was nothing."

Jon-Jon puts his phone down on his right knee and claps five times, slow, like this—clap, clap, clap, clap, clap.

"Yeah"—I sort of smile—"yeah, you know." I laugh.

"I could have made some money. We all could've," Jon-Jon says.

See that's what's been happening with Falter and Meadows students. You go there and run on a bet. No one talks about it and no one really makes any bets, but whenever people plan on actually running, more than a few people show up. They show up and Jon-Jon's always there.

I can see why he's disappointed.

Jetson barks at me.

Jon-Jon looks at the dog. "And?"

Jetson growls. I'm not doing anything. I take a step forward and the dog charges at me. Jon-Jon tugs the leash back.

We all look at the dog.

We're all thinking the same thing, but only I really know the real deal.

Still, I'm not telling. I don't want the last thing people remember of me to be that I caught one, showing symptoms and all.

Jon-Jon glares at me. "Didn't catch anything?"

Brad tries to speak for me, but Jon-Jon raises a hand like he's some mob boss and a single gesture commands the entire scene.

Then again, it's kind of like that, actually.

"No," I say, "unless you call insomnia demonic."

"It should be!" Brad laughs. Brad is so fake.

I want to say it—*I don't know why I hang out with you*—but I won't. I won't.

Enough's enough.

Jon-Jon doesn't laugh. No one does.

He says something like, "Fair enough," right as the lunch period rings out in the distance. I give this kind of weird, awkward gesture—"It calls"—and then I burst out of the scene too quickly, like I'm trying to tell Jon-Jon that I'm hiding something. I manage to say, "Catch you later, man," as casual as I can.

Jon-Jon says something like, "Yeah. We'll talk later."

The way he said it, it sounded insincere, like a mob boss who's already read a victim's future. He knows. Or he doesn't know. Maybe no one knows. Even I kind of push it aside. It's easy when there's so much stuff going on.

It isn't until after school that the activity continues.

Like it waited patiently for me to return home.

Last thing I want to do is have to sit and eat dinner with the parents. Mom's cooking is all Shake'N Bake, out-of-the-box premade stuff. She's got all those clients to worry about, and when you're lawyering it up, dinner and family and all that stuff isn't top priority. And Dad, don't get me started on Dad.

Even when he's pretending to care, in the back of his mind he's thinking about the latest cancer patient of his.

It's not just money with them. It's like, well, it's like what I've seen in so many movies. The job becomes you.

So when I get back from school and all I want is to crash for a few hours, Mom calls me into the kitchen like a home-cooked meal is a surprise.

"Son, dinner's almost ready."

I watch her pull out meat loaf from the oven.

"It's four thirty."

"Early bird special," she says, and chuckles.

I head up the stairs, but she's not letting me get away easy today.

"Where do you think you're going?" she says from the foot of the stairs. She's still wearing those oven mitts. Makes her look ridiculous.

"Getting a hoodie, Mom." I point in the direction of my room. "It's cold in here."

"Are you feeling all right?"

Enough with that—but she won't stop with the questions. Like she really cares. Whenever she's around, she tries to be supermom. Whenever she's around, it's usually because she lost a case, so she's feeling depressed. Feeling depressed for my crazy mom translates to: smother Hunter. Turning up the parenting to 150 percent hurts everybody.

At the dinner table, I can't sit still.

Mom asks me if I feel okay.

"Just cold, Mom."

She doesn't seem to be having a problem.

I look at the placemat she set for Dad.

"He showing up?"

Mom makes excuses: "Dad is busy saving lives."

Yup, saving lives, like some kind of Superman. I take a bite of meat loaf, dry and bland like any other store-bought thing. But I know what'll happen if I don't eat it.

Mom asks me about school.

"It was like any other day."

"Getting close to graduation!" Mom grins, bringing a piece of food to her lips.

"Yeah." I pick at the food. Watch as even Mom pretends to like the food, that small piece going in her mouth and back out into the napkin. She does it when she thinks I'm not looking.

I look down the hall, the one leading upstairs, expecting to see something. I don't know what, but my eyes keep floating back to that focal point.

Meat loaf, eat another piece of meat loaf.

"Refill, hon?"

This is the kind of stuff that bothers anyone. I can get my own water. I can pick up after myself. I'm eighteen and she's treating me like I'm ten.

I get up from the table without saying a word.

As I do, my gaze floats back to the hall. I do a double take when I see it. It's not really, um... let me try to explain. It's still the hall, and the stairs, and the little side table thing my mom put there for decoration. But what I saw was something else. Kind of like a blotch where evening light should pass.

Course, I could have just said it was a shadow.

Shadows are one of the symptoms. But it's more than that. When I look, I feel something looking back. It's you, isn't it?

It's got to be you.

But I don't want my mom to suspect anything, so I refill my glass with water from the tap, which is nasty but I'm not really thinking straight right now, and I sit back down to eat.

A chill runs up my spine.

I chew, looking at Mom while I'm sure you, whatever you are, look on at this pathetic scene. It's really sad, you know? No dad and some depressed mom about to take enough pills to feel fucking fine.

I zip up the hoodie.

It's a different kind of cold. You'd think "cold spots" means what it sounds like, but it's kind of different. My mom isn't cold. But I am. My mom isn't shivering. But I am. My mom isn't being watched. But I am.

My inner stupid's excuse is that I'm just really, really tired. It's common to feel more sensitive to temperature when you're tired.

Yeah, but this is different.

This is the start.

It's not just broken vases and doors opening in the dark.

I focus on the meat loaf because it's all I can do to block out what's happening. You kind of just want to ignore things when they're so intense, you know? You just want it to go away.

Mom looks down the hall. "Son?"

Stop calling me "son." I have a name.

I don't say anything. Another chunk of dry-as-hell meat loaf. I point to my mouth: *Can't talk. Eating.*

Mom asks me about Becca. Oh, shit—Becca.

We were supposed to meet up before classes started today. We do that every day. I was supposed to meet her at the water fountain after school. She needed a ride home...

So you know how it feels to have lost track of time? That's totally how I feel. I'm kind of scared, not because Becca will be mad—*she will*—but because I *didn't even notice*. The entire day passed by and I didn't even notice.

Another shiver.

Never even thought about her all day.

"Son?"

"Huh?" I'm staring and stabbing at my plate. "Yeah?"

"I was asking about Becca. She hasn't been to the house lately. Are you sure you're all right?" Mom being Mom.

"Yeah, I'm fine, really." Another mouthful. Like she'd know the difference. Becca was here the other night. But Mom wasn't. This isn't anything new. It's a fact that I'm the one who got used to Mom and Dad being so fake about how our family works and they *didn't*. Years and it's all still the same.

It's beyond annoying.

I look down the hall, eyeing the area near the stairs, like it's impossible to look away.

Mom maybe says more, but next thing I know, I'm bringing my plate to the sink and Mom's saying from the table, "Just leave it in the sink."

The sponge in hand, I tell her, "I'm washing my own dishes, Mom. Like I do *every single day*."

Turning the faucet to warm, it feels so damn good, the hot water on my freezing cold hands. I let the water run through my fingers. Feels so good. The best. I close my eyes and get lost in the feeling until Mom shuts the faucet.

She has her hand on my forehead. "Oh my, you're freezing."

"Mom"—dropping the plate in the sink—"trust me, I'm fine." Mom follows after me, but I stop her. "Don't."

It's easy to see why she acts the way she does, but the last thing she needs from me is another problem.

"I've got a lot on my mind, Mom," I tell her. "If you want to help, give me a little space."

Mom knows that she's crossed a line.

I wipe my hands on the sides of the hoodie. "Okay?"

Mom sighs, starting on the dishes. "A shower might help, dear."

"Yeah." I start up the steps. To myself, I whisper, "It just might."

It would be cool if I could just get a little hot water, but no. It's always like this, and Dad should have gotten it fixed already, but maybe I don't complain enough because I have trouble caring. That's probably how a lot of stuff doesn't end up happening: everyone gets caught up in putting it off. Put it off long enough and you have to take cold showers. This is not going to be fun.

I mean, I can get *some* hot water.

Wait a minute. Let me try something.

Okay, see? Now there's hot water.

If you just turn the knobs left and right, hot and cold at once, you get hot water. Dammit. Okay, I think if I just give it a little more...

This should be on a test.

If I get it right, do I get some points?

I need as much as I can get, really.

How about extra credit?

Ah, there.

Under the shower, I can almost let the hot water knock me out. I hear that it's actually kind of common for people to fall asleep in the shower. I think the trick is to be ready to stick your arms out in front of you so you don't crack your skull on anything when you fall down.

So I do that. I mean, why not?

But dammit—I get maybe a minute of hot water and it's back to cold. That means I need to jump away from the shower stream. That means I have to mess around with the water again.

It's usually not this bad.

I bet I look like an idiot. I'm the idiot who got in the shower naked before I even checked to see if there's hot water.

I mess with both hot and cold but nothing works. The water is ice cold.

I think about shouting for Mom, but then I'd be proving that something's wrong, that I can't do this myself. I've done most things myself; why would I need Mom's help now?

I watch the water. Maybe if I just wait it out a moment it'll warm up. The pilot light might need to warm up, whatever the hell that means. I reach for my towel and wrap it around me.

It's probably funny to anyone not in this situation, seeing someone in the shower afraid of the water.

I test it again, sticking two fingers under the jet stream. Nope.

It's getting colder in the bathroom too. I can see my breath.

But it's not hard to push it aside, paying it no mind.

I probably wait a few minutes, which seem like forever, and then I try it again. The water isn't as cold this time, which is enough to lean in and try playing with the shower knobs again.

I toss the towel back on the rack.

Yeah, okay, so in the corner of my eye, I saw it.

I saw it from the moment I got in the shower. It was kind of like a shadow, a mass or blotch that you can barely see; but it's also not really either of those things. Behind the shower curtain, I thought of it as just something I made up, something I imagined.

But you see, my towel didn't make it back on the rack. It slipped off and hung in midair, forming a shape that waited for me to see it.

Chilled, you care most about getting warm. Getting warm is, like, the only thing you need when you're fucking freezing.

I'm shivering.

I look at my hands—they're shaking.

I'm really shivering.

This isn't cool.

I have trouble taking it all in. I see it happening but, you know, it's happening and I keep myself out of it. I'm like, "Oh, okay, cold spots now, great." But I'm not like, "Help me. I'm being haunted."

It just doesn't come off as totally true.

So then when I'm under the water with my eyes closed, I get a shower going. Not really hot water but not cold either. It feels good enough, and I stand there, letting the water run down my shoulders. I like the way it feels on my penis. I wouldn't ever mention it to anyone, I'm not a pervert, but it really does feel great, the warm temperature just dripping off the tip.

But it doesn't last long. I start to feel the water changing. Going to be cold as hell so I reach for the towel but it isn't there. I feel the air around where it should be and then—

Well, I still don't know how to really explain it. But it got my attention.

Eyes opening, this is what I see: my towel draped over an area of space, forming the shape of a human figure, but that isn't really right either. It looked off. I—I don't know how to explain it. The head was too small and the shoulders too broad. But it lasts only as long as it takes for me to see it. Then the towel falls and gets drenched in the water, and I'm stuck without a dry towel.

I stand there, in the shower, shivering for a long time.

I'm still not able to get warm.

I keep thinking, "So that's it, huh?"

But it carries its own weight. It isn't as simple as saying that I'll think about it later. I guess seeing it, seeing something that shouldn't be there, kind of changes the way I perceive everything else.

You know how it's never a problem saying you believe in something, but you really don't accept or believe it because it's never anything more than some random concept? That's kind of how this is. I've heard about it since I was a little kid—people being haunted by demons—and about how it's gotten to be so common that there's a whole industry around getting rid of them. But it all comes off as fake.

It doesn't seem real until it's staring right back at you.

And it's watching. It really is.

It's watching me right now.

It's always there, this feeling that I'm not alone.

It gets me thinking about everywhere I'm not looking. If I'm looking straight ahead, is it watching me from behind? If I'm looking everywhere for it, is it everywhere I'm not, watching?

That's the kind of stuff I think about.

And I sort of fixate on this, because it's a problem, a real problem. And I'm—I guess it's fine admitting it now—I'm getting a little worried.

Not afraid. I'm not, I swear.

But something, everything, is starting to feel different. Everything's changing and I'm not sure I understand what that means.

I'm still shivering, damn.

It takes getting under the blankets, napping for, like, an hour—or at least trying to nap—to stop shivering. I want to get online and read about people's experiences with demons, but I can't type. My fingers keep hitting the wrong keys. So yeah, I get under the covers, keeping the lights on even though it really doesn't matter if they're on or not, I hear the haunting continues no matter what. If it needs to, it'll zap the lights. But it feels, you know, reassuring.

I pull the sheets over my head, just enough so that it's kind of hard to breathe. I don't really sleep though. I just listen to the sound of my breathing, the sound of my voice, but I'm not talking. I'm not saying anything, which takes all the comfort out of being under the covers. I try not to think about anything, but that doesn't really work.

So I make a run for the other side of my room, secure my laptop, making sure it's plugged into a power source, and get back in bed.

Before I really do anything, I get a message.

Becca. I'm actually a little relieved. This takes me away from what's been happening since I got home.

"I'm like so angry at you right now you have no idea."

I read the message twice before replying, "I have some idea."

"Then you know that I had to walk home. Walk home."

"Becca, I'm... sorry?"

"How sincere, ugh."

Fess up, Hunter. Admit that this isn't going to just go away. And I'm not talking about Becca.

"Look I am sorry, okay? Lots going on. It's crazy."

Becca types and erases and types. I watch the cursor flicker. I look around the room. I don't see anything wrong, but the feeling is still there. I wish it would just lay off for a little bit—just a little fucking bit.

Becca's reply: "I'm still angry. I want you to know that I'm angry. Things are crazy yeah but that's not an excuse for leaving me at school."

Either I tell her or I don't. She isn't going away.

"It's not that."

"What? What are you talking about?"

"Something happened, okay?"

Becca types, "Oh my god..."

I know she's thinking I got with someone. That's how Becca thinks.

"No. No it's not that."

"Then WTF are you saying????"

Say it. Just fucking say it.

"I ran the gauntlet the other day and..."

"No..."

"And yeah. Things have been happening."

"You"—Becca's cursor flickers—"you've got to get this gone ASAP."

Just say that you know.

"I know."

"When did you go? Hunter, you're so stupid sometimes. Why would you go to Falter?"

She'll pick you apart if you talk about it.

Becca blasts me with messages, many of them about how stupid I am for running and that it's even worse because I didn't tell anyone.

Then I tell her I went on Friday.

"Last Friday???"

"Yeah."

That sends her over the edge. Well, she's already fallen over the edge, so it sends her over another edge, somewhere. The edge after all the other edges.

"Hunter. Hunter..."

"I know."

She's worried. I'm sort of worried too.

I think the lights in my room have dimmed.

Here comes Becca with all her so-called wisdom: "You have any idea what a demon is?"

It goes on for paragraphs. I think she copy-pasted them from other sites. I was going to do this anyway, so it works, but Becca's not going to let up now. But I needed to tell someone. I already feel better for having told someone. It's kind of like, "Why didn't you tell anyone?" But at the time, knowing what would happen, as in what's going to happen from this point on, it makes you dizzy. Like you want to faint. It'll be easier to just faint than having to see it all pop.

Becca tells me that demons aren't people. They never were people. They're unclean and dark masses. They look for hosts and try to make the host theirs. They populate the earth and maybe come from other planes of existence. No one knows about that part, but demons can take the shape of you or something else who's close to you.

Then she lists out the symptoms.

She lists out the symptoms, and I swear:

They happen right as I read them.

Becca says it's common to see doors opening and closing.

My door opens but no one's there.

It remains open until after she lists out "cold spots" and "noises."

My room gets really fucking cold, so cold that I can't really type, so I go and get another hoodie—I have a lot of hoodies—and put the hoodie on top of the hoodie I'm already wearing. Zip the fucker up, hood over my head. I feel like I've gained twenty pounds, everything's so tight and packed in, but I'm still going to get under the covers. I'm sweating but at least I'm not that cold.

There's sort of a banging noise, but I can't be sure where it's coming from.

"Hunter," Becca types.

I haven't been responding, whoops. "What?"

"Are you having trouble sleeping?"

"You know I've got insomnia," I reply.

"No, like, do you wake up at three A.M. every night?"

I think about this, but I don't really know. "I wake up a lot at night. That tossing and turning deal."

"Think about it. Three A.M. Are you waking up at three A.M.?"

Shit. I don't really know, but the fact that she's stressing it is getting me worried. I ask her, "Why?"

"Because..." but she doesn't finish.

"Don't get stuck in other tabs, Becca. Tell me."

"I'm reading about it. It's like three A.M. is significant. Dead time, they say."

I watch as my bedroom door closes. "Do you believe in this stuff?"

"In what, demons?"

"No, not demons, but where they really come from, the whole spiritual thing?"

"I do, Hunter. I have to."

"You don't have to do anything."

"You have to get this taken care of. We need to call an exorcist."

I feel dizzy. And cold. And I hear footsteps. Listen to how they seem to go from somewhere near my desk to the foot of my bed and then stop.

I think, "Okay, that's kind of scary."

But again, it's hard to take this as real. It's hard to take it as really happening to me.

I type out whatever comes to mind: "I'm just really tired all the time. Like more than usual. It's like I can't stop thinking. But I'm not really thinking about anything."

Becca doesn't reply for a long time. It shows that she's seen my messages, but she just doesn't reply.

I start searching for stuff on my own. There's a lot of stuff out there.

There's this one guy who had three demons competing for his approval. And another person—she's kind of hot—who is haunted and documenting the entire thing. She's already gotten a film option for it.

I watch an interview with her. She's pale as hell and keeps forgetting the questions they ask her. Her agent or whoever, the person with her, answers for her more often than she can. She looks like shit.

The agent says that the demon has already begun infestation. It's only a matter of days now. And the interviewer asks if they plan on full possession.

The woman speaks up: "It's too late for Suz now..."

Kind of weird how she says it too, there's a sort of monotone way about her voice.

I search for the term "infestation," and I get thousands of results. No way I'm going through all of them. I click on the one at the top, the wiki entry for the term. It goes on about how infestation is only the first in three "prominent" steps in the circle of demonic possession.

It's what's happening to me right now. The haunting part.

Symptoms: the cold spots, the footsteps, the...

What literally just happened: a whisper that sounds like my voice saying my name. Kind of like, if I can explain it, "...unterrrrrrr..." Where the "H" in my name is missing and the end of my name, the "r" runs out long. Like a growl, maybe.

I click around, ending up on a wiki overview of the entire circle.

Three main steps—the first is infestation, which I know. The next is oppression, which is where "the host is broken down" and it looks like a lot of crazy and really scary stuff happens. I start reading about it but—

"Hunter, I left a voice mail with Father James, the best in the entire parish." Becca goes to church. She goes to church every Sunday. I think she's gone to a bunch of exorcisms too. Religious people like exorcisms; apparently at the end, after the demon is gone, there's a feeling of unity in everyone there. I only know this because Becca tells me about it a lot. Never thought much of it until, you know, this started happening to me.

"That's good," I reply.

"What else are you experiencing?" Becca asks.

I skim the article about oppression, but maybe it's better to not read it. I scroll to the top of the wiki entry, reading the last word, "possession." Three big steps and the final is, like, *final*. It's all over by then.

The article says exorcizing the demon is best during stage one, but it is possible up until the end of stage two. But by stage three, the human body is so run-down that an exorcism, "though possible," ends with "the host in a critical state." Damn. How do you take that information?

I'm having a hard time even making sense of it.

Demons. They're all around us. Happens all the time.

But never to "you." Until it actually does.

And then you're...

I...

A cold shiver runs through my entire body.

"Hunter?"

I watch Becca blast me with more messages.

I sense it somewhere, watching, and there's nothing I can do about it.

In bed, I'm able to feel a little bit safe, but three A.M. will arrive, and even if I do sleep, I'll probably wake up.

Becca says, "Keep chatting with me. I'll stay up all night."

And she would and I tell her how much it means to me, but in fewer than a dozen messages, I think I fall asleep because everything goes blank and I don't wake up until it's morning.

I WAKE UP LATE. I'M GOING TO BE LATE FOR CLASS. BUT
maybe that's a good thing. I don't get out of bed, even though I feel
like shit, stinking of late-night sweats. First thing I think about is
how I was talking to Becca before, I guess, I fell asleep. Thing about
that is I don't really feel like I slept at all. I yawn and feel pressure on
my forehead—a headache coming on. I look at the laptop at my side,
on standby, and press a key to wake it up. I check our chat history.

After around one A.M., it's all Becca, mostly saying things like:

"Hunter?"

"Hunter what happened?"

"Hunter you're scaring me."

I scroll up to the last thing I said: "Something's in this room with
me."

I stare at what I said. I... don't know what to think.

Other messages include more about what happened in the shower, how my phone disappeared and ended up with my dad. The
whispers.

And I ask her at one point, "Do you really love me?"

Wow, that's just embarrassing.

Like, really?

Anyway, I look at what we talked about and feel strange because I don't remember any of it. I wonder if this is normal. Does this happen so soon? Another symptom?

Hey, but Becca came through as always. She's going to get this taken care of. This is what I'm talking about, I think. I mean, I despise her most of the time and I wish I could just break up with her and enjoy being single for the rest of my senior year, but that takes so much effort, you know?

I know I think about this a lot. But unlike most things, I don't find it any easier the more I think about it. I don't see it happening. She's there, and she's been at my side for as long as there could be anyone at my side. It helps when you've got someone who does everything for you.

But at the same time I feel bad, because that's also what my mom tries to do, smother me and stuff, and it's kind of like saying, *I'll let her but I won't let you.*

But feelings are like that. They are complicated.

I don't know what to feel about what's going on. That's a good example.

Another complicated situation is the shower situation.

No way I'm going back in there.

I'll brush my teeth at school.

I'll use the gym showers during lunch period or something.

I'll boycott that bathroom.

Guess I shouldn't—facing your fears is important, right?

But then I'm rushing to get to school on time because I've been absent a lot.

First period's already started when I pull into my parking space, but she's right there, sitting cross-legged on the sidewalk. I shut the engine off and walk over, sit next to her. She doesn't say anything. I don't say anything. When I try to hug her, she pushes me away.

"It's just..." Then she stands up. "The way you touch me, it's different. Like colder or whatever."

I guess it's to be expected. She was going to do this.

"Don't be mad, 'kay? Like, it's just my imagination but I... want us to keep some distance until we get this fixed."

I shrug. "Sure, whatever."

"You sound mad."

I'm not mad but I go with it, because I don't have to even say why I'd be mad, it's all laid out for me. "Maybe."

"Hunter..." She kneels next to me. "I just don't want to be near *that thing*. And if it's attached to you... if we, like, do anything... even a kiss, it's..."

It's hard to explain, I know.

"You know?"

But in this case, I'll pretend I don't. "Whatever."

Becca brought to her knees...

"I'm sorry, so sorry." She hugs me but there's nothing to it. Like she hugs me in a way where her arms wrap around me but there's no feeling.

I sit here until she leaves, swearing that nothing's changed.

But everything's going to change.

I think that long before I even realize.

Walking the halls is different today. But this isn't really surprising. Tell Becca and the whole world will know. That means I need to figure out how to explain it to Jon-Jon. That means I need to get ready to never hear the end of it from Blaire. That also means, ah, shit, Brad being Brad. He's going to be an asshole about it, I'm sure.

But the school, it changes shape. Becca wants to keep her distance and suddenly I walk the halls and people... I don't know all their names, but I think one girl's named Stephanie and that guy saying, "Hell yeah, man," is named Raul—I think we talked a little when we had summer school that one time back in... junior year? Anyway, word gets around, yeah. And real quick, like anything else.

Everyone at Meadows, including the teachers, knows that I ran the gauntlet and I succeeded.

Meaning, I'm haunted.

But that's kind of the point people are trying to prove when they decide to run. They face the darkness of that tunnel and they face the fears of Falter Kingdom. They run because, if they do, they'll be remembered for it.

I want to believe that I ran for the same reasons.

I've gone on about this, I think, but it's hard to do much of anything today. The halls are full of faces that congratulate me on what happened.

What did I do, I mean really?

From a sophomore who says he ran it too but lasted only, like, five minutes: "You rule."

From another senior from last period, Greg I think is his name: "Never thought you had it in you." I never knew that we knew each other, just saying.

From a freshman new to the high school game: "Like, what was it like? You've got it made if you run and nab a demon. Can you teach me, man?"

From a junior who plays on the Meadows varsity basketball team: "Motherfucker, now that's big!"

From another senior, but someone I don't recognize: "Yo, it's Chris. We know each other from somewhere, right?"

From Blaire, who I meet on the way to the restroom just because I couldn't stand sitting in class anymore: "I knew before even you knew. I want you to know that. Tell that demon to really mess you up, make it count."

"Blaire!" I try to talk to her, but yeah, trying and doing are two different things. She'll come around eventually. I'm not going to bother. This is what usually happens. Since grade school, one thing sets her off and it's a week of not talking and then, suddenly, it's back to normal.

I wish things would go back to normal.

From the start of the day, it goes on like this. It's overwhelming but also kind of cool. But then lunch happens, and that means Brad.

I'm standing in line for food, not making eye contact, while Matthew, a guy from last period, chats with me, but really it's that he's chatting to me, and I'm not really listening. I'm not even trying to hold a conversation. He's talking about music. A local scene or something where there's a lot of cool basement shows. He's talking to me about it like he's trying to sell me on going to one.

"We're still auditioning members and shit. Maybe you wanna...?"

Know how that goes. I nod but kind of stare at this space between the sign showing today's "specials" and the back of a person's head.

And then it's Brad's voice from the back of the line, getting closer with every word until he's slapping me across the shoulder. "Bro, I fucking knew it! You liar. JJ's going to have your balls chopped off for this. Dude!" But he's happier than I can be. Same as anyone else, I guess.

"I'll be all right," I tell him.

"Jetson had you figured. Bro, animals are better at sensing that shit."

I don't want to talk about this so here's my reply: "Yeah."

"So, like, is the 'd' with you right now?"

The "d." Only Brad would say that. Ugh. I tell him, "How the fuck am I supposed to know?"

Brad looks at the music kid. "Who the hell are you?"

I point at him. "He's recruiting band members for some band."

Brad gets in the kid's face—"Go recruit somewhere else!"—and there he goes, but Brad doesn't stop. "The demon's supposed to stick around, bro. You feeling disturbed?"

I turn to him. "Man," I say, "shut up."

"Bro, I don't know why you're so bummed. This is going to make you. For real, man, you're golden. Your yearbook bio is going to read 'Winner like a motherfucking sinner.'"

Not listening. The line is moving. Soon: chicken fingers.

"What about the symptoms?"

Even Brad's asking about the damn symptoms. "I'm a little annoyed by all the questions, if you want me to be absolutely real."

But today Brad's not going to be as big of an asshole. He actually listens to me. I know, it's crazy. "Fine man. You're tired. Bet you're really tired. I bet a lot on the fact that you're... really tired."

"Not going to be your next wager," I tell him.

"Cool, it's cool," Brad says. "We got to see JJ."

"First, chicken fingers."

"What's with the chicken fingers, bro? Every day it's those deep-fried strips. You get sick of those or are you eating for two now?" Brad laughs.

I look at him. He seriously stops, animal shot dead in his tracks. Totally dead mid-laugh, maybe even a little standoffish.

"Hey, bro, just playing."

"I'm just hungry, okay?"

"Cool, cool."

We wait in line, I get my order, and we make a beeline right for the exit. I don't look at anyone because everyone's busy looking at me. Today of all days, the name on people's tongues is "Hunter Warden."

I can't get past how Brad reacted a second ago. I wasn't that mad. I mean, I don't think I was that mad. He's just obnoxious, that's all. I can't stand him. But yeah, he didn't need to be afraid or something.

We're talking and people wave. Everyone's like "Hunter, yo!" and "So awesome" and "What was it like?" It's what almost everyone wants to know: What's it like? I mean, it's a common thing right?

People have demons and then they get rid of them.

I ask Brad and he says, "I dunno anyone that did. But there've been a bunch, yeah. Ask JJ. There's a tally going on."

Another group of people slow down to congratulate me. It's the thespian crew, and they're all like, "You got to be a part of our play before you get rid of it. We'd kill to get some authentic activity on-stage."

Yeah, yeah—everyone wants some part of it.

Brad says, "Bro, you're a celebrity."

I can't take it at face value. I'm too preoccupied with a previous thought. How many people have gotten a demon while running the gauntlet? But anyway...

I like but also hate what's happening. The reaction. It's great to see that doing something crazy gets a few likes, but at the same time, I'm like, *Do you really care?* I know maybe two in every twenty who I've talked to, but we don't have anything in common. Really we don't. I like the attention—would be kind of weird not to—but it's also sort of fake. Like Brad being Brad—it's really fake. If I really said anything to them other than "Thanks" and "It was wild," they'd shut off and not listen anymore.

It's all the effect, I guess, of being one of the, like, 5 percent who actually ran.

Jon-Jon looks up from his phone and actually stands up when he sees me. "Well, well, my demonic friend..."

"Hey, about that..." I start to apologize and explain why, but Jon-Jon won't have anything to do with it. It's like I'm the guy he's trying to, I don't know, swindle... that's a word, right, "swindle"? I'm the guy who's being swindled into some new scheme.

"Jetson sniffed it on you after sixty seconds," Jon-Jon says as he walks back to where he always sits, picking up a growling, sneering Jetson. He tries to get the dog to stop but gripping on to the dog only makes it worse. He tells two girls, "Walk him 'round back."

They comply.

He adds, "I'll text you when we're done." Jon-Jon turns and grins at me. "First piece of advice—stay away from animals. They go right for the jugular." Jon-Jon taps the side of his neck.

I ask Jon-Jon what I asked Brad.

"Well"—Jon-Jon looks back down at his phone—"it's a short list."

He holds out the phone and I almost don't want to take it. Jon-Jon rolls his eyes, stands up, and puts it in my right hand, points at the screen: "There's the list. Twelve names. It was eleven until I added your name."

There I am, number twelve.

"You keep a list?" I ask Jon-Jon.

He laughs, hands going through his stylized hair. "Like I told you before, I could have made a lot of money on you."

I sigh. "Well, I'm getting the exorcism."

Jon-Jon nods. "Naturally. When is it?"

Brad chimes in: "Bro, get it soon, but not before, you know, having some fun."

What fun?

Jon-Jon with that weird grin of his. "We'll plan a few... events. A few parties. We'll make a killing and everyone you know will treat you like a fucking rock star."

I don't know what to say.

"You like that?"

I guess I was staring at one of Jon-Jon's accessories, a ring on his index finger. Jon-Jon's decked out in a lot of fancy shit. I don't know where to get half of what he's got, but the guy's doing his best to be some character out of a detective flick. I've said it before, yeah, and I'll say it again—every single time I see the guy, he's trying to look the part of a gangbanger.

"Yeah," I say. Why the hell not?

That grin. "You'll make the dollar signs and buy yourself shit like this."

Brad says, "Bro, you got to throw a party."

"I'm not having anything at my house."

"Shit, man, really?" Brad shakes his head. "Then have it at mine!"

Jon-Jon likes what he's hearing. "It's a start."

I'm not so familiar with all this demon stuff, okay? I know what everyone knows, but none of the specifics. So when I tell them that it won't work, they ask why. I say something like, "It's back at home."

"What is back at home?" Jon-Jon asks.

"You know..."

Brad's like, "What? What is it, bro?"

"The demon."

Then there's laughter.

And then Jon-Jon talking down to me: "The demon's right here."

"Yeah, bro, the demon is attached to you, not some house."

Jon-Jon takes his phone back from me. "We're going to make a lot of money. And you owe me for that little fib."

I guess he's got me there. I owe him a lot. Not just talking about the money I haven't paid him back yet.

"There's a party," Jon-Jon tells me, "it's for the upper crust. Talking the heavy buyers, heavy hitters. It won't be just Meadows kids. You're going."

"I'm going," I say.

Brad asks, "Am I going?"

Jon-Jon clicks his tongue. "I think you'll sit that one out. Our friend here is going to help me out."

I want to ask him what he's got in mind, and I start, but he interrupts: "We'll talk about it later."

Reach for an excuse or something. Think, think, think: I don't want to be a part of whatever local ring Jon-Jon's got going on. Think...

"You know I'll have to bring Becca."

Jon-Jon looks at me straight-faced. "Don't let the ball and chain know."

I don't really know what to say. I'm speechless. And then the bell rings.

Brad says, "Bro, I... think we should go, know what I mean?"

Jon-Jon watches me.

Here's where I have to ask, just to get it out of the way, and in this moment, it's almost like I need to ask: "What's your deal?"

Jon-Jon blinks. "My deal?"

"Yeah, your deal."

"I deal drugs. I deal vice. I deal what needs to be dealt to survive."

"Why here, why to us?"

Jon-Jon clicks his tongue. "Every circle needs its line."

I want to be like, *What the hell does that mean?* but Brad grabs me by the arm and says, "Bro, seriously, quit this shit."

Jon-Jon says, "Listen to Brad. Brad isn't always stupid."

Brad's like, "Man... that's low."

But we got to go, he's right.

Jon-Jon says, "Remember—be fashionably late. Only way this works."

There's a party—one that I would never be invited to if I was just Hunter. But I ran into a tunnel and I'm being haunted by something insane, and probably becoming insane all at once... and people love me for it. I can feel myself tensing up. I can feel myself snapping. It's so damn strange to see.

I can feel everything changing. The weirdest part is that, besides what makes me feel... what I can't even really explain...

I'm starting to like it.

There's this one video that I keep going back to. It's only a few minutes long and it's actually not an unboxing video or whatever. I'm not sure what makes it any different from the others, but after, like, four million views, people seem to have made it something totally different. In the video, there's a person in a rabbit costume flailing around like an idiot. At first you think the person's drunk, but then you see them cough up blood, like a lot of blood, and then you are like, "Okay, I know what's happening." Lots of these videos online. Lots of people call it possession porn but I don't see anything pornographic about it. It's not even really shocking. It's sad. That's what it is. Sad.

The video is only a few minutes long but it doesn't really get good until the end, when the person holding the camera turns out to be the person in the costume. It doesn't make any sense, but sure enough, that's the case.

I've read some of the comments. One calls it an example of "late-stage possession," while another comment calls it "hot." The comment that caught my eye is the one that explains how this is "late stage, usually the last, when disembodiment is a common occurrence."

So this is the kind of stuff I have to look forward to?

I end up watching it twice every time I go back to it. Not sure if the site counts repeated viewings into the tally of views. If so, I'm probably responsible for, like, three hundred of those views.

I have to turn the volume up so that I don't hear the scratching sound coming from inside the wall.

Even with two hoodies on, it's still really, really cold in my room.

No, you never get used to it.

I found these gloves in my parents' room. It makes it kind of hard to type but at least I can type. Before, my fingers would have trouble hitting the right keys. Oh, and blowing into your hands and rubbing them together totally doesn't ever work. It's a waste of time. Hands don't get warm that way.

I watch the rabbit video a third time, mostly because the music drowns out the scratching noises really well.

It's kind of why I'm watching videos right now. I mean, I watch videos a lot. So what? But it's also really easy to stare at a screen and block everything else out around you.

I keep thinking about today at school and feeling strange because I know that they're all paying attention because of what happened, not because we actually know each other. I'm just a guy in the yearbook like everybody else. But it's like they'll remember me for being one of the people who ran and "won."

I don't think I've won anything.

This part isn't fun. The cold. The fact that stuff in my room is moving around. I'll find things where I didn't leave them. Kind of like what happened with my phone, but yeah, that hasn't happened again. Fingers crossed it won't.

But I'll leave, um, like a book on the bedside table and I'll wake up and then I'll be at school, putting stuff in my locker, and the book will be in my bag. It happened with a *Penthouse* I had too. Actually, that happens a lot.

Hmm. Well, okay. What else am I going to say?

Porn's around. It's there. I shouldn't feel weird about it. But yeah, I do. I don't want anyone to know that I actually own issues of *Penthouse*. That's, like, really trying... next level stuff because everything's online now.

People, yeah, they text me a lot. It's like I got into the college I wanted to get into and everyone's happy for me.

Okay, it happened again.

I don't dig this. It's the worst part so far.

The footsteps around my bed and the feeling that I'm being watched—both of those symptoms combined make this really horrible. Make me almost not want this to go on. Make me almost question why I was stupid enough to let this slide for a few days.

The footsteps are loud and near, so even when I listen to full-album streams, I still hear it. And it's not even just "hearing" it, you know?

It's like I can sense the footsteps.

They feel like shivers without the actual shivering.

Doesn't really make a lot of sense, I guess. But that's how it feels.

Hey, look, a new unboxing video for that new video game console. This is something to savor. I kind of don't want to watch it right away. I want to save it, open it up in a new tab and leave it there for later. Like there might not be another good unboxing video, I just want it to be there, something to look forward to, something that isn't more footsteps.

But the footsteps start walking toward the door.

The footsteps sound like they are coming from above.

The volume's as loud as it's going to go. My ears should be hurting. I think they are. Maybe. But I'm really focused on ignoring the symptoms.

Sure, I know, demon, you're there. But you can't keep me from living my life. And I have a life. There's a fuck-ton of videos I haven't viewed yet.

Like this one here that I couldn't care less about but I'm going to watch it because it's going to be really, really loud.

This haunting stuff is so annoying that it's making me deaf.

But okay, the video isn't any good.

And I'm kind of curious, actually. I crack my knuckles and think about it, think about if I've ever been up to the attic. I don't think so. I didn't even know the house had an attic. The footsteps are in twos, one-two, stop, one-two, stop... I pause the video and listen with my headphones still on.

Are you hearing this, Mom? Dad?

But no, they probably aren't, because they're not even home. Go figure.

The footsteps continue until they stop. And where do they stop...?

Takes a second to get it right. Put two and two together, or whatever the saying is. When I figure it out, I wish it wasn't true, or that I even paid any attention to it. The footsteps stop right above me, above my bed. I look up and it's like it's looking down at me from above. It's trying to get me to go up there, like a dare or something. What's in it for me? I mean, really?

Beyond everyone suddenly paying attention to me.

Beyond everything strange and confusing that's happening.

I want to still be me. Not that anyone around me would understand what that means. I just want to be able to sit in my room and watch videos. I want to be able to jerk off without the door opening and closing. I want to be able to take care of myself without my parents or Becca telling me what to do. I just want to be me, you know? And that might not be very cool or interesting, but then I kind of think that most people aren't really very interesting when you break them down. They do the same couple of things and that's it.

But yeah, I have to go up to the attic.

I have to because I just know I'll keep thinking about it, wondering about it, until I do. I mean, it's right above me. How am I going to sleep? I already have trouble with that, and now I've got something, like, I don't know, looming from above.

Next question then is if I should take my laptop with me. I feel like I should, but then I think about how bad it'll be on the battery if I unplug it for, like, the ten minutes it'll take me to check the attic only to end up plugging it back in. That's how battery life dies.

So then I think maybe the phone. Yeah, the phone because I'll need light up there. Attics probably don't have light, especially at night.

Okay, so I'm heading up there.

Living my life.

I am. I'm heading up there. I keep all the lights on in my room, in the hallway, every room. The house is lit up like Christmas but it's still dark in the attic. Random thought: Why is every ladder to every attic made of cheap, creaky wood? It creeps me out. I'll admit it. It does.

Living my life.

There's nothing in the attic.

I shine the light around and see nothing, shining it quick, like a once-over, because deep down I don't want to see anything. Worse is I don't want to feel anything. Still, I make each step and I end up in the attic.

Apparently I'm not alone.

There's something in here.

The creaky floorboards match the creaky ladder.

Each step echoes out, not like a usual echo but like there's something taking a step forward whenever I do. It's coming from behind me, the steps.

I won't look. I won't look. I won't look.

The area above my room, my bed, is right over there. But that's where Dad dumped all the boxes of old VHS tapes, movies, albums, and other junk no one uses anymore. Maybe I got it wrong. Maybe it's over there...

No, but then shining the light across the dark attic, I start to see things.

I'm going to say that it's my imagination messing with me, but that's a bunch of bullshit because it's obvious what it is.

I've seen it as a shape out of the corner of my eye, seen it in the shower. Now I see it standing not three or four steps away from me. I shine the light in that direction, thinking I'm fearless, but when I do that it's gone. It was a shape though. Some kind of dark mass.

Living my life.

I'm leaving the attic.

That's enough; there's nothing here.

No more, no fucking more.

I'm hating myself right now. I'm really hating the situation. It's messing with me, that's what it's doing. When I leave the attic, the lights are off in the house. All of them, every single one, except for the lights in my bedroom.

I mumble, "You're messing with me," because I don't want to shout it out. I read somewhere that demons feed on your energy. If it's negative, they feed on the negativity and turn it into their own counterattack.

I'm not up for a fight. I just want everything to stay the same. But I also like that things are different. I'm confused.

I stand in the hallway for a long time, gripping on to my phone.

It's just... well, I know something's going to happen if I walk into that room. The lights are on for a reason. In the dark of the hallway, I feel safer than being in my bedroom. But then again, I can't just not go into my room. It's *my* room. If I let it scare me out of my own room, then I'm not really living my life and everything's changed. My future involves going back into this room.

I know I will, but right now, it's just so hard to step inside.

I'm letting it all get to me. The symptoms are at their worst when I'm home alone. Being home alone is the most frightening thing imaginable.

I'll say it. Might as well say it.

That's the truth. Better to be lost in some big crowd or something than to be in a house all by yourself.

Then it makes a sound. Sort of a whisper, but I don't know what it's saying.

I'm not alone. I'm not alone in this house.

It's in my room, isn't it? I know it's in there, but I'm not going to lose it. I'm going inside like it's just another night.

Living my life.

First thing I notice when I finally stop being a wuss and I walk inside: it's not cold in my room anymore. The cold has shifted. Don't know where it is, but it's not here. Also, my laptop.

I'm kicking myself for it because I sort of knew it would happen. I mean, I remember thinking about taking it, like I subconsciously knew something would happen if I left it here. So it's sort of my fault. I knew it, I knew it, I knew it. But that doesn't change the fact that it's gone.

My laptop. Where the fuck?

Here's what I'm talking about when I say it's exhausting.

I have to look everywhere. There are so many places where the laptop could've gone. Then I think about the possibility that it broke the laptop or banished it into the ether of some kind of hell or something.

My life is in that laptop.

I can't live my life without it.

Just thinking about all of it...

Okay, I sit down on the bed. I take off one of the hoodies because I'm legit sweating now. I maybe close my eyes and maybe fall asleep.

Whenever I start searching for it, like a half hour's gone and I'm exactly the same: tired, just really tired. Also a little afraid. Definitely confused.

I keep thinking about what the demon might look like. I'm surprised that the more I think about it, trying to form an image out of the bits and pieces I've seen, I'm more interested than scared.

That's normal, right? I really don't know.

I want it to be normal.

I start from the basement. I hate the basement. Not because it's scary—it's really not—but because it's where my mom has all of her whatever-you-call-them, collectibles, I guess. They're so stupid but she loves collecting them. They are all figurines of different fantasy and science fiction characters. She doesn't read and she doesn't watch any movies, but she buys all the memorabilia. It's all in this basement. But not my laptop.

I check the kitchen; the dining room; the room some people call the "family room," which is dusty and has a very cool TV that we never use; every stupid closet (there are too many closets in this house); all the upstairs rooms, including the drawers jammed full of stuff I don't need to know about; and not the bathroom because fuck that bathroom.

I go back to my room. I go online via my phone and just kind of try to think about something else.

When something like this happens, it's not like all the movies where the character fights back and everything just falls into place. The laptop is missing and I'm out of options. I've looked everywhere and it's gone.

I start thinking about what to do next. Did I back up my files? Any very personal data on there that I don't want anyone, or anything, to know about? I think about stuff like that, and it makes me really, really tired.

I sit in bed and then I lie down in bed and then I'm remembering where I'm supposed to be. I'm remembering the party, Jon-Jon's thing, and I'm remembering something else.

I check my phone. There's still plenty of time.

Back out in the hallway, I keep the lights off because it's creepier that way. Actually, I keep them off because I'm too lazy to feel around for the light switch. I go down the stairs and out the door to the recycling bin shoved to the side of our garage.

I pick my laptop up—nope, not wasting any thought on how this could have happened or how I could just know where it was all of a sudden—and I look to see if it's been scratched, messed up, broken. It's like it just flew here.

Back in my room, it's cold again.

Where's my hoodie? There. Okay.

I open up the laptop. It looks like the screen froze, but no, actually it hasn't, hmm. Tap a few keys, click around, and the window starts playing a video I've never seen before. It's not something I was watching.

Two guys in a skit, both of them overreacting and freaking out over the simplest things. It's actually kind of funny.

I pause it a moment but the pause button isn't working.

The video's got a mind of its own.

The two guys in the video seem like great friends. I like this video. I hover over the subscribe button and figure, "Why not?"

They practice their secret handshake and it soon gets out of control, one of them being punched in the face. The punch goes right through the other, and that's where I definitely laugh out loud. Almost no one ever actually does that when they type "LOL," but in this case, I did. I didn't even need to type out the acronym.

When the video's done I try playing it again but it won't work.

Then the browser crashes.

"Fuck," I mumble, but thankfully my session is restored. But that tab's—go figure—missing. It all makes sense even though it also kind of doesn't. But right about now, I don't want to be alone with a demon in this house. I know it's early, not time for that party yet, but I think I'll just go to a coffee shop or get food somewhere.

I suddenly can't stand being here, alone with it.

I shiver and am confused by the fact that I can go from being curious to completely afraid just by the way everything feels around me. It's like... the weight of the air shifts, and at the same time my senses are all out of order. Not like I can feel what I taste, not that sort of thing. Um... it's more like I can just feel everything more, and my nerves are extra sensitive to anything that happens. My mind is racing too, and that's really why I want to leave.

It feels like something's sorting through my thoughts, rearranging them.

I want out. And I guess, this is my opportunity to do just that, even though I won't really know anyone at the party, and they really want to hang around me only so that they can know more about the demon. What do you tell people if you, yourself, don't even really know what it is?

Then I get scared again, by the lone thought that lingers like it was handed to me, dropped right in my brain:

You will.

JON-JON WASN'T JOKING ABOUT BEING FASHIONABLY late. When I walk in, everyone's already watching. They're like, "Hunter, holy shit, look at you!" And I'm like, "Yeah, you're looking right at me, what's up?" But that's the extent of most of our exchanges. The place is pretty swank for a high school party. But then Jon-Jon said it's more than that. A lot of people, yup. There's no way I'm going to be comfortable here. You know that it's a bad sign when the first thing you think about when getting to the party is how you desperately want to leave.

Ha, and I want to even more when Jon-Jon spots me.

"Hunter, excellent," he says, and gestures for me to sit with him at a table.

What is this place, I mean really? That's what I want to know. It's a ballroom but it's also a club. It's a club but it's in someone's house.

"Money, isn't it?" Jon-Jon asks me.

I'm like, *What?* But really I say, "Yeah."

What else is there to say?

I'm still thinking about the laptop thing that happened.

I'm thinking about that video.

I'm thinking about the way the two guys acted all genuine, cool, like longtime friends, and for some reason I think about it as fiction instead of it being something real. Those two guys are definitely real but I can't take it as that. They might as well be comic-book characters or something.

Jon-Jon tells me, "It's okay. This will be easy money for us. I'll get people to hang around us, and you just keep them entertained."

I snap at him, "What am I, a prostitute?"

Jon-Jon laughs. "That's good. Be just like that."

He leaves me at this table. I stare at empty plastic cups. I could really go for something to drink right about now.

I don't look around the room like I probably should. If I do, I'll end up making eye contact with people. I find it kind of strange that I'm overwhelmed by this kind of reaction, but at the same time, it's still very flattering.

I am flattered.

This is all fake flattery but it still hits. It still sticks.

And I want that attention like anyone else.

A guy named Jeff sits next to me. He has a drink for me. Now this really does feel like some kind of prostitution thing.

I'm getting really nervous.

"Be cool," Jeff says, "figured you wanted a drink."

"Thanks," I say, and then, "So what's this party all about?"

Jeff takes a sip from his cup and I sip from mine. The beer is kind of lukewarm and tastes watered down—bottom-of-the-keg beer.

"The guy that's hosting it is being all *Great Gatsby* about it."

"Huh?"

"Never read that book?"

I shake my head. "I guess not."

"He's into a girl that he can't get. They have a history. That's what this party's about."

"Oh," I reply. I'm really not doing well at this. I think it's because I'm being forced to hang out with people.

"Anyway," Jeff starts, "how's the demon thing going?"

"It's... going," I say in a surprisingly monotone way.

"Yeah"—he nods—"I had one too."

"You did?"

"Yup." Jeff takes another sip, which sends the signal for me to drink too. "But I didn't do that Falter thing. That's crazy. It's a cool legend, but no, I'm too claustrophobic for that."

"How'd you get it?"

Jeff shrugs. "I just got it one day. Woke up and everything had changed."

"Damn." I take a gulp of beer.

"Yeah, but I didn't wait around for symptoms to really kick in. I had the exorcism two days after I started being haunted."

Shit, makes me think about how long I've been holding that off.

"But I guess you're planning on going through with it?"

Through with what? Do I play dumb? Do I actually know what he means?

Jeff's like, "If you do, be ready, man. People do it but it's basically like saying, 'Yeah, I'm ready to die.' Some people think it'll make them transcendent. That there's life beyond the body."

"And what do you think?" I said that not because I want to know but because by asking that question, it'll cause Jeff to carry the conversation, and I don't have to say anything.

"Me? Well—"

But Jon-Jon interrupts us. Someone else, a girl named Melanie, wants to say hi to me.

Jeff shakes my hand. "Good luck with it. With all of it."

"Yeah, thanks," and then he's gone, back into the crowd of the party.

Melanie smiles a lot and giggles. She asks me more about running than the demon. She says it's really, really hot, a big turn-on, dangerous situations like that.

"Do you go to Meadows?" I ask her, just to change the conversation.

"I'm going next year."

Her hand is on my leg. Oh, man...

"Next... year?"

"I'm almost done with eighth grade," and then a giggle.

Oh god, hand off crotch now. Now, now, now. "Oh, cool," I say.

She giggles, drinks more, and I want to ask her how she got into the party, but there are always ways. It's not like there's anyone paying much attention.

Thankfully this train wreck doesn't last long.

Another group shows up and starts lecturing me on the ins and outs of demon hauntings. All sorts of stories about how demons can travel through time from one "unclean" place to the next. They talk about religious stuff, the fact that demons are from hell.

I don't know much about it, but they are talking and I don't have to really do anything but occasionally nod my head and say "Yeah."

So it's okay, but it's also so absurd that this is happening.

That this is all happening.

After the group finishes, Jon-Jon sits down and asks me in that way he always does: "How much money do you think you made in the last hour, on a scale of one to ten, ten being raking it in like a fiend? What do you think?"

It's hopefully enough to stop. I tell him, "Eight?"

Jon-Jon laughs, hands me a beer—not keg beer, but an actual bottle of IPA, some craft beer I don't know. "You're off the hook, friend."

I stare at him. "So... I made money then?"

Jon-Jon tells me, "You're off the hook. Debt paid. Next thing we do, you'll be raking it in. But I got to take everything I'd give you as repayment and handling fees."

"That's bullshit." Shouldn't have said it but...

It's okay because Jon-Jon just laughs it off. He must have made a lot. He's happy. I haven't really seen him like this before, all mellow and laughing, not playing up that crime lord crap.

I stand up and ask, "So I can go now?"

"Don't forget your beer." Jon-Jon hands me the bottle.

"Yeah, okay. Yeah," I say. I sound drunk even though I'm not.

So I walk around the room once, determined to leave now, totally not digging this atmosphere; everyone's trying so hard, you know? It just feels... wrong to be at a party like this, where everyone's all about being amazing and dressed up and trying to get laid. It's so much effort, for me it kind of takes it out of caring. I usually care. I'm here, aren't I? I cared enough to make sure that they still notice me. Now I feel empty.

I really feel empty.

I just want to...

Oh.

"Hey," I say, forgetting the concept of pickup lines.

Nikki Dillon walks up to me and hugs me like we're dear old friends.

Of course Nikki Dillon is at a party like this. Of course.

"Hunter, so great to see you!"

It sounds so genuine it makes me blush. Probably doesn't look like I'm blushing though, in this dark light, which is good, because I feel really nervous all of a sudden.

All of a sudden, it's happening, what I could never bring myself to doing... talking to Nikki Dillon. No secret to anyone and I really don't need to say it now, but here it goes: it's no secret that she's a longtime crush. I think she knows it as well, because in the past we've had too many encounters where we cross paths and exchange glances, do that thing that is everything about saying you're interested but without actually putting yourself out there.

We do that stuff.

But now it's finally happening.

She's talking to me, doing all the work, and I don't know what to say.

I don't have to say anything.

I grin and forget everything.

She tells me, "You're a hit."

"I'm a... what?" Too nervous, and stupid, to think.

"Everyone loves you." Nikki raises her eyebrows in a cute way as she brushes a strand of hair from her face. She does that so perfectly. I bet she practices these kinds of gestures in the mirror for hours.

"I guess so, yeah." I laugh all nervously.

Stupid, so stupid.

Then she says something that I think she lifted from a romance film, or a spy thriller, or maybe I'm just thinking that she did.

"We keep trading looks. I feel like it's time we trade numbers."

That was so smooth I can die happy now.

And then we do. I trade numbers with Nikki Dillon.

Nikki hugs me again, plants a kiss on my right cheek, and says, "Call me."

This party's not so bad after all. But it's peaked, it's over.

I'm glad I'm here. I'm glad I showed up. I'm not going to think about how she's into me maybe just because of the demon.

She's always liked me.

That's what I choose to believe.

But I get the hell out of the room, posthaste. It's like if I stay there, everything will be second-guessed and ruined.

In the back of my mind, I'm thinking, "When is it time to trade photos of ourselves naked?" Then I hate myself for being an asshole. That's something Brad would do.

I drive around aimlessly, up and down the neighborhood streets. I'm actually just happy, feeling like everything is perfect. Like life can be the shit sometimes.

I can't believe it.

I drive for what feels like hours until she texts me.

She texts *me*.

I pull into the driveway, seeing that Dad's home. I stay in the car and text her back. We have an entire conversation in text, with me sitting in the car, avoiding the fact that I'll have to go back inside. I'll have to face it. And every night it surprises me with something worse. I don't want it to ruin this feeling.

So I think about this instead.

Reread every single line of the conversation we had because I can't really believe it.

"Hey H."

"Glad I bumped into you tonight."

"Me too." Winking smiley.

"You still there?"

"Left after the keg was tapped."

"You up for something this weekend?"

"I'm up for anything." Heart emoji.

"You up for something *tomorrow* night? 7ish?"

"Mmhmm. Sounds good."

"Sounds great."

"Sounds perfect."

Here's where I respond with a stupid regular smiley.

"Buh-bye babes."

"Night!"

Could have done without the exclamation point. Also, I don't like that I was the last to reply. But still. There it is—proof that everything's changed. Proof that it happened.

Please be enough proof to steel my mood until I fall asleep tonight.

I look up at my window and see that the lights are on. I turned them off when I left. Beautiful. But you know who's beautiful?

Nikki.

I have a date with Nikki.

Friday night.

"Mr. Warden to the principal's office." The way Halverson's office goon says it, I don't know, it just makes it sting so much worse, you know? I was in second period doing my best to just be myself, but since word got out about running and the demon on my back, I can't focus on anything else. I feel like all eyes are forever on me, so I have to put up appearances like this is a twenty-four-hour reality TV show. That's enough pressure, especially when you kind of want everyone to keep watching, but then someone gets on the PA and says those things. If you think being dropped off at school by your parents is embarrassing, being called to the principal's office like some sixth grader is worse. I can't look people in the eye on the walk to the office.

But then everyone's buzzing about what Halverson might want with me. I hear in the halls their whispers, gossip already starting.

There's talk about me being expelled.

For running the gauntlet? Really?

I hope not. I also don't care. But then I remember what happens to people who are expelled, especially this late in the school year. Starting over at a new school for, like, a few weeks or something is like being sent to prison. If that happens, I'm finished. Like totally done. I won't be able to go on.

Think about something else.

Think about something else.

I have nothing in common with anybody but I still want them to like me, especially now that it's all like this. They're all watching.

That's a scary sentence: They're all watching.

Almost scarier than having to go home and face a demon that's getting worse with each day.

Last night... yeah, I'm not thinking about it.

I'll just repeat the excuse I'll give Mom if she asks: *I decided to rearrange my room. It was getting boring and dull the way it was.* Things didn't move, exactly. It's just that things went missing and I wanted to keep all the things I really need close to my bed, like I'll be able to grab the thing before it tries to nab it. I kept my laptop in my arms when I slept.

It's getting kind of ridiculous.

The office goons make me wait like they didn't just announce my name over the PA for the whole school to hear. Rush me in here but then I have to wait.

I shiver and start worrying that it'll start messing with me during the day. Then again, is "messing" the right word for this? Haunting is a form of hazing, right? I guess so. Not like I'll ask anyone for clarification.

That's just asking for more attention.

Maybe I want more attention.

"Mr. Warden—"

Doesn't sound like she's asking.

"If you'll step right this way..."

Yeah.

I walk into Halverson's office. The place is cramped, full of books, stacks and stacks of books everywhere. Halverson's this kind of pudgy guy, probably in his late forties. He's got bags under his eyes. Eyes are bloodshot too.

Bet he doesn't sleep well either.

"Hunter"—he gestures toward the seat facing the desk—"have a seat."

"Yeah," I say because I have nothing else to say.

I sit down and wait.

Halverson looks at something on his computer—click of the mouse, typing something out—and then he turns his attention to me. "How are you on this fine day?"

It's a fine day? I say, "Fine. I'm fine."

"Good, good." Halverson nods his head.

"Yeah," I say, nodding my head too. I don't mean to, but when you watch someone nod his head kind of like a bird, you end up doing the same thing. Sort of like how if you watch someone throw up, you get nauseated too.

"I called you into my office today because, well... frankly we're concerned."

I'm concerned too. I don't say anything though.

"We have received reports about a Falter Kingdom incident." Halverson goes back to his computer, typing something out, still talking to me though. "Frankly, I have heard everything there is to be heard about what happens in that tunnel."

"Yeah," I say. I'm actually agreeing. Falter's got a whole lot going for it. I think.

"I obviously don't condone what kids your age do there, as it's quite dangerous."

That's also kind of the point.

"Frankly," Halverson says, turning back to me, "more than a couple parents of students attending Meadows have called in, concerned with, well, you, Hunter." Halverson leans forward. "I want you to be honest with me. Are you experiencing symptoms of a haunting?"

Frankly, I am. Instead I say, "Yeah."

He leans back in his chair, folding his hands. "Well, that's unfortunate."

What's unfortunate? I mean, what's unfortunate besides what I already know?

"Frankly, my hands are tied, Hunter. You're a good kid, but I must operate in accordance with the school board's guidelines. Due to your condition, you are deemed ill and unfit to attend school."

I'm nodding. I'm agreeing with him. "Yeah."

"Don't take this harshly, because I am more concerned with your well-being. Have you"—he searches for the right words—"seen a specialist yet?"

I shake my head. "Not yet."

"Then as of now, there's nothing else I can do."

"Yeah."

"I'm going to have to suspend you until you get checked."

"Yeah."

"Frankly, I don't want to do this, but as principal of this school, I am forced to act outside of compassion. You do understand, right, Hunter?"

I nod. "Yeah."

"You're free to return the moment you are seen by a specialist."

Someone walks in, one of those rent-a-cops, the guys who linger around like guards with no weapons around the school.

I stand up and walk over to the guy.

"Oh," Halverson calls out, "I'll need a note from the priest. Proof, understand?"

I nod. "Yeah."

Halverson leans forward, resting his elbows on the edge of the desk. "Don't take this personally, Hunter. And please get checked out now. Today. There are plenty of places that will help you. Do you need help finding one?"

I shake my head. "No."

"Are you *sure*?" The way he stresses "sure" seems so strange, like he doesn't have confidence in me.

"Yeah. I'm sure."

"Well, all right then." Halverson gestures to the guy. "Ben will walk you to your car. I know you're capable of doing that on your own but, frankly, it's a formality."

"Yeah," I say.

And we walk out into the hall.

Halverson probably said something else but I'm done, no longer listening.

I don't know how to feel about the whole thing. I guess it should be bothering me but it still doesn't feel real.

And I'm kind of excited about how people will see this. It's going to be good. Suspended for demonic possession. Everyone will be talking about it. About me.

And then I'm thinking about Nikki. My date with Nikki. It's hard to take in just how bad it is to be suspended this late in my senior year when everything else is going so great.

Well, you know, outside of the whole demon thing.

Ben the rent-a-cop guy doesn't say anything to me. He walks behind me and seems kind of afraid.

I bet I could lunge at him, pretending to punch him, and he'd wince. That's also kind of cool, I have to admit: you know, how there's this sense of mystery and almost fear surrounding me. The older people are the ones worried. Everyone else finds it exciting.

And me?

I think I've mentioned it way too much. I go back and forth on the whole thing. But Halverson is definitely right.

I need to get checked.

How the hell do I do that? I don't know...

Maybe I actually do need help.

I sit in my car until Ben the rent-a-cop guy leaves.

It's not even noon yet. I can't go back to school. I'm not sure I want to go back home. Then I daydream about how word's getting around. Soon my phone's going to blow up with text messages and calls.

Everyone will be buzzing about me.

And Nikki, she'll be one of them. Imagining Nikki talking to her circle of friends, all impressed with what's happened. Forget what Brad and Jon-Jon and Becca and Blaire think. They can think what they want. I'm sure I'll get word from them. But Nikki, I bet she's really into what's happening.

Maybe turned on.

I can't help it. It's so awesome to think that I'm the one being talked about, all the way up to the "it" people, though I don't totally know what that means. I've always had some names in mind, the people you know of but never really talk to. Those kinds of people. They are talking about me, maybe the way I'm thinking about them right now. Their talk is all curious and wondering, being like, "Hunter's possessed. He's been kicked out of Meadows because of it!"

But I guess I'll go home.

I'm feeling really tired all of a sudden.

I have no idea how to go about this stuff. Know what that means. I need to call Becca. It's kind of strange to think that as I talk to Becca, I'll be thinking of Nikki. Of course, I'm also sort of worried about Becca finding out.

But I also don't care.

You don't just say no to Nikki Dillon.

I drive home slowly, taking detours and back roads, listening to nothing, deep in thought about my date at the end of the week. You do what you need to do to shut out all the bad. Feels kind of like it's going to take a turn for the worse, you know?

I know, but I also don't want to think about it. I shut that out and replace it with a well-constructed fantasy, I'll call it practice, where Nikki and I go on a date and really hit it off, if you know what I mean.

I'm sure anyone would.

When you're human, you got to just, like, know that you're going to have these kinds of thoughts.

I'm human. And...

I wonder what it really is. Demon, sure—but where does it come from?

If I ever get a chance to, like, flat-out ask it a question, that'll be the first one, right at the top of the list.

Where do you come from?

I read somewhere that symptoms shouldn't start until nightfall. I call bullshit on that because it's one P.M. and I'm hungry and locked in my room. The doorknob won't turn and, yes, it's unlocked.

It's messing with me and getting stronger and bolder and meaner every day. I send everything above as a text message to Becca, who immediately replies with this exclamation point, three of them actually, and then:

"I heard! That's like such bullshit!"

Duh. I text back, "I'm home with it."

"Are you okay?"

"See previous message."

"Wait, like, you're stuck in your room?"

"Yeah," and I add, "It's cold in here."

Becca texts back, "We need you to meet someone today."

"Ditch school and help me. I'm clueless with this shit."

It's true. I can't believe it, but yeah, I really do need Becca's help. But everything I just said feels so fake, and wrong, and nothing at all sincere. But it's there, so that's something.

"I'll leave at lunch period."

Good. I want to text back, "I'll be stuck in a room haunted by some demon, waiting for you," but instead I text, "Thanks." And again with the "Love you."

We both text the same two words to each other.

It feels as strange as ever.

But Becca doesn't ask about the party the other night. She doesn't even act suspicious. Maybe she's caught wind of the Nikki thing but she won't say anything about it. I think it has a lot to do with how she's reacted to what's been happening. For being someone so close to me, she shouldn't have done that, keeping her distance and stuff. But then she's also skipping school and she never skips school, so...

I'm confused. What else is new?

I know you're there, yeah.

I can sense it nearby, but it's weird because I can't get a make on where it's standing. It feels like it's everywhere around me. But it's also not doing anything. It just wants to keep me here, in this room.

Like if I left the room I'd do something stupid.

I look up from my phone and shout, "Are you protecting me or some shit?"

I hear a creaking coming from the floorboards, kind of like how the floorboards creak when I shift my weight from one leg to the other. A low creak, and then there's nothing.

I get a text from Brad. I don't read it.

It's probably just a bunch of "Bro, you got suspended?! That's fucking wild! You the man!" kind of stuff.

I try the door, still not budging.

I sit on my bed, laptop open, and I start scrolling through blog posts and other stuff. Just wasting time.

Blaire texts me, "Halverson's a douche."

I text back, "Yup. Douching it up."

Blaire replies, "You'll be okay."

"Yeah, I think so."

"Talked to Becca. She's on her way."

I read that text again and again. Something about it...how it makes me picture everyone I know soaking in the drama that's probably happening, and they're all running around, exaggerating their concern, so that they also get some attention. That's probably happening. And then I think of Nikki, picture her sitting at a table in the cafeteria, watching as Becca and Blaire make a scene. Everyone knows what's going on.

And here I am, freezing and stuck in my room.

I get a call. When I look, it's a number I don't recognize.

Well then, ignore.

But the number keeps calling. I put my phone on silent. I go online and focus on something else.

This is all getting so overwhelming.

Becca messages me online, telling me that I'm not answering her texts.

"Yeah, getting overwhelmed by things."

"Gotcha," she types, "on my way. Father James is cutting us like a huge break. I think he's going to be the one that sees you."

"Great," and then I add, "Yeah, that's really great."

Becca asks, "Still locked in?"

"Yup," I type back. Then I add, "Might have to leave via the window."

"That's like so fucked up," she says.

"It is, yeah. I don't understand what's going on."

"But we do know what's going on though."

I try to make sense of it, put it in words that would make sense to her: "No, I know, I mean... well, it's just like everything people said about being haunted but it's also very different."

Becca doesn't type anything.

"Let me try to explain." But the explanation doesn't come. I type out something that doesn't make sense so I delete it. I'm at a loss. Then I ask, "Who's driving you?"

Her reply: "Jon-Jon."

I should have known. I mean, it's not a bad thing, I guess.

I type back, "Cool."

She knows me well enough to know that when I reply "Cool" it means the opposite of cool. She knows my mannerisms but she doesn't know how I'm really feeling. And that's what makes me think of Nikki as the real reason I'm going to keep doing this. I'll break up with Becca when this is all over and Nikki and I are together.

Becca types back, "We're heading out now. Be there soon, like ten minutes."

"Okay," I reply.

I lean back in bed, laptop on my stomach, hands in my pockets to keep them sort of warm.

I wait—wait for something to happen.

I look at my phone next to me; the screen's lit up, people reacting. People are always reacting.

If anyone's confused by this, just think of how confusing it is for me. I'm full of mixed emotions. I want it gone but I also know that none of the attention would be there if it weren't for the demon.

I think, "You are the reason I'll be remembered."

I expect something to happen, but nothing does.

I stare at the screen, watching the social media feed scroll with the latest from hundreds of people I follow.

Nothing happens.

I start to count each breath I see.

Then there's the sound of someone messaging me.

I blink, realizing I hadn't blinked in a good minute. Hands out of the pockets, I lean forward and read the message.

"They are outside."

I look at the name of the sender but the name is mine. It's my name.

I don't know what to say, so I say, "Thanks."

"The door is open."

I read the message and then look at the door, wander over and give the doorknob a tap, then a slight jostle.

It's open.

I look over at the laptop, breathing out a sigh that I see as a little plume, a cloud in front of my face.

When I look back the sender appears as "offline."

I don't have time to react though because whatever that was, it was right. They are outside. Jon-Jon's car parked behind mine, Becca looking up at my bedroom window, waving.

I look at the phone and see a few missed calls.

Oh yeah, it's on silent.

I switch the ringer back on, notice over two dozen missed calls and more than a handful of text messages. I run downstairs, taking along my laptop and the power cord too, because, well, I've learned my lesson.

At the front door, I shove the laptop in my book bag and I leave the house without looking. I don't get a real chance to think about what happened until I'm sitting in one of the back pews of the church, waiting to be seen.

I put all the pieces together. And then it sort of makes sense, but not really. I was messaging myself?

Was that you?

JON-JON TELLS ME THAT THE EXORCISM IS THE REAL
payoff. At first I don't really follow. Sure enough he explains that
first there are a series of meetings.

"Only, like, three," Becca corrects him.

Jon-Jon brushes the comment aside. "Yes, three, but you see, there
will be time—plenty of time, in fact—to milk this for some serious
money. The payoff will be the exorcism."

This bothers me. Jon-Jon isn't a friend. He's a businessman. He
lives well as long as he makes money off others. He sells, sure, but
he's also got the betting thing going on. And I'm becoming, I think,
his main prize.

"Why are you here?" I ask him, just because.

Jon-Jon with another one of his questions: "How confused are
you, on a scale of one to ten, ten being amnesiac?"

I don't answer.

Becca doesn't like Jon-Jon either and tells him to leave the church.
"This is a spiritual place, like, take it outside!"

Jon-Jon raises his arms in defeat. "Fair enough. I'll be in the car."
To me he says, "Big money, think 'big money.'"

When he's gone, I ask Becca, "Why did you bring him? Of, you know, everyone you could have asked for a ride, you chose that guy..."

Becca's embarrassed. She's staring at her phone, compulsively refreshing her social media feed. "He asked me, okay? And I thought, 'Emergency,' so I just said okay instead of looking for someone else."

I don't want to even look at my phone. Forget that it's there.

Everything's exhausting. Everything's also very, very good... but I won't mention that. Not now. Not here.

We wait in the last pew for, like, an hour, but not really, it just felt like that long, before a priest who isn't Father James introduces himself as Father Albert, greets us and apologizes for the wait.

"Okay," I say.

Becca leads the way. "Thank you for seeing us on such short notice!"

Father Albert sort of bows. "My pleasure, my pleasure."

On the path to becoming a priest or a deacon or a nun or a monk—spiritual people—I guess you learn how to have a crap-ton of manners. Like, this Father Albert is incredibly nice. Like, too nice. So nice it makes something deep inside me angry. It feels insincere. No way Father Albert is really this glad to see us. I've got a demon attached to me; why would he be "delighted to see us"? Wait, did he even say that? Maybe I made it up.

He's excruciating though.

Look at the way he walks. All pious and calm, like every day lasts forever and there's nothing more important than seeing and speaking to Becca and me.

Father Albert's office is really neat and tidy. Of course it's neat and tidy. Why wouldn't it be? Look at the guy.

Becca does all the explaining.

Father Albert folds his hands and listens all calm and contently.

He's really bothering me. I mean, yeah...

Ugh. I just can't stand it. People like this.

He can't be serious.

Father Albert apologizes for a second time. "Unfortunately, Father James will be unable to perform the exorcism. Yet I am able to accommodate you and happy to complete the task."

Becca smiles. "That's great. I understand."

Father Albert asks me a series of questions, starting with "How do you feel right at this moment?"

I should be honest, right? I should just say what's on my mind. Yeah.

Well, here it goes: "I'm kind of annoyed. Annoyed at you, at this whole thing."

Becca's like, *Hunter, the fuck?* But she doesn't say that; she just looks at me in a way that says something along those lines.

Father Albert nods. He's so understanding.

I say, "And see, that makes me even more annoyed."

Father Albert says, "That's fine. Next question I want to ask: Has the unclean spirit contacted you directly?"

Unclean spirit? I think about this one... but then I go with: "I don't think so. I mean, I've heard things. Whispers. My name, maybe."

"Mm-hmm, mm-hmm—this is quite normal."

But then I remember the messages. I kind of stop myself, second-guessing it, but then—why the hell not?—I tell him. I tell him about the messages.

"That does sound like direct contact." Father Albert starts writing in a Moleskine journal.

Becca looks freaked out. "What does that mean? Like, what does it mean for us, I mean Hunter, if the demon's contacted him, like, directly?"

Father Albert takes her question like target practice. "It implies that the unclean spirit—we prefer not to label them 'demons'—is increasing in presence."

"Like, getting more powerful?" Becca says, all confused.

Father Albert nods, not even looking at us while he writes in that stupid journal. "That is correct. The unclean spirit will begin breaking down Hunter."

I'm already broken down, what else can happen?

Becca, she doesn't have to try so hard. Her face is flush red and she's biting her nails, "Oh no, oh no. That means... what does that mean?"

Father Albert is Mr. Cool. "Calm down, my dear. There is still plenty of time. Naturally, the parish encourages a timely exorcism. This isn't true in Hunter's case. But, well, one more question, Hunter—do you feel like you're being watched at all times?"

I shake my head. "No, only when I'm home alone."

"In a certain room, or everywhere?"

"Mostly, um, my bedroom."

Father Albert goes back to writing.

We sit there in silence, a real waste of time.

"I am going to expedite the next meeting. From here, I will visit your homestead and bless it."

Becca again, all nervous: "And then what?"

"After blessing the house, we will arrange to have an evocation, or summoning. I will act as lead but Father Andrew will accompany."

"Evocation..." I say.

"Yes, it can be an unpleasant term, but that's how Father Andrew is recognized in the parish. It is quite clear, Hunter, that you have attracted a spirit that doesn't wish to linger. Some are more aggressive than others. By the looks of it, you attracted an unclean spirit that seeks to possess you as quickly as it can. Now"—Father Albert waves a finger—"do not attempt to contact the spirit. You must ignore its advances."

"Yeah," I say, having trouble hiding how pissed off I am at this whole thing, "I've been doing that. Been wearing, like, two hoodies and gloves and all kinds of shit, basically staying in bed, but I'm 'ignoring' it."

"Excellent." Father Albert doesn't even seem to notice how angry I am. "The spirit will soon commence with expending more energy."

Before Becca can even ask, Father Albert has an explanation.

"The spirit will become more aggressive. We must push up the exorcism to a week from today."

I lean forward. "So that's like..."

"Next Wednesday."

Becca's happy all of a sudden. "Oh wow, that's, like, perfect!"

Is it? I don't know why but I feel weirded out by how soon it is. And also how Father Albert's all casual about something that's so serious. I don't know if I can trust him. And even after we shake hands and go back to the car, Becca filling in Jon-Jon with the details, I still can't shake the feeling that I can't trust him.

I realize that it's because of the one thing he said, the one thing he saved for me, whispering it in my ear when we shook hands:

"Your anger isn't your own. Be vigilant with your emotions. You are the only one capable of understanding the difference between direct feeling and conjured, manipulated senses."

I'm angry because he told me that and then just let me go. I didn't get to ask why or what he meant.

Jon-Jon looks at me in the rearview mirror. "Why are you so moody? Everything's rolling well."

I don't say anything. I don't trust Father Albert.

I don't like that I might not be acting like myself. I don't like the idea he put in my head that this anger, and pretty much anything that happens, can be something doubtful. He's making me doubt everything now.

What is real and what isn't?

Are these emotions the demon's manipulations?

Becca and Jon-Jon are getting along all of a sudden.

What the hell just happened? Not a half hour ago, Becca loathed the guy. Okay, maybe not loathed, but she definitely felt the same way about him that I do. Now she's laughing and making plans. I hear the words "haunter party" and it's Jon-Jon's wise idea to make more money off me. It's also Becca's idea because she wants to probably piggyback on all the popularity I'm experiencing.

Jon-Jon says, "Forget what we had planned with Brad, we've got to have it at Hunter's place."

"No," I tell them, "no fucking way, guys."

But I've been vetoed. Some friends I've got.

The entire car ride back to my place, I can't concentrate on what

Becca or Jon-Jon talk about. All I know is by the time I'm alone again in my house, there's a party and there's a price. There's a bunch of people involved, and I'm losing whatever little faith I had in these friends of mine.

I've lost faith in being sure of anything.

I say I want to fit in, but why do I just want to curl up in bed and forget that all of this is happening. But my bed is in that room, and you're there. I know you are...

I go into the family room, turn on the TV, and watch some sit-com. I grab one of the blankets left draped on the side of the couch. I fall asleep here, I think. Either way time passes. When I wake up it's night and Mom's there, hovering over me all creepily. She says she's made dinner and that she's sorry she hasn't been around.

Yeah, what else is new? At least I can count on my parents being clueless 100 percent of the time.

I think about ripping up the note Father Albert gave me. It's not even a thing until I see it gripped in my hands. This one note is a big deal. If I don't have it, I don't go back to school. If I don't have it, I'm free. Still, I think about the possibilities. Could I? Should I? I'm not. There's no way; I won't. I'll just put it back in my pocket. It'll never leave my side. Just like my laptop.

But for one flicker of an instant, I feel like I actually still have complete control over what's happening. And then I go back to watching TV and listening to my mom try to do everything for me.

This is the night that proves a real turning point. It's the night that puts the "m" in "man," or whatever that means. I'm just trying to get excited about the date. I'm just trying to feel something other than nothing. I'm trying to get out of bed, because I'm still wrapped in these bedsheets and I'm supposed to be in that shower, getting ready. That's the problem though. I don't want to step inside that bathroom. Not after what happened.

But I'll have to. I know I will. I mean, I could use my parents' bathroom. Yeah, I could do that. But that'll mean having to talk to Mom. It'll mean she'll find out somehow. She'll find out about the date. And then she'll try to help, which won't help at all.

It'll just make things worse.

So it's either the bathroom or getting Mom involved.

Guess there's no choice. Well, I could stay in bed. I could blow off the date.

I could, but I'll have to kill myself if I did. Leave Nikki Dillon hanging? How would I be able to live with myself? Actually, I don't even want to think about it. Okay, out of bed. Got to get out of bed. One foot after the other, walk into the stupid bathroom and get this over with.

I guess I'm just annoyed that I'm not actually excited. I should be nervous but I'm not. Probably a good thing, sure, but I kind of feel like something like this should really have me on edge. I should be thinking of all sorts of things I'll say, things we'll do, and pretty much be at that point where I'm creating all kinds of backup scenarios if the typical dinner and then a show falls through. There's a lot that can go wrong tonight but I'm not even thinking about it. See, that's what kind of makes me feel strange.

I really do feel like it's true: I'm not myself.

Something about how I feel...

It feels like any other night.

It feels like I'm being forced into this date.

Big moments like these ruined because of not feeling into it, not really being myself... now that is the biggest bummer.

At the bathroom door, I breathe in and then out.

Kind of have to just say: *Fuck it. Do it.*

Open the door and it's as cold as my bedroom, maybe a little colder. Showering when it's cold, ugh. This is going to suck. But this time I keep my clothes on until I get the hot water running well.

It's easier tonight, but I'm not going to count on it. Not even going to think about it. Anything can go wrong in a single instant.

In the shower, the water's warm the entire time. I start to calm down, maybe getting a little excited about the date, but then when I dry my hair, I see that my hair spray is gone.

And it's always where I leave it.

I don't know what to do except to not acknowledge it, so I sit down to use the toilet and think about ways to make my hair not puffy and stupid looking without hair spray. It's all I've ever used so I'm kind of lost.

Here's what really messes with me. The hair spray, sure, okay, it's missing; I'll figure something out. But this...

I finish and reach for toilet paper and there's nothing left. Like one little sliver hanging to the cardboard roll. No one uses this damn bathroom but me and I replaced the thing last time I used it.

I know it's you.

I know it. It has to be, and it's trying to ruin everything.

I'm not going to say what I did to make do with the fact that there was no toilet paper, but I'll say that it wasn't pretty and that towel is now in the garbage outside. I go back to my room to get dressed.

Good dress shirt and these designer-style jeans, the kind of jeans that are faded gray, yeah. They're simple but I think I look good in them.

This is me actually trying.

I go back into the bathroom, looking for something else to use in my hair, go through the cabinets—random cold medicine and old prescription pills, cleaning products—but then I see a thing of cologne I've never seen before. I don't remember buying this. Did I get it as a gift? Push that thought aside until I find a bottle of hair gel that I definitely didn't buy.

Yeah, so maybe my reaction wasn't right, especially if today—of all days—I wanted to just ignore the symptoms and feel normal.

"Stop fucking with me!"

My words, which I didn't really mean to shout, seem to hold there, right in front of me, instead of echoing out the way normal sound does. I can't explain it, but it felt like the area around me sank lower, packed in so that sound wouldn't travel the way it usually does. I wish I'd paid more attention in class. I feel like we learned about the speed of sound and other frequencies.

But the important thing is that it's definitely messing with me, and I was stupid enough to lose my cool.

I took Father Albert's words about being true to myself in a way where I have to keep everything I care about, everything I know, close. That means pushing away all the other activity, the stuff that's supposed to get a reaction from me.

So here's what I'm going to do—

I'm going to use this hair gel.

I'm going to use this cologne.

I'm not going to admit that the hair gel works better than the hair spray ever could.

I'm not going to mention anything about how good the cologne smells.

I'm not going to notice that I'm locked in this bathroom.

No.

I'm not going to notice.

I'll just try the doorknob. Once. Twice. A third time.

So what if the lights go out and I'm cold, really damn cold? I'll shiver and keep trying the doorknob until it opens.

When it does, I head out, turning on the heat in my car, just for a little, to warm up. I don't leave it on for too long though, because Nikki won't like that. And I also don't want to start sweating.

Along the way, I feel better. I was able to just keep cool and not get worked up when activity started to really get in the way. Maybe that's all I need to do. I can't be sure, but at least it worked.

All I want to think about now is what's ahead. All I want to think about is Nikki and making sure this date goes well. Oh shit, I forgot the laptop in the car. Minor problem. But I don't think it got hot enough to scramble the chips and stuff. I'll have to try it later.

Maybe a little worried, but not going to think about that right now. Nope.

I park in front of Nikki's house and I text her, figuring this is probably the better way to go about it. Really, I don't want to meet her parents. That's just too much pressure.

She texts me back: "Be there in a few."

Thinking: "Good, this is going to be good."

Really feeling: nothing. I'm not nervous. Well, kind of nervous about the laptop. If it's dead, that's going to cost me more than I have to spend. I don't work a job and I've always been a little sensitive about that part. A lot of people at Meadows have part-time gigs. Some are full-time. I don't know how they manage it, but they have money to spend. I don't have money to spend. I don't like talking about it. Really don't. Worse is the fact that I still get an allowance. I used to quantify it as my mom and dad's way of saying, "Sorry we can't be around. But here's money for food and stuff." Like, that makes a lot of sense. But I'm eighteen now. I'm about to graduate, and yeah: Still an allowance? I can't let Nikki know that this date is being funded by my parents' money.

What time is it? She said a few minutes. It's been fifteen.

I think about turning on some music but I don't really want to listen to the radio. Nothing on the radio is any good. I sound bitter. I guess I just don't like the type of music everybody likes.

Waiting, not letting my thoughts wander. This is hard.

First thing I'll say to Nikki: "You look great."

No, that won't do. Um, how about "You smell nice."

What am I, a serial killer?

"It's a nice night, huh?"

Yeah, that's better. Casual, kind of like I don't really care. Just being myself. Man, I'm really trying hard to be nervous, excited, or something. But yeah, this will be good.

I don't even see her walk up to the car.

She's right there, tapping on the glass, smile on her face, looking amazing—what else should I expect? Nikki's wearing a pinkish-red dress. It looks like she's ready to go to some lavish restaurant when really I'm taking her to a franchise place. Hope that's not a problem. The way her house looks from the outside, and the cars in the driveway, her family is probably loaded.

When she opens the front passenger door, turns out she gets the first word: "Hunter, oh, Hunter, so excited!"

She leans in and kisses me lightly on the lips. It's closed-lipped and kind of like a tap, a peck.

I fall back on the least weird of choices: "It's a nice night, huh?"

Nikki nods, energy on high. She's acting different tonight.

"So what do you wanna do?" she asks.

I tell her that I planned to go to this restaurant, then either a show, some concert some kid told me about at school, or maybe just a movie.

She seems to dig the idea but then says, "Wanna just get a quick bite and then go for a walk?"

A walk? In a dress like that?

"Sure, if that's what you want."

She winks. "I'm simple. And a concert isn't my thing."

Well, all right then. I do my best to drive all cool and casual, making small talk, but really I can't help noticing that she keeps looking in the backseat. I don't want to say anything but I also can't help but, well, notice.

We end up at a fast-food place, her choice, and I order one of those family-feast-sized combos. She laughs and says, "It'll be our little secret."

I park the car in the back of the fast-food parking lot, as far away from the other cars as possible, because, like I tell her, "We can't let anyone spot us."

She calls the fully loaded nachos. I pretend to make a big deal out of it so I get two extra tacos than her share. We're fighting over who gets what and it's kind of funny. I know I'm laughing, having a good time.

Nikki and I look at each other, sharing the guilt, as we scarf down stuff that should never be called food.

I ask her, "How're the nachos you stole from me?'

She makes a face, mouth full. "Those tacos worth stabbing me in the back?"

Laughter and more eating.

She turns on the radio and tells me, "This song is, like, everywhere.

Every single station. Watch..."

Nikki scans the other stations, stopping only long enough to hear a couple beats. But she's right, two stations down the line, the song is playing.

"See?" She sips from a big plastic thing of soda.

"I don't get it," I tell her.

Nikki says, "I love the song. It's so... *now*."

I guess so. A song that defines this moment?

I start on another taco.

She jumps up in her seat, leaning forward, which makes me drop the taco all over my lap. She laughs and says, "Come on, let's do something else!"

I'm like, "Yeah, sure," and then, "Of course, I've had enough to feel guilty for a long-ass time."

Nikki touches my arm. "Wanna go for a walk?"

You know I do. But let's not seem too eager. I tell her, "Sounds good." And then I ask, "Where?"

She narrows her eyes, knowing well that I won't be able to say no. "You know where..."

At first I think she's joking. Then I begin to see it all. Everything. I see it pull back, like one of those movie shots where it starts zoomed in and then zooms out to reveal a huge landscape.

In this case, I'm focused on her so much that I forget to even notice everything that makes her even want to be around me.

Zoom out and I see.

Zoom out more and I can't help but feel cheated.

Zoom out to the point where I'm parking the damn car at the fields, and we're both getting out into the dark of the night, walking the fields with our phones used as flashlights, me shining my light over her shape, Nikki shining her light in my eyes, blinding me, laughing—it's a wide zoom that makes me feel, well, kind of sick.

I know. I know that she is like all the others.

I'm quiet and she's all happy, giggling and doing her thing, what she probably uses on any guy she wants.

Hand in hand, but my arm is limp; she's swinging it as we walk closer and closer to the real cause for all this.

Do I need to really say it?

Do I really need to say anything?

Zoom out enough and it's all so obvious. But from this distance, it seems like everyone would get it instantly. I'm the stupid moron who thought that she actually liked me.

I see the spray-painted black crown from far away.

The moon is high in the sky.

She's leading the way.

There it is—root cause. And I think I'm going to be sick. All that fast food's going to end up under some tree.

Nikki pulls me in close. "Tell me," she says in a whisper.

I got to play up the conversation. I can't stand it, but that doesn't mean I'm a wuss and won't go through with this, like maybe I'll still get to make out or round the bases with a one-of-a-kind girl like Nikki.

But come on, I know that I won't get that far.

Still, I say in a perfect even tone, "Tell you what?" Say it in a way that's as sexual as possible. Flirting, I guess.

I don't know what I'm doing.

Nikki's eyes glow. "Is it here?"

Do I play dumb or do I fast-forward, zoom the hell out to where I can be sick and everything that seemed worth it ends up being wrong?

I push it aside, mostly because I don't want to believe it, don't want to believe that it's just the same as anything or anyone else.

I tell her, "Yeah."

Nikki kisses me. It's a real kiss. I want it to be because she likes me, not because she wants to be near it.

When I pull away, she says, "Keep kissing me. I wanna know what it feels like to kiss you."

We kiss and then she runs away from me screaming, "I wanna know what it's like!"

I run after her. "What are you doing?"

She runs toward the opening, as if she's going to run too.

I'm saying something like, "Are you serious?" But it doesn't come out as a question. She stops near the opening of the Falter tunnel and then kisses me again. She pushes me to the ground. "What does it feel like to never be alone?"

A kiss.

"I just, like, wanna know what it feels like to be around."

I tell her, "This is what it feels like."

"It's watching us right now, right?"

I nod.

She giggles. "I wanna make out right here, right now."

"W-what?" It's a genuine stutter. She's kind of freaking me out.

She's unbuttoning my shirt, her face near mine, breathing heavy, eyes wide and really bold. "I know you wanna."

I don't.

Nikki pulls her dress up. "I wanna be as close to it as possible."

I really don't.

Nikki bites my lower lip. "Make it do something."

I really can't.

I'm frozen in place, shocked by what's happening. Nikki kisses me hard, driving her tongue into my mouth. She keeps asking me about the demon—what it's like to be haunted by it, what it's like to be so close to possession, what it's like to never be really sure of what I'm feeling—and then I push her away when she finally comes out with it: "Make it latch on to me."

I tell her, "Stop."

But she doesn't, not at first. She keeps trying to kiss me, forcing her will on me or something.

My stomach churns. I jump up to my feet, knowing that it's all coming up. I don't want her to see it, so I run into the tunnel.

She doesn't follow.

I hear her call out my name, but I run until I can't see the entrance anymore.

I run and then somewhere around there, I feel better. I feel fine. The sickness disappears. I stop and just stand there, wherever I am, in complete darkness. I'd look around but there's nothing to see, nothing to feel either. The air around me heavy, but really, I feel fine. I feel... safe.

I think about what might happen next.

How I'll have to go back to that.

"That" being the failure of a date, the failure of everything.

I'm confused but here, in the tunnel, it's strange, almost comforting. The fact that nothing is there, literally nothing at all, not even sound, makes me feel great. It's comforting. I stand there, absent to everything.

Until I know that I'll have to face it.

So I walk back until I can see the opening. Nikki is sitting on one of the rocks, her dress wrinkled. She looks depressed.

When she sees me, she runs to me, and it's clear that she's still not convinced that this—whatever's between us—is over.

"Hunter, what the hell?"

All I say is "I'm heading back."

"But..."

She follows. She doesn't want to be abandoned at Falter, not with the legend being so true and real and mysterious and fun and awesome and attractive.

On the drive back, Nikki tries to talk to me, tries to apologize, but she doesn't know why any of this has happened. She feels vulnerable, and you know what? She should feel that way. If only she knew how insane this feels for me. And then she looks in the backseat and asks me if it's there.

"I just wanna know, that's all."

Ugh. I'm not going to tell her.

I'm never going to tell.

She gets dropped off at her fancy house and I drive home. I park the car in the street because my dad's home and took my spot, and I wait in the car until they're both asleep.

I count the windows, looking at every single one. I swear that one of the lights flickers on and off, but I don't care. Even if it is you, I don't care.

I don't know what to think. Everything's broken, ruined, and I feel absolutely nothing. It's times like right now where the car could lift off the ground and I would be able to ignore it.

Reality is, I'm hurting. I've been hurt. I said I wasn't nervous and I wasn't really excited about this, but yeah, truth is I was. I just couldn't feel it going in. I felt nothing because that's what I've been feeling since this stuff started. I feel mostly nothing, even when I'm angry or afraid.

Everything's, like, some kind of other object. My feelings aren't really mine. They're just there, and I can feel them if I want.

But I don't. Especially now, I don't.

I sit in my car for hours. At some point, I reach into the backseat and get my laptop. It's the one thing I care about right now. Work, damn you, work. There's power. It's definitely on. Black screen for way too long. It's like it's holding back, not wanting to actually work.

What does it take for it to work? Me caring? Even a little? Then fine, I care. I really care.

It's kind of sad to think that this laptop is my real window to anything I like. I have no other real connection with anything living or dead. This stupid laptop is my gate. It lets me seek out what I'll never get to see if I didn't have that access. Yeah, I know it's sad. But a lot of things are sad.

It'll be sadder if this thing is really broken.

I leave it sitting on the front passenger seat and I stare up at the sky. I don't see any stars. Maybe I don't want to see any stars and that's why things look so miserable. Nothing to see up there or around me, so I rest my head on the steering wheel. Things happen, I guess, but I'm right here, sitting in my car.

But then I hear it—the sound of the computer starting up.

And it's almost the kind of sound that I could map to the feeling of things getting better.

But instead, I take the laptop and sign in.

I avoid signing in to any social media. Instead, I go right to a video. I click on the one at the top of my recently viewed, which is, ironically, the one with the two guys, the one that is a skit but it seems like they are both actual friends. I forget where or how I saw it until the second viewing. I remember that night when my laptop went missing. I remember the video that was open when I got it back.

This is the video.

This is the same video.

What does that mean?

Maybe it doesn't mean anything. I don't know. But it's cool, the video. Both guys get what's going on. They don't pretend to be anything they're not. It's a skit, but I feel like it's, um, what's the word, improvised. Yeah.

I open up a new document. I notice that the laptop battery is at full charge, but I'm too tired to take it as real. It goes into the big group of stuff that I'm not thinking about. I scroll through the various notes I've typed to myself, wasting time. It really feels like there's nowhere else to go from here.

I'm looking at notes, notes I type to myself because I know I'll never actually look at them again.

There's nothing else left.

Seriously.

Like here's one: "yearbook bio/what you'll be remembered for."

I still haven't written one. Well, I'm going to write one now.

Here I go, typing out the truth:

"I won't be remembered for being haunted. I'll be remembered for being like everyone else, but maybe a little more sincere. I'm not fickle like everyone else who latched on to me when really they should have just, like, gotten away. Let me get the help I need. I'm Hunter Warden, a senior at Meadows, who hasn't declared what his major in college will be. I'm Hunter Warden and we probably had a few classes together. I'm Hunter Warden, and yes, I drive a shitty Japanese car that's, like, eight or ten years old. I'm Hunter Warden, and no, I don't find that new hip-hop artist interesting. I'm Hunter Warden and I don't like football, basketball, or any of the other sports all of you guys are so hyped and happy about. I'm Hunter Warden and I don't want to join your band. I'm Hunter Warden, and what makes you think we are the same? I'm Hunter Warden and I'm actually a nice guy, if you actually talked to me about something other than the stuff you always talk about. I don't want to be any different from anyone else. I don't. I'm like you: I want to fit in. But, like, I don't like the same things you do. And all anyone talks about is the stuff they like. It's all stuff, stuff, stuff. There's got to be more to talk about than just stuff. When it isn't stuff, it's who got into the better college, who got the better SAT score. I'm Hunter Warden and we could have been friends."

I read it back and, man—this is bad. It's all wrong when I just want to be right. It should be a bio, not a rant. It should be written so that I'm not saying it, right? It should read, like, "Hunter Warden is a B+ student, set to attend State in the fall." Something like that. Yeah, that's better.

I'm going to close this document now.

Save and exit?

Yeah, whatever.

I know. I know: The truth is they will remember me for what's happening now. They'll never let me live it down. I'm the one in the middle of it, stuck with having to live with it. I mean, it'll go away sometime, right?

People will forget. They always forget.

There's always State. Bigger group of people. A fresh start.

So then I just have to wait. Something about that seems depressing—really, really bleak—like I won't make it that far. Won't make it past graduation.

I'll be stuck in high school with everyone acting like I'm the shit for something I shouldn't have done. Most don't even know my full name.

There's really something wrong about being remembered for something you had no part of, something that's actually trying to hurt you, you know? That's what's really scary. I think I'm going to stay in the car tonight. There's no way I'm going to be able to walk inside.

I'll stay here all night. No problem.

I'll find something to do online. I'll fixate on something that isn't my situation. I don't want to think about it. Maybe I'll actually fall asleep. Either way, the laptop stays at full charge all night. It doesn't even dip below 90 percent.

I don't realize I'm asleep until I fall twenty stories from the top of a building and I'm able to stand back up without a scratch. I look like shit, but it's only because the dream is right out of a movie and the main character in that movie gets ripped up, bleeding and bloody, but keeps running.

I keep running, being chased by what I won't see until later, when it's that part of the movie where the main character ends up cornered, dead end, and he's frantically looking for some other exit.

But there is no exit.

The only way I really can leave this is if I wake up. When you're in the dream, you think that you can just think, "Wake up," and you'll wake up.

I think that but it only makes the dream seem more real than it is.

I shouldn't be running. I shouldn't be shooting at the unseen enemy. I shouldn't be saying the lines that the main character says in the movie—stuff like, "If you want me, you'll have to kill me!" and, into a phone that I didn't have until it appeared on-screen, "Fourth and Front Street! Fourth and Front Street! Five minutes! If you're late, I'm dead!"

I should just wake up because my dreams are never like this. My dreams are never this interesting.

Never this... real.

But I keep running.

And I love this.

It goes from one city street to the next, and I'm running up walls, doing parkour like a pro, and my heart just has to be beating like crazy. I'm sweating in bed and it's cold as hell in my room. I mean, I know what's happening.

This is from one of my favorite action movies.

If I follow it to the very end, talking right to that gunshot, I wonder if I'll die too. Or just wake up. Something about this dream is just too real. I pinch myself and I feel it. I'm not waking up.

Run then, right? Nothing else to do but run.

It's all so exciting, even though I know how it'll end.

At the next corner, I turn left and end up dodging traffic. Going against all these cars, it's a display of athleticism that I could do in my sleep. Ha, get it?

Anyway, one truck makes it hard to just duck to the side, so I jump forward, grabbing the grille of the truck, and run up the windshield to its roof. I'm lying prone, riding the truck until I see a bridge.

The best part of the movie is when the main character does this huge jump from the moving truck to a bridge, hangs there, and then free falls to the street in, like, ten seconds.

Being the one who does all this is insane. It happens so quick it's like a slideshow of various pictures. It ends with a roll forward, a look in the direction of another wave of traffic, and then a sprint down the way I came.

This time it's a mad rush all the way up some steep incline. This city is swarming with people who shout at me. The main character's on the phone the entire time, shouting at people. I like that I get to shout at people.

Sweat drips down my forehead like it's been raining like crazy. It's all for effect, but it seems so real, especially when I have to make a sharp right turn around one corner, into an alley where I run up a brick wall, grab on to a ledge, and start climbing the ten-story building.

I'm not really afraid of heights, but looking down the way the main character looks down in the movie really makes that sinking-stomach feeling intense. Really intense.

Part of me wants to drop again, just to be able to do that free-falling thing again, to get to stand back up and not be hurt at all.

But that's not the way the scene goes.

I'm on the roof of a building. From above, a helicopter shoots at me, *Enemy of the State* style.

Run, run, run—I get that tunnel vision when I put everything in the next jump, the one where there's that awesome shot of the main character bridging the gap, jumping across. It's just like that in my dream. That shot from the ground floor, looking up so that you see my body fly across, barely making it to the other side.

It's almost that part where the main character gets shot.

I climb down the side of the building, Front Street intersection right there, and the person who was on the phone, the car, is right there. Just like in the movie, my dream zooms in to show the car parked and the person waiting, all anxious, to drive off and start the car chase part of the movie.

But in the movie, it doesn't happen with the main character.

The main character gets shot and it's this big deal, big twist, that some people love and some people hate.

In my dream I run down that alley.

I keep running, but when someone points and shoots their gun, I'm not in the alley anymore. The sides of the buildings blur into a sort of darkness. I see trees and then I see nothing.

I keep running but the dream's taken a weird turn. It's really not the movie anymore. It's a tunnel. It's that tunnel. It's nothing but that one moment when I ran and felt everything change in an instant. I know where I am but I can't say the name.

But the dream keeps going, running in the dark.

It's like that until I don't feel like I'm running anymore.

And then it's just me and something else, and we're sitting at a table. It might as well be the kitchen table at my house. I'm sweaty and achy, and I'm feeling as if I really fell from a building and somehow survived just so that I can be in this kind of pain. But the pain is distant enough that I can kind of say, "Wow, this sucks," without actually having to be rushed to the hospital.

I'm sitting at the table alone. Sitting there, realizing that I'm sitting and doing nothing at a kitchen table. In a dream. There's something wrong about going from an action scene from a movie to sitting at a table.

But that's how this goes, I guess, and it's now that I realize that

I don't have a lot of control over my dream. I'm being led by the dream.

Facing me is an empty chair. The chair is empty until it's not.

And then I'm staring at a mirrored version of me. But something about it is different. It has the same voice, my voice, but it doesn't have to use it. It speaks without speaking and it breathes without needing to breathe. It matches me as much as it can, but it also wants to be me.

Then I really look and see what it is.

I'm kind of scared, yeah, but if I keep looking, keep thinking about it. I get kind of curious too. I can't help myself.

I ask a question, and I can hear myself say it aloud.

The question, it's the one that comes to mind first, the question maybe everyone would want to know the most: "Where do you come from?"

I'm talking in my sleep.

It kind of all just happens, the answers falling into place like stuff I already knew but forgot up until asking the question. It's here, and it doesn't know where it came from. It only knows where it currently is, and in this case, it's in my dream.

It tells me, "I'm standing next to you."

Part of me wants to say, *But you're sitting across from me.*

It breathes just to show that it's real.

I can hear the sound of scratching even though I'm still sitting in this chair, hands folded on the table.

It tells me, "I saw you running."

And then it tells me, "I ran after."

I hear the bedroom door open and close, then the words, "I want to know why you stopped running."

What do I say to that? I don't really know what to say.

It says, "There's an end to the tunnel."

I have to ask, but this time I just think the question instead of saying it: "Is that where you came from?"

It doesn't seem to want to reply.

More breathing, and then the room gets even colder.

It says, "You will wake up soon."

I'm saying aloud, "What time is it?"

I should be getting more scared the longer I speak to it. Those pieces of information—stuff told to me by Father Albert and others—warn me not to make contact with the demon. Don't make contact. Don't speak to it. But does a dream count? What about a nightmare?

And then I'm thinking, "Can it hear my thoughts?"

It tells me, "Yes."

Then I think, "What is your name?"

The name it gives, it's pieced together from a half-thought I had once, when I thought it would be cool to drop my name and just go by a single letter.

I used to think it would be cool to be called "H Warden."

It calls itself "H."

And I know it's only because it looked into my thoughts and picked out something as close to my own name as possible.

One thought keeps pulling me aside. It keeps telling me, the thought, to be afraid. Be so damn afraid. And wake up. Stop contacting it.

But H is right there, looking as close to human as possible.

I hear myself ask, "I take it you're all about causing shit, right?"

H doesn't seem to give an answer.

We sit there—the dream frozen, paused—but I find it still kind of awesome. It's nothing I've ever experienced before. It's like talking to yourself, but instead of just getting the thoughts you know and the words you've already said, you actually get something in return.

New information, new ideas, new feelings jump into the spaces between your own thoughts.

H then tells me, "You are going to wake up now."

But before I do, I have one other question: "How is this possible?"

H says, "It's possible because it just happened."

And then I wake up.

My sheets are damp. I touch and smell them. Nope, didn't piss my pants. It's sweat. I look around the darkened room. I check the time.

Three A.M.

I feel tired. That's nothing new. I yawn and sort of say out loud, "Does this feeling tired shit get any easier?" And then I hear a scratching noise coming from the other side of the wall, almost like I'm getting an active response.

I sit up in bed, wondering if I should be worried.

Out of breath and really kind of lost, I don't want that dream to stop. I want to sleep but I feel like it won't be possible. No matter what I do to try to sleep, it's that same sort of tossing and turning where I end up sort of asleep but not really anywhere close. And then it gets to be morning and, you know, back to school.

Another day, but I can't help but feel like I'm taking back some of what's changed since running the gauntlet. I can feel my grip on giving a shit really finally... faltering. And I'd like to think that it's a good thing.

HALVERSON DOESN'T EVEN LOOK AT FATHER ALBERT'S
note. Makes me think I could have folded up any sheet of paper and
said I got checked out. He kind of just says, "Frankly, I'm just happy
to see that you're going to be okay," and then lets me get to class. I'm
late to first period because of him though. After last night's dream,
most of my day feels like one long stretch, like a high I didn't know
I was having. It's all blurry and nothing I do really seems to mean
anything.

In third period, we take a test that I didn't study for, but then
again, I'm starting to think that everyone's given up studying this
late into the school year. But during the test, I look at the questions
and read them over and over again, but none of them make any
sense.

I read question number one and I see my own question typed out:
"Where do you come from?"

A, B, C, or D. D is always all/none of the above.

I answer D, none of the above.

Next question: "What's your name?"

A, B, C, or D. I can't read the options so I go with D.

Down the line, all thirty questions are a mixture of questions I want answered and answers that don't seem to ever show.

I catch myself staring into space, chewing a pencil. The teacher seems to notice too, makes a face. I shrug and go back to the test.

The last question kind of freaks me out:

"Are you good or bad?"

It's right out of those haunting flicks. There are so many of them. The documentary ones are the worst because they try to get real footage of possessions. It's always that question—are you good or bad?—when priests and other experts try to make first contact.

It's like they can be only one or the other.

I'm both scared and kind of interested. It's mostly because I know that H wouldn't answer that question. H. I almost don't realize that I'm calling it H now. Funny and weird how it feels like the dream wasn't a dream, was as real as anything else, but then I can forget about certain parts. I just take it as plain truth, reality, and then I start using the information—H—and I'm caught off guard by it. But just for a moment.

I hand in the test and the best I can probably hope for is a D.

Probably failed though.

Then it's lunch and Brad and all his stuff that today, of all days, I really can't take. I don't even try to be a part of the conversation.

Blaire shows up, asks me, "How are you feeling?"

I didn't know I was sick or something, but I say, "Fine."

Today's the first time I don't buy lunch. I sit there and sort of listen to Brad talking about how his team, meaning the baseball team that he decided to like and follow this season, is going to totally dominate. On no real grounds, of course. It's something to talk about. Brad's all into it. But then again, I don't know anything about the sport. I never really cared for it.

I find myself thinking about the dream.

The kitchen table part.

I analyze it like I wasn't actually a part of it: What did this mean? What did that mean?

It's not really about getting anything else from the dream. It's just fun to analyze it. To think about it, you know?

It feels like a totally different take on the world, a world that normally doesn't seem like anything but a plain truth, obvious and kind of dull. There's so much out there and it feels like it's all defined. Just like college. Just like careers. Just like networking. Just like society to be that segmented.

This is where I should go see Jon-Jon, but fuck Jon-Jon. I can't deal with his betting pool and opportunistic ways.

This is where I think about maybe going to the bathroom and just sitting in a stall for a whole period. It seems attractive. I really feel like everything's wearing thin, all the people being nice to me, all the people talking to me all because of H. All because I did something they all pretend to do and the only difference is I actually did it. I went through with something, and H happened to run after me on the way out of the tunnel.

I don't know.

I just feel like H is becoming the least of my concerns now.

Everything else feels like homework, like something that makes every day a bummer, because I have to do and feel and act in a way that I don't want to. But maybe it's always been this way and it's only now that I've lost any and all cares about it.

No, I'm not going to talk about Nikki. She's just another face in the crowd. A pretty face, but no doubt ten times shallower than most. She just wants what she wants and has a big enough ego to go through with it. And thinking about crossing paths with Nikki is enough to make this day end.

Forget the bathroom stall. I walk right back to my car.

I sit there sometimes staring at my phone. Becca texts me a few times but seems really busy.

I expect word to get out about my date with Nikki, but no one cares or it's really that Nikki doesn't say anything, although if she really were the cliché I know she is, a fucking stereotype, she would make up some story that ruins me.

Go ahead and ruin me.

It would get people to stop talking about me like they actually care about me. People who sometimes get my name wrong, calling me Hunter Warren or Hunter Walden like that book. I'd really dig just driving into the woods and just building a house there. Thoreau had it right. It was the one book I actually read a lot of when almost everyone else couldn't get past the first ten pages. That book is more than the words in it; it's all the ideas, the whole life outside of society, outside of all... this. It comes down to being different, I guess. Or something. That was my interpretation of the book, anyway.

Man, I'm tired.

But I can't sleep. Not in this car.

I look down at the phone, another text. Someone.

Then a text from Brad, who just says, "Bro we're going to party hard man." And then that reminds me about the party. The one that is now at my house. The one that is now really happening.

And soon. Like *this* weekend, not next weekend.

Yeah, just want to sit in this car.

Then I get a text from Blaire.

She's thinking about skipping and I text back a two-word answer, "Do it." Just not feeling up to chatting about anything.

She texts back, asking me again, "How are you feeling?" She knows I was lying before.

"Blah," that's my response.

I watch the cursor blink. She must be typing something long. I sit there, eyes closed, until the phone buzzes.

"I understand," she says, "first you think you're going crazy and that you shouldn't be annoyed at everyone. Everyone's paying attention to you, treating you like you're popular. I know you wanted this. You feel weird because now you're living for two. You're going to go through a lot of changes, maybe quicker than most. I just worry about you, Hunter."

"Don't. I'm just tired."

A few minutes pass before I get another reply. "It doesn't get any better." Her message, it shouldn't annoy me the way it does. I can't help it.

"How would you know?"

But she doesn't reply. I text a question mark. I can tell that she's getting my messages.

"You don't understand, OK?"

Still nothing.

"You're just like the rest, wanting a part in this without actually being held accountable. You say you worry about me. Don't. I'm going home. Fuck this."

I drive off just as the bell rings, signaling the end of classes for the day. It's like getting out before the flood washes me away or something. It's this adrenaline rush that I get leaving before anyone sees me.

It's kind of funny actually, looking back on it later.

And it's strange when I think, "Wonder what H is going to try today," and I'm almost excited to get back home.

Really strange how that is, huh?

But that's my day. As time goes on, things start to change shape.

That's today, and tomorrow, it'll be maybe different or exactly the same. Only thing I'm sure of is that it'll be one step closer to that party.

Yeah, I'm really not looking forward to that party.

The weekend arrives quicker than I wanted it to. It feels like one second I'm driving home from class and the next thing I know I'm standing in my family room, the one room in my house that's never ever used, and people I barely know from Meadows are filling that space.

They all want me to say something like, "I know all you people."

Really what I'm thinking is "I don't know any of you."

But that's kind of wrong to say too. It's mean-spirited and it makes me feel like shit. Maybe that's my problem; I'm becoming withdrawn. Over the past few days, I've thought back to the dream. I've thought back to what happened, and I have started to look forward to the next dream because part of me just knows that it'll happen.

It hasn't happened yet.

I'm starting to tell myself that the reason for being so withdrawn is because I have started to look somewhere else. Where? That's kind of the problem. I'm looking around for something that even I'm not sure of. I'm not finding whatever it is I want to find in the people who look at me like I'm exactly what they are looking for.

No, I don't know what the hell I'm talking about.

I only know that this isn't going to work. I mean, look at this. Check it out:

Jon-Jon charges ten dollars at the door. Brad lingers around me at all times. Becca, who tells me what to do via text message, is too busy hanging out with people she never gets to hang out with; it's because she's in the same room as them—guess who drew in the popular crowd? yup—that she gets that chance.

She's making the most of it.

Blaire isn't here. She'd never show up for something like this. It goes way over her head. Also, she's sure as hell still holding a grudge. The other day, when she stopped by the lunch table to ask how I was doing, she left before I could really say anything. She goes and texts me later like I'm a charity case, like she knows something I don't. I haven't bothered to text or call—figure she wouldn't answer even if I did.

Brad speaks for me: "Yeah, bro, here's the man, the main man!"

Jon-Jon takes bets for the big séance or summoning that's going to happen later.

People walk up to me, usually one by one, but also there are times when it's a whole group. By now they aren't even remembering the running part. They're all focused on H. Well, to them it's just "the demon." They are all fixated on the demon. They start by saying stuff like, "What's it like?" Some flat-out ask me stupid stuff like, "Can you get it to slap me in the face?" One girl who said we were in a class together last semester keeps asking me whether demons are like people and have all the same organs, limbs, and, yeah, "genitalia." Sick, I think, but I say the one thing I say to everyone: "Yeah."

"Yeah" to the question about experiencing a cold chill.

"Yeah" to the person who asks me if it's true, that being haunted means things go "bump in the night."

"Yeah" to the one who asks if they can get drunk around me (i.e., the demon), hoping that being drunk or something will make it easier for the demon to mess with them.

After all that, some stick around making "conversation." But since we don't have anything in common, and they don't really have a lot to say, it usually ends up with a bunch of gossip or talk about hobbies and news.

This one guy wouldn't go away.

Brad would leave after introducing me to a person, and this guy just sort of latched on and started giving me a lesson on poker—not just any kind of poker, but Texas hold 'em. When he asked me if I'd ever seen a game, I said, "Yeah," and that launched him into a long, really energetic sort of explanation of this one time he made almost a thousand dollars playing.

Here's where I could've questioned if it was true, because he's young and probably couldn't get into casinos yet. What's the age requirement, anyway?

Here's where I could've helped the conversation by actually saying something else, but instead I sipped from a glass.

But I chose the glass, and that's what I end up thinking about the most.

I think in distant commands—listen, listen, take a sip, listen, listen, look around the room, nod, take a sip—and it's all I can do to keep from walking out on the entire party. This is supposed to be my party, you see, but it's really none of that. It's a number of things, but at the very bottom of the list is me.

I catch Nikki Dillon talking to some guy I don't know.

When I look over at her, she catches me and looks away. So that's how she's decided to treat what happened between us. Nikki's going to ignore me. Makes it easier on me, I guess. I could go over there and strike up a conversation, but that's not me. That's never been me, especially now when I know why she even bothered.

At some point, Becca texts me, "Where are your parents? Should we be worried they'll show?"

I look at the screen blankly, longer than I need to, but it's good because for as long as it looks like I'm texting, I don't have to pretend that I'm interested. I type slowly, "They aren't here. Work."

I'm not lying. It's true. My parents are at work. They have their own lives. I'm just a small part of it.

Brad runs around the house once, shouting, "Everyone, attention please!" And I know what's about to happen.

Jon-Jon wanders over to the coffee table. Along the way, he grabs my arm, says to me, "How excited are you to make money, on a scale of one to ten, ten being a future millionaire?"

But he doesn't give me time to reply, because he sets down the board on the coffee table. He gets Brad to do all the talking, but Jon-Jon stands there, next to me, all smug and cool and people know him as exactly that: a smug and cool guy. People seem to think it's still all Jon-Jon's thing even though I'm the one haunted, I'm the one who is "hosting" this party.

I sound like I'm bitter but I'm not.

I'm just observing.

It's all kind of insane, really.

The fact that people will pay attention only when you've already sort of stopped trying to get their attention, yeah... I don't know, doesn't it sound kind of fake?

I look around the entire room at everyone who's here. They've gathered around close. Body heat makes it easier to want to drink, thinking that it'll cool me down.

There has to be, like, a hundred people here.

Brad shouts above the noise, "We will attempt to make contact with the presence!"

Brad's talking in a way that's not like him. He got it from that investigative haunt show. It's ridiculous. I want to be like, *Brad, are you serious?* Instead, I don't say anything.

"We will bring our collective energies together"—Brad raises his hands—"by bringing our thoughts to the board."

People focus on the board, the little device that points to different letters, which I hope will be spelling out "Brad you asshole."

No, I'm not bitter.

I just don't really feel like I'm a part of this—this event that's really just about everyone feeling better about themselves, everyone wanting to meet up and feel important.

Brad asks everyone to "hold the hands of those next to you. Let us bind together and begin our discussion with the demon that has chosen our dear friend Hunter as a host."

"Dear friend." That's something to note. Well, I note it at least.

The way he says "friend" makes it sound like it might be an insult, but then again, Brad is an asshole. He can't help it. I think he's maybe the only person in this room who might actually believe that we're friends. So what does that mean when you look at how he treats and talks about me? Yeah, I really don't know. I'm not so sure it needs to be something I think a lot about.

I'm busy not thinking about what's going on.

Everyone lowers their chins, looking down at the board.

Brad says, "Now we call out to the presence! We call out in hopes of reaching you!"

Jon-Jon leans in and whispers into my ear, "You're up."

Up for what? I didn't know I needed to do anything else. You got the party. You got them to believe that this will work.

Jon-Jon nudges me with his elbow. "Go sit at the board. Grab the pointer."

I don't want to but I do. I sit down and I put my hands on the pointer thing.

I look around at everyone.

They're mystified by the whole process.

People love these types of things. I know they do because I used to as well. It always makes for a great time. I'm jealous. As I look into the eyes of these strangers, I'm really, really jealous. They will have a good time. They are having a good time. And it'll get better, the longer this party goes on. I won't be able to have as much fun as them. I know more about H and what's happening than they ever could. Even if they did... even if they knew more about what it feels like to be near a demon, they wouldn't experience it the same way I am. And I keep going back to Nikki, to all the things people have said to me, all the enthusiasm, all the kind words that simply couldn't sound any weirder and off-putting, like they're all meant as an insult.

I keep looking at everything as the opposite of the true intention. Someone says that it's great that I'm haunted and I take it like they're saying, *I don't really know you or care to know you, but I'm fascinated with the fact that you are being haunted so I'm going to pretend that I really want to get to know you, even though we have nothing in common and I won't ever try to listen to what you have to say!* Wow, that really does sound bitter.

Okay, well, here I am.

Right here and now.

I look down at the board when Brad starts asking H questions.

Fingers on the pointer, waiting for the reply, I think, "Don't do anything, H. Don't even bother. Sorry for this. But maybe you understand how I feel." It makes some sense, you know? What does a demon get but a lot of fear and a lot of curiosity from people? So many people are driven to wanting to know. And, I mean, I'm one of them. I can't help but want to know more.

But this isn't the way.

Brad asks, "Are you here, in this room, with us right now?"

Brad says, "Give us a sign that you are here."

Brad commands, "Move a chair, make a sound..."

Brad asks, "Can you make a noise? Can you turn this room cold?"

I'm repeating it over and over like I have some command over H: Don't do anything. Don't do anything. Don't do anything. Don't do anything.

I know that I don't have a clue.

At the same time, though, I kind of want them all to freak out the way I did when the symptoms started showing. I'm thinking it'll be good to give them a scare.

I'll move the pointer if you make the room cold. It's a sauna as it is, everyone stinking the place up with their BO. At least we'll get a moment of cool air.

I take it back so that when Brad starts repeating the same questions like they do in the show, repeating them until they get a response, I move the pointer so that the answer to "Are you here, in this room, with us right now?" is a definite "Yes."

There are gasps.

There are sounds of people gagging, freaking out.

Some people laugh.

One guy shouts out, "Holy shit!"

Like they didn't see this in a movie, on TV, on the news, maybe even at another friend's or family's place. Then again, maybe you never get used to it. Priests always look nervous at the start of the exorcism.

When Brad says the next question—"Give us a sign that you are here"—the room goes cold right when I know that it'll happen. It's hard to explain but it's a lot like the conversation at the table in my dream. I didn't know until I knew, and it was because I knew, at that precise moment, that made all the difference. The room chilled like a meat locker; people are shivering for more than one reason. And I look at them, kind of amused by the whole thing.

They are the ones being used, for my amusement and maybe for H's.

I know that H did it.

I know that he did. I know, but I cannot confirm because I only know that "H did." There's nothing else that comes to mind to support what just happened. If I ask why, there's only the one answer for when you don't have anything else to say: "Because."

I spot Nikki to my left, shivering, more than a little freaked out.

She looks right at me, and I understand that look.

It's straight-up guilt and regret.

It's like this one event, a simple sign that H is around and maybe watching, is enough for her to lose her cool.

I can imagine Nikki wanting to apologize, wanting a second chance, but then again, I won't let her. I won't give her that second chance, even though I like thinking that she'll ask.

She would, wouldn't she?

I know she would.

Brad stutters, "W-will you move this chair?" He points to a chair. He's losing the audience. He's not talking in that voice anymore. Brad looks at me and says, "Bro, this is crazy..."

They all just wanted to be near, not directly involved.

Jon-Jon looks happy. Yeah, he's happy. The fact that it's cold in here means he probably made a ton of money.

How much of that will I see?

What kind of cut am I going to get?

Part of me cares, but the other part just wants to see the party fall apart.

Brad ends up asking, "So you're not going to, like, move the chair?"

I watch people exhale all nervous, seeing their breath, which they also see, and because they can see it, some leave the room. Maybe leave the party.

I think, "That's how it's going to happen. This is how the party can end."

I think, "Crash the party."

Brad's is the only voice in the room, barely a shout now: "Give us another sign, uh, that you're here with us."

Someone can be heard whispering, "Dude, you're going to piss it off."

It's so quiet in here...

Crash the party.

Jon-Jon's having a wonderful time.

Crash the party.

Becca is nowhere to be seen. Later I'll find out via a text message that she wigged out and left the room around the time it got cold.

Crash the party.

It's okay, I don't want them to get what they want, but maybe this isn't really what they want. They only want to think it's cool.

Most have no clue about the capability of a demon. I'm still figuring it out.

Crash the party.

"Are you still, uh, here with us? Bro?"

Real smooth.

In the quiet of the room, we see it. We all see it at once.

It's so simple, I find it great. This is hilarious. Really funny.

"Nice choice," I think. And then I immediately second-guess myself, finding it odd that I'm sort of, like, working with H on this.

But it still happens. And it happens beautifully.

It's so quiet that the creaking of the door's hinges gets their necks turning. All in that one direction, there it is, the closet door creaking open slowly. They get enough time to look and see and get what's happening.

In the quiet and cold chill of the room, when I know what will happen, I can't help but look on in fascination as the door completely opens and then...

... holding on for one, seemingly tense moment and then...

Slam! The door slams shut so hard that it rattles the wall.

People trip and fall. They shout and scatter.

Brad's repeating the words "No fucking way" over and over again, while grabbing on to my right shoulder.

Jon-Jon stands in place, putting on that cool performance, also loving every second of this.

I'm leaning forward, laughing.

I'm not laughing because I want them to be afraid.

I'm not laughing because I'm bitter.

Really, I'm laughing because it's funny.

I find it really funny. I don't think it's wrong. Right? It's actually funny. It's maybe the funniest thing I've seen in a long time. They played right into the joke, a joke that wasn't even called a joke until I knew that it was supposed to be a joke. And then I'm whispering to myself, "Good one."

And it's then that I know:

H saying without speaking, "They wanted a party."

I'm laughing, laughing really hard.

Brad's like, "What the fuck, bro? This is insane," and then nearly bashes his head against the corner of a wall on the way out.

I watch as everyone filters out of the house. The only one left, Jon-Jon, says to me, "How successful do you think this was, on a scale of one to ten, ten being free booze and weed and whatever you want for a whole year?"

Course, I know what he's saying.

He won't be giving me a cut. He's just going to make me go to him when I need more beer or liquor or weed. I breathe out and say, "Three."

Jon-Jon's already made his decision though: "A success. A complete success." He walks out of the house, casual stroll and all.

I watched everyone leave, and now I feel like I can really breathe.

I'm in bed when I get a call from Blaire. I don't second-guess it. She's a friend and maybe she's not angry anymore. Then again, was she ever?

Yeah, I pick up.

She's the first to say something: "How did it go?"

"It went..." I don't really know how to explain it, so she starts speaking for me.

"I know. It's happening so fast. It's hard to describe."

"Yeah," I say, trying to hold back a shiver.

"Can I come in?"

"Huh?"

"I'm outside," she says, really more like a whisper.

"Everyone left. There's nothing left to see."

"That's okay. Good, really."

I sigh. "Yeah, whatever. Door's open."

She knows the drill. She knocks on my bedroom door and I'm reminded of the fact that she might not be allowed in the room, but then she's already turning the doorknob and she's inside.

"Hey." She gives a little shy half-grin.

She knows not to annoy me, sitting across the room instead of next to me. For a while she doesn't say anything. She isn't shivering, cold like I am.

"You cold?" I ask.

"I'm not supposed to be cold."

More time passes like this, nothing really said, just both of us in this room, dealing with whatever there is to be dealt. She asks me about my dreams.

"What do you mean?"

"The dreams, they're probably really vivid, right?"

I don't say anything.

"Yeah, it'll just be like you can't tell what's a dream or actually real, but then you won't care either." Blaire isn't looking at me as she talks, her head down, hands folded in her lap. "It feels so much like you're dying while at the same time everything you've ever dreamed of coming true is actually happening. It's becoming reality."

"I don't think so," I tell her, probably just because I don't want to admit that she's right. It feels that way, doesn't it?

She looks up at me, finally. "You're not going through with it, are you?"

"Huh?"

She shakes her head. "If you don't, then you don't. It's just that most people don't go through all of it. They get up to, like, what you're experiencing now and then they freak out, get confused, get the exorcism. Everyone wants it gone before they really understand what the kingdom is."

The kingdom?

"They don't really see any more than a small glimpse, and the first time you see anything from the other side, it's scary as hell. You're going to react like it's all bad. People react and get it done. They throw a party, get high, get drunk. They never get what it is they passed up."

It looks like she's starting to cry, but before I can ask her, she's wiping away the tears.

She keeps talking, and it's clear that she just wants me to listen.

"The kingdom is as big as our world. It's basically the same, except they avoid us, and we avoid them. I guess what I'm trying to say is... I don't know what I'm trying to say. I just want you to know that if you don't go through with it, I won't look down on you. Okay?"

I clear my throat. "Um, okay."

"I won't think you're stupid or insane or whatever."

"Thanks." I sound insincere.

"Things will get really, really bad before it gets any good." She pauses and then adds, "And even then, it's not like they'll stick around either."

I don't know what to say, so I don't say anything, and we sit in silence for a while. I'm surprised that I almost start to nod off. She brings me back when she gets up and starts to leave.

I ask her, "Why?"

She raises an eyebrow. "What?"

"The things you said, how do you know?"

"Oh." She opens the door, looks back at me, and says, "I used to have one." And then she leaves.

7

"THAT'S THE THING ABOUT CONVERSATIONS, THEY ARE almost always two-way, especially when there's more than one person talking. I mean, look at how a person makes eye contact with a person they're talking to. It's straight on, you know? If they can, that is. A lot of people just kind of look around and then occasionally look at the person they're talking to. But, anyway, you could have, like, ten people in a circle, talking, and even though it's like everyone's a part of the conversation, there's only one or two people talking. If any more talk, it gets all crazy, like any other party, you know?

"You know what I mean?

"Right? You saw it tonight, how it'll be someone talking to me and then Brad, or someone else will walk up and try to be a part of the conversation. Almost one hundred percent of the time, they'll end up listening. Only way to really be a part of it is to butt in, and I mean really... just flat-out start talking over the other person.

"It happens more often than it doesn't; people are talking, two people talking about whatever, and a third person walks in, says something that gets the attention of one of the other two, maybe both of them, and then it changes the dynamic of the whole conversation.

"I see it all the time. It's like there's a pattern to how people talk. And if you look at the pattern, it makes all the information that fits into that pattern kind of, well, lame. I think it kind of makes almost everything that happens between when a person says hello and good-bye kind of predictable.

"You know what I mean?

"It's just that I think it's all filler.

"It's like a song you buy on a whim because it's recommended to you and you listen to the whole thing expecting it to be better but it's not as good as you thought.

"That's what most conversations end up being, I think.

"I've listened to so much music I don't like, just because it's there, and it's too hard to get up and find the right music.

"I don't know. I really don't know. I don't know what I'm going to do now. What do you think?

"It's a wreck, huh? I know. No one cares about the place where the party is; they trash it with beer bottles and cups and food everywhere. I don't remember anyone buying pizza but there's a slice of pizza facedown on the kitchen tile. I take one look at all of this and I get tired.

"This is rude, right?

"I mean, you aren't human but you have to think this is rude. The word 'rude' makes sense to you, right?

"Yeah.

"It is rude."

Ugh.

I don't know where to start.

"I think I'll just sit here in this corner for a while. Parents won't be back until the end of the weekend. Or whatever. They could be back already, it wouldn't matter much. I'm still sitting in the corner of a room, cleaning up after other people.

"No, they aren't back.

"What time is it?

"I'm not tired. Not anymore.

"Think I should just leave everything this way?

"Yeah... I should.

"What is Dad really going to do? Mom's just going to think that I'm sick or something. I'm not sick. You know that. I know that.

"I'll be fine. No problem.

"And even if it ended up becoming a problem, I could definitely get by. I know how my parents think. Even if I didn't, I'm good at playing the right part of a conversation. It's like you can talk your way out of anything. Just say something that doesn't let the other person say anything in response.

"You can be, I don't know, talking about a test.

"Yeah, let's say we're talking about a test. It's you and me, we're talking about what answers we got. Comparing notes, basically. I wouldn't really be as confident about my answers, so I probably wouldn't have remembered them. So you would be the one asking and directing the conversation. I've noticed that most conversations have one person really aggressive, talking more, and another who's reacting more than talking. Words are said but both people usually don't stay at the same level. Really good conversation is different. I think it's when two people get along and they just can't stop talking so it keeps going, and the conversation goes back and forth but both are aggressive. Both are talking just as much. I can't remember the last time that happened. Most of the time it's one person and everyone else reacting.

"Same thing, just different size.

"You'd be talking about the answers.

"I'd be like, 'Yeah, I think I got that one right.' But see, I wouldn't be sure. I'd be either confused or just not that interested in the discussion. Maybe worried, because if I failed, I'd be pretty certain that the answers you got weren't the ones I got.

"That's how most of the conversation would go. You talking more and leading the direction—what is talked about and when—and I just kind of fill in the gaps with reactions, with replies. That's how the conversation would go. It's the typical kind of conversation. It's why I can just say something and people either will notice or not—it's up to what I say, how much of it is just agreement and how much of it is actually statement. If you disagree, it's just fuel for the aggressive one to keep going and going and going...

"Thinking about this"—oh, man—"it's getting me worked up."

Maybe I'll—I don't know.

What do I do?

Am I really going to clean?

Hmm.

Do I go upstairs?

Do I grab my laptop and go online?

Do I go to sleep?

Do I at least try to sleep?

"What do you think? Think I should go online? Yeah?"

Hmm.

"What time is it? Yeah, I think I'll check online. See what's up."

I go upstairs, find the laptop where I left it, plugged in and charged, resting on my unmade bed. I don't bother making the bed, not when I'm under the covers 100 percent of the time I'm in my room. Jesus, it's cold. I hold back that shiver like it might be an insult to H, run back downstairs with the laptop, because why not?

It's warmer downstairs.

"Let's get rid of this fast-food garbage. They just left it on the couch, beautiful."

And... let's...

Watch videos.

"It's like opening a gateway of content when you sign in. There's always new uploads. New stuff.

"Huh?

"I haven't...

"What is this? I've never heard of this kind of thing before.

"ASMR?

"I don't remember subscribing to this guy's channel. Damn, he has a lot of these ASMR videos.

"What does ASMR stand for? It's an acronym, right?"

I'll look it up. Yeah. First search result, boom: It's an acronym. It's an acronym for Autonomous Sensory Meridian Response. I could read more about it, but the first line says as much as I need to know. This stuff is supposed to calm you down. Soothing voice and stuff.

I like that.

I need that right now.

"I think I'll... click on the one here."

It's a red-haired woman with really, really bright blue eyes. She gazes at the camera in a way that makes me not want to look away. She speaks in a low, breathy whisper.

"I think they manipulated the sound or something... everything seems really close. Like she's..." I'm looking for the right words. "Yeah, that's it—like she's whispering right into my ear."

It really does work though.

The more I watch this, the calmer I am.

The calmer I am, the more aware I am of what's going on. I'm curious about how I've gotten so used to the symptoms now. I'm so used to them that I can't imagine what it would be like to literally be alone. I'm so used to them that I always dress in layers. I'm so used to them that I've been online twice as much because there's nothing else left in my room except for clothes, furniture, and this laptop.

And then I kind of just stop thinking at all.

"This is really working..."

And I sit here, watching the entire twenty-minute video.

During it, I can't help but think that you are watching it too.

When it's done, I yawn.

"That's really great. It works. I think I'm going to... subscribe to more ASMR videos."

I do that, clicking around, subscribing to the more popular ones, the ones that also have a bunch of collections videos where they talk about various things they collect. There's one channel that has a bunch of videos of a guy who just repeats words over and over again.

"What do you think? Should I subscribe to the repeating-word guy?

"I don't really know why I'm talking to you.

"I think I'm hearing you say something but I can't really tell. It kind of feels like I'm just talking to myself, all these thoughts. Makes me feel a little insane. I guess that's kind of the point though."

Could be one of the symptoms. I'm not really sure.

"Are you there?

"It's okay; you don't have to respond. I don't really know why I'm even doing this. I don't really know what you are, H. A demon, duh, but what's a demon, really? There are speed demons and people called demons in video games and other sports, but they are just people who are insanely good at things.

"I'm curious, that's the thing.

"I'm curious, even more so after today.

"It's like I want to ask you questions and be the aggressive one, the one talking, but when I do, I'm not sure I'm talking to anyone.

"It's like, it's like... I'm talking to a wall sometimes.

"But then I can also sense that you're near.

"What time is it?"

It's almost three A.M.

I didn't look at the clock on the desktop. I didn't look at my phone. But I knew. I just knew—nearly three A.M. Then I look and it's true. It's 2:58 A.M.

Is this frightening or exciting?

What's happening, I can't help but let happen. I can't turn away from it; I tried ignoring it and that didn't work.

I look around the house, the mess.

"Oh, fuck this.

"You agree, right?

"Yeah. Yeah, exactly.

"I don't want to be in this house right now. I want to be somewhere else. I'm not cleaning this shit up. No. I'm not.

"I think the only choice I have is to go for a drive."

And it's just like that—it seems right to leave.

I leave the laptop sitting there, a flicker of trust. I know that I've left the laptop there, just like I know that I am basically just talking to myself.

I won't say that was something else.

But at the same time, it's exciting that it could be.

When I pull out of the driveway, I don't have anywhere in mind to go. I just go. I start driving down one street until I end up on another street. This late into the night, it's pretty cool to pretend that I'm the last one alive. Or that I'm living in an alternate dimension where I can start and stop time and there's nobody but me and my car, and whatever it is that I want in my life.

It's fun to pretend it's the end of the world.

I end up merging onto the interstate and I count how many semitrucks I see. It's the wide-open road and I'm the one little dinky car sharing it with all the other semitrucks.

I don't know where I'm going until I take the exit.

That exit.

I make a right at the first light.

Another right at the second stoplight.

It's like I knew where I'd be going but kept it from myself, until I'm driving fast down that completely pitch-black back road.

They really need to repave the road.

The asphalt is chipped and really hard on the tires. But that doesn't get me to slow down. This drive is mine, and it's all about the speed and night air brushing past my face.

When I get there, I drive down that dirt road because I don't want anyone to see my car. No one's going to see my car, but still, I don't want my car to be seen.

It's funny how I can just pretend like I don't already know what I'm doing. It's really funny how I can just stay in the moment, thinking, "This is happening," and pretend like I'm not actually heading over there, pulling the car into park, shutting off the engine, sitting in the dark, listening as I say, "Here we are."

I said it but I stay in the car for a long time.

Guess it's because normally this would be kind of freaky, in the middle of the forest, dead end of night, and after all the stuff I know can go wrong, I'm still here. By myself.

A rush of ideas comes to mind.

I'm thinking a family of serial killers about to attack me.

I'm thinking a big-ass feral St. Bernard with rabies about to make it so that I'm stranded in this car for days, weeks, starving to death.

I'm thinking of all kinds of stuff that I'm pretending I didn't see in movies. But no, that's also all just padding, stuff I have fun thinking about, before I make that long walk that's really not that long.

It's just for effect.

Yeah, I'm on that long walk...

It's actually not as quiet as you'd think, being out here at night. You hear all kinds of noises—bugs, animals, the wind blowing stuff around—and that really does help.

For a while, I don't use the flashlight on my phone.

I just walk the path I've walked so many times, in complete darkness.

If, like, Blaire were here, she'd be impressed. Becca, she wouldn't care. She's already created some image of me in her mind.

Around the time the path opens up into a big field, I start shining the flashlight around. I step on empty cans and other junk—guess there was a party here recently.

I listen for people's voices but I don't hear anything.

It's an interesting image, thinking that someone's nearby, maybe passed out drunk and sleeping under the stars, and here I am, the definition of late to the party.

I keep on walking.

Soon it's back to a narrow dirt path.

Past that, it's pure forest.

This is where it's tricky, but somehow I know where I'm going.

When I get there, I shine the light up at the crown, staring at the tunnel. I stand at the opening, tuning in to the noises surrounding Falter Kingdom.

I don't hear anything.

The moon hides behind clouds, making it hard to even see the ground at my feet. I sit down cross-legged at the opening of the tunnel.

I stare into the darkness.

I say that I don't know why I'm here but it's a lie.

I've been holding it back until it's appropriate to just say it.

And that moment's right now: I'm here to see you.

I'm curious. I want to see what you look like, H. And I mean really what you look like. I figure this is the place where it's most possible, the place where we first met. I don't know a whole lot about how this works, how energy is used and transferred and stuff, but I figure if it's near a weak spot where demons can and will exist, then this is where I might see you.

I'm right here, H.

"I'm right here," I say aloud.

Breathe in.

Breathe out.

Listen to the quiet.

I have to be patient.

I have to calm down my nerves. I'm shaking. I've been trying to focus on other things to avoid the fact that my heart is beating so hard it's like it's coming out of my chest. This isn't easy for me. I have to believe that I'm here for a reason. It's the only way I'll be able to calm myself down.

And I'll wait.

H, I'm right here.

I'll say hi first.

"Hey."

I wait—wait for some kind of noise.

I sit here, back straight, staring into the void, trying to remain focused on what I see—which is nothing—but my mind quickly goes to different things. The word "void" is one thing. Is it really the right word to use in this situation? I've always liked the word "void." It has this eerie kind of connotation. I hope I'm using the word "connotation" right. I think I am, but I can easily doubt myself the more I think about things.

I look up at the stars. You can't really see them so easily from back home. But out here, you can see every single one. Some of them twinkle. More than a few just stay there, all bold.

"H, you there?"

I feel a cool gust of air escaping the tunnel.

Then nothing happens for a really long time.

It feels like forever, and I watch it go light, then dark, and light again, as clouds roll past in the sky. Mostly it's just the moon and me.

I know H is nearby, somehow.

I don't really know how it works, but I want to know. That's why I'm here. I have to know. It's either be curious or be a fucking pussy. It's easier to be a pussy and just run away from what's happening, but then I'd never be able to forgive myself, because what I'm seeing and feeling is nothing I've ever experienced before. It's both crazy and cool. I don't know how to describe it. That's basically why I'm so curious.

Life can be so dull when every day it's school and then home and then parties and everyone acting like some concert or football game or dance is like some big deal. When it really isn't. It isn't. I have a hard time finding interest in what's already there, everything laid out in front of me like it's already been lived, prepackaged for all of us graduating high school. We go through steps and never really make our own footprints in the ground.

We just step where everyone else has stepped.

No new paths.

I don't like that. I hate it, really.

But this, what's happened, it's different. You hear so much about demons and hauntings and possession, but it's just like being in a movie or becoming a rock star: it never really happens to you.

But it's happening to me.

See? I can't just be afraid.

What's happening is worth understanding as long as I keep my distance.

I've thought about it and I've made up my mind: I want to understand; more than anyone would want to understand me, I want to understand this. Everyone around me just wants to be around me, like some entourage.

I want to care.

Most people probably don't care about anything other than themselves.

So what, then, if I sit here all night?

It gets lighter around me, but it remains dead-end night in that tunnel.

I hear footsteps nearby, but it passes.

Just someone, a person, or maybe my imagination.

But I'm here. I'm here to say hi.

I'm here to understand.

I'm here to see H.

Shortly before dawn, I stand back up. My legs ache like hell, but I stand there for, like, another hour.

I talk into the tunnel: "How are you feeling?"

When the sun finally replaces the moon, I say into the tunnel, "Good morning."

But there's nothing there for me to see.

I'll walk back at some point, but I know that it was right to have gone here. It was the right choice. I needed to sort things out. Not everything is sorted, but I'm beginning to understand where my priorities are. There'll be an exorcism and there'll be all the usual stuff, step by step, that will end up being my life... but something is happening here that doesn't happen to everyone. Only, like, 40 percent of the world ever experiences stuff like this. It's common enough that you know all the symptoms, but it's special in that way that you end up on a short enough list.

It's true, though I didn't want to admit it:

I will be remembered at Meadows as the guy who was haunted.

I'll be like the others who ended up the same way.

But I really don't care. I don't care what they think because what they think is clearly what everyone else has already said. Nothing new there.

I understand all of that.

So I'm ready to understand everything else.

Before leaving, I say into the tunnel, "See you around."

And I make the not-so-long walk back to my car.

I don't realize how tired I am until I'm almost home. I start to nod off while driving. It's bad, yeah, but that's why I drive slower, and I keep things under the speed limit. I look at the time on the dashboard, and it's early enough that only the morning people are really going to be out.

The sky is a shade of blue. It's more a mixture of the end of night and the first couple blinks of new day.

It's dark enough still that I need my headlights on.

Funny to note: I didn't have them on the entire time I was on the interstate. I thought the trucks and cars honking at me were just doing me a favor, trying to keep me awake. I'm okay though. No accidents.

I pull into the driveway and rub my eyes.

Yawns can feel so good sometimes, you know? Same way there's nothing like a good stretch. I glance up at my window the way I always do and I'm surprised to see that the lights are on. Not only that, I see a figure in the window. I blink and it's gone and I'm kind of like, "Was that you, H?"

Maybe I made that part up.

I am pretty tired. I probably just imagined it.

I leave the car where it's going to be left and head up the walkway to the front door. Inside the house, I don't notice the change right way. It's kind of like a slow burn, how sometimes you light something on fire and it doesn't flare up the way you expect, not right way. I notice the laptop first; it's right where I left it, but it's been opened. A video plays, an ASMR video I haven't watched.

All the empty bottles and garbage, even the board and its pointer—it's all gone. Went missing or something. I'm not playing stupid. I know what happened. I can put all the pieces together.

So I might not completely understand it, but yeah, I know what just happened. Scratch that—I know what happened while I was gone. There's no mess and no sign that there was ever a party.

I sit down on the couch. I laugh. "But I like the version where the party still happens because, like, everyone still gets a good scare." Then I add, "And we get a good laugh."

I lie down on the couch, laptop on my stomach, and I start up the ASMR video from the beginning.

Just as I'm beginning to nod off, I hear it.

It's my voice but it's not me who's saying it. It's different from the other times.

The voice says, "Welcome home."

And I know it's you. It makes me shiver but I let it pass.

Keeping my eyes on the video, right before I fall asleep, I say: "Home sweet home."

I think that's supposed to be funny.

I wonder if H laughs, or if it's possible for H to laugh.

I've been waiting for this. It's so sudden—know how sleep sort of pulls over you like a sheet, like you're a body being covered but you're not actually dead? Yeah, that's how it starts. Pure sleep, the kind that just works, and you don't have to work for it. It just comes. Just sleep. Guess it's there, waiting for me. I find it even though I don't really know what I have. It is sleep in the most basic kind of way. It's nothing and everything until I see it open in on a familiar setting. I can't put my finger on where I am, only that it's happening again.

Like I said, I've been waiting for this.

It feels like before. So real, I can sense that this is reality, but then I know I'm dreaming. If I really need confirmation, I can hear myself breathing. I don't know how to really explain it all but it's there. I'm just outside of anything real. I'm in this, right now, and I recognize these people.

Here's how it all comes to me:

I see the bright blue sky first. Second, I see the trees, the forest, and I hear the various trappings that make a person know immediately that he's out in the middle of nowhere. I'm talking the sound of birds, the bugs biting at you, the smell that's supposed to mean that there's no smog, none of the usual pollution. It's all there, and it wraps around me like I've never left.

Then we're walking.

I say "we" because there are three people with me.

There's a girl and two guys. We're all talking, daring one another to jump into a nearby river. We're talking usual talk, the kind of stuff that's all about toys and games and the stuff that's supposed to fill a young person's mind in movies. But see, I'm right in the middle of another scene.

The movies never really get it right. They make some things so much fancier and prettier than it really is.

The people with me, they get along.

And I'm not saying I don't get along with other people; that part is easy. What I'm really saying is that people usually don't have such perfect conversations. They don't just go from talking to arguing and back so smoothly. I'm not sure what I'm trying to say except that I think... I think that the movies get it so right, get it perfect, and because it's perfect, it comes off fake. Yeah, that's it. I'm walking with three characters from an adventure movie I watched when I was a kid.

I watched the hell out of this movie.

We're about to find a dead body.

It's the discovery that defines our summer.

But it's also the discovery that defines our lives. Some of us never make it past this discovery. It kind of warps our minds.

But we're living a perfect moment. It's summer and we're kids and we're friends. What gets better than that? In this dream, the dream I'm gripping on to, just waiting for its strange turns, it doesn't. We walk through that forest to the rocky line where it slopes into a gorge.

One character says something.

Another character says something.

A third character says something.

And then I say something.

But there's no overlap unless we're supposed to be arguing. There's a rhythm to the way we talk. We're friends. That's how we're defined. I don't know anything about them—let's just say that I don't even though I've seen the movie a thousand times— and we're best of friends, looking for some great adventure.

It's just like that Friday when I ran. There was Brad and Blaire and... that other kid. Steve, yeah, that's his name. I barely knew him and he barely knew me. It's just like that day, except the characters here are written in the script to get along.

I walk with them and I say my lines.

I walk with them, but I'm more interested in the knowledge that this is about to change. I can almost sense it coming. In my dream, I'm able to think my way through the events as they happen. It's so cool that I can, that I know how this will come together. I should be bored, but it's like I'm walking through the scene of the movie as it's being filmed.

I'm like, "Where's the camera?" right as it all changes.

Instead of the gorge and the dead body, it's Falter Kingdom. I can see the crown, the dark tunnel, the sort of doom and gloom that you always feel around the place. One second I'm in a movie and the next second it's me, standing there with the rest of them; I'm talking about Blaire and Brad and Steve. We're as we really were, and there's Brad talking to Steve.

This is how real people talk. It's not pretty. It's more annoying than anything else.

I hear them talking about Nikki. It's just like the usual, Brad always bringing up the gossip, Nikki at the top of the list.

"You guys hear?"

No, I didn't hear, Brad.

And then there's Blaire. Blaire looks miserable. She's always so focused on school and the future. All that stuff. Then there's that kid Steve, but let's just move on because whatever.

Who's left but, oh yeah, me. I'm drinking beer, downing them one after the other, which makes Blaire kind of worried; she notices while Brad gets competitive.

I knew that he would and there I am, knowing just what to say to make it not be about me. But on this day, it becomes all about me. Everything turns and the dream does too. It turns all on me. Eyes on me, like I asked to be the main character. Even *I'm* looking at me. But then I start tossing and turning in my sleep. Something's weird about this.

The details are different. They don't add it up.

It's not just the details either. It's the perspective.

I'm seeing from somewhere else... and it's not until I'm walking up—that's me, walking up to Brad and Steve—that I get it.

I get it now.

I'm not really listening to them and I'm drinking and then it kind of just happens before I even realize it. I tell them that I'll do it.

Funny how one stupid thing can turn everything upside down.

Everything's upside down and I'm seeing it all happen.

I'm running down the tunnel like it's so damn easy. I'm running all drunk, almost tripping on my toes.

I'm running toward you.

And then I pass you by. It's like you're running after me. It's like you're the camera and I'm the main character, being filmed.

But this isn't anything like that. This is what you saw, right? This is what you're trying to tell me.

You leave me though. You let me run and you turn and look back at what happens when their timers go off. First it's Blaire, who says, "Oh no..."

And then it's Steve who says, "Hunter?" He sounds insincere, kind of worried but clearly doesn't care.

And then it's Brad who starts freaking out: "What the fuck?" But that doesn't stop him from shotgunning a can of beer.

Blaire tells him, "Something's wrong."

"Shit," Brad says, beer running down the sides of his mouth.

Steve starts backing away from the opening of the tunnel.

Brad notices. "Shit, how long's he been in there?"

Blaire doesn't have to check. She knows exactly how long.

But I don't hear that part. You decide to move on, back to me, running. You join me where you left me, and it's only at that point that I am able to move forward. I was running in place? I start grinding my teeth. I never grind my teeth in my sleep.

Back to Blaire, who's the only one left.

I know where Brad went. Like Steve, he was scared. He didn't want to be involved, thinking about himself first. When Blaire called him out on it, he shouted, "We'll get help!" They were both so scared they couldn't move.

I know because you know.

It's the only way I'm able to know.

You reach out to me and touch me, but I don't see your hand and I don't notice you when you do; but that gets me to stop. That sends the signal to go back. But you're with me the entire run back.

You're at my side when I walk the trail back to my car.

You're right there, in the front passenger seat, when I pull out of the Meadows parking lot.

You're right there.

My body and mind are telling me that this is bad. I'm starting to shake in my sleep, but something else, the fact that the dream keeps going... it keeps me from just pushing away. My curiosity makes me turn the next corner. But instead of driving home, I'm driving back.

It's three A.M.

I know because you know. It's three A.M. the previous night and I'm driving. I make that exit and I end up on that dirt road. I sit there for a while and you stand outside, watching me from the front of the car. At one point, I look right at you and I'm able to see what I look like. I look different somehow. I don't know.

Turn another corner, on foot, and I walk toward you.

I turn my attention to you.

It's the darkness of night and it's like that person standing at the opening of Falter Kingdom... it's like that person isn't really me.

You look at me and I look back.

I see what you see.

That person sits down. That person seems to be really patient, like he has nowhere else to go.

For a while, there's nothing, one watching the other.

But then there's the familiar voice: "H, you there?"

And then I hear you say, from deep within the tunnel...

Yes.

The word hangs there, and it's my voice. But it doesn't register as a real word. Like everything else, even in the context of a dream, you sound like me and you send everything in the only way that's possible. It makes complete sense but, at the same time, things don't seem to add up.

They don't need to add up.

They just are.

And then the words "How are you feeling?" they reach the very back of the tunnel. I can hear them in this dream, which means you could hear them when I said them.

I hear a rumbling noise, a low voice.

It seems like you're getting closer to that person, to me.

I'm sitting there, all deep in thought, totally not seeing you in the dark of the tunnel. You get closer and closer and closer.

When I move to leave and say, "See you around," you're right there with me.

I see what you see and from where you stood: you could see my breath in the air, chilled, but I didn't seem to notice that night.

You watch me walk back.

You watch and I watch.

And then you say...

See you around.

Next thing I know I'm on the couch, awake.

I WAKE UP HAPPY AND IT'S WEIRD, YEAH. I REMEMBER
everything and it kind of, well, it gives me something to think about.
It's all going to end at some point, right? Like, I could be like everyone else and just be like, "The exorcism is next week." I could be like
that but I think I'm way beyond that kind of stuff. It'll happen, yeah,
I'm not forgetting that, but really, this is my chance to learn more.
This is my one chance to explore. I mean, seriously, after what happened after the party, after that dream, I'm so excited.

I wake up refreshed, feeling like I have a ton of energy.

Also bizarre, but I'll take it. Can't wait to see what happens next.

I go to my room, looking at the time on my phone and, damn, it's
early. But not early enough to see that H has changed some things
around. I look in my closet and it's kind of like, "Um, I used to have
more clothes than this..."

But the laptop's still there, on my desk. I walk over and look. I
google some possession porn videos because maybe they'll give me
some understanding, I don't know, and I end up watching this one
that shows a before and after of someone's possession. It's mostly
about the person's exorcism. They don't even go far enough to have

any of the dreams, any of the lapses in time and consciousness and shit. They get it done quick, and the fact that they did really makes me feel better.

I say, "This one's like all the others."

And it's not like I'm talking to myself. It really isn't.

I don't realize that I'm shivering, goose bumps on my arms and everything. I'm wearing only boxers and a T-shirt that's been sweat through.

Again, I have to be like, "Um, I used to be wearing more clothes than this..." I scratch at my palms, some sort of rash maybe, but I push that to the side when I hear a car door close outside. I don't want that person to see me at the window, so I do that thing where you hide at the side of the window and take short glances, not even, like, ten seconds each. I see a white car. Not Mom's or Dad's...

Second time I look, I see a familiar man.

Then the doorbell.

"Who the hell is that?"

But then I know. It clicks—Father Albert. It's like the information was given to me.

You did that, didn't you?

I stand there a second, curious to see if I'll know... but nothing happens. The doorbell is pressed a second time.

Dammit. I put on some clothes, whatever I can find.

Running down the stairs, I say something like, "Does your kind actually get hurt by all that religious stuff?"

I'm in for a surprise when I open the door. One look at Father Albert and you tell me. No. It, like, holds there, as if right on Father Albert's forehead, the word "no" hanging there. Like it's you, trying to make me laugh.

"Greetings, Hunter," Father Albert says.

The way he looks at me, I notice.

I can't help but get angry when I see his face, how he just kind of judges me and acts all fake. I know that he thinks I'm sick and falling apart because of what's happening. I know that it's his job to be here, to help me, but the first thing he could do is just be real. Say it, man. Say it: *You look like shit.*

I reply, "Hi," and I feel like shit when I say it.

Funny how it all switches when someone like Father Albert shows up.

He walks into the foyer, hands folded, Bible pressed against his chest. He looks around, and I just know that he's trying to sense where H is.

"He's looking for you," I whisper.

I think about what might happen. I really don't know what's going to happen. I wonder...

"How are you feeling on this fine morning, Hunter?"

What do you want me to say? I shrug and say the first thing that comes to mind: "I'm really tired but I'm, uh, fine. Just fine."

Why is it so hard to speak? Like, it was really hard to just get that out. It's like I don't even want to keep up appearances. It's like, whatever.

Father Albert with his fake grin. "On this morn, we will begin our process. First, I'd like to bless the house. This will not take long."

"Okay," I say, and Father Albert leads the way.

I whisper, "What does this do?"

I kind of expect H to respond, but then Father Albert's like, "This will help cleanse your place of rest. A home should not be invaded. It is a sacred place, for it is where you have chosen to occupy and place meaning. This is the reason an unclean spirit will attach itself to a location. It will try to get your attention. Once it gets your attention, it will attempt to make contact. Once it does that, as we have discussed previously, during our meeting, it will begin the principles of infestation."

"Infestation," I mumble.

"Mm-hmm." Father Albert nods, walking into the kitchen. "You will experience a variety of advanced symptoms. One of the most popular symptoms is a late-stage sense of lethargy. Additionally, cognitive dissonance."

Father Albert stops, puts a hand on my shoulder, and I want to slap it off. I want to say something like, *Stop being so fake. Tell me how far gone I am. Just tell me and you'll still get that payday.*

He leans forward. "Pray with me."

I'm not praying with you.

He makes the sign of the cross, folds his hands together, and starts on some prayer that I really can't stand to listen.

I'm mumbling stuff like, "This really works, yeah, really?"

But when I hear a rumbling from deep within the house, I start thinking that maybe H is wrong. Father Albert really can hurt him. It's kind of like... a double take. I'm like, *Wait? What's happening?*

Father Albert walks into the next room, the family room, and starts making hand gestures.

He doesn't stop praying.

I hear the same rumbling. It's getting louder.

I close my eyes and I don't know why. My bottom lip starts to quiver and I don't know why. A lot of things happen and I don't know why.

But the fact that I don't know doesn't seem to bother me.

Father Albert says my name, and I open my eyes. He wants me to follow him upstairs.

As we do, he continues the prayer. He blesses every room, but we step into only mine. Right as he walks in, he stops praying. Father Albert notices the drop in temperature but doesn't say anything. He kind of looks around my room in a weird way, and I can tell that this isn't normal. I watch from the hallway, completely separate from the fact that he is in *my* room, judging my things, and more than all of that, he's judging me.

It makes me feel like I'm the one who's at fault. Like this is my fault. Father Albert looks at my bed and it's like he's thinking that it's pathetic.

It makes me mad.

Really mad.

When he looks back at me, waving me in—"Dear son, please, be by my side"—I want to punch him. I want to push him to the ground. I come up with a dozen things I want to do to him and they all end the same way: he leaves and never comes back. I'm like, *Why do you get to judge me? Can I judge you? Can I tell you how fake you are? How you probably never had one single original thought in your head?*

How you probably never did anything interesting in life? You just followed the same footsteps and ended up where you are, Father Albert.

But there I am, standing at his side.

He places a hand on my forehead and I'm surprised by how warm it is. It's like almost scalding hot.

He starts reciting another prayer.

In this moment, I start to feel a little sick.

"Hunter, stay with me, son," Father Albert says.

I want this to end. That's what I'm thinking.

I want this to end.

I want this to end. I repeat it in my head, like some kind of message that won't send. I want this to end.

I start shaking.

I want this to end.

Father Albert says, "In the name of the Father, the Son, and the Holy Spirit..."

I want this to end. Now.

Suddenly the bedroom door shuts.

Father Albert stops praying.

We start hearing the scratching sounds.

It gets colder. I remember the cold. I see my breath and Father Albert's too. I can still feel the heat on my forehead. I know that you never left, and then I also see what's about to happen.

I start to feel better.

Father Albert keeps telling me, "It will be okay, son."

He holds on to my hand. The look on his face, the way his lips still move, he's reciting the rosary. I see the beaded necklace in his hand. Oh, so that's what it is. I didn't know until just now what that was.

Then we hear the rumbling again.

Father Albert closes his Bible, tells me, "It appears as though the situation is far more advanced than previously specified."

Like that's my fault. Right? My fault?

"I told you what I knew."

Father Albert nods.

I ask him, "What are you going to do now?"

Just because I'm curious.

Does a priest get afraid?

Father Albert keeps cool. Of course Father Albert always keeps his cool. I kind of want him to just be real. I want him to jump in fear. I want him to start praying for his own safety. I want him to be like, "Damn, man, this is bad."

Something like that.

Instead he tells me, "Perhaps it's best to leave before we provoke the spirit any further."

I know what's going to happen next.

He tries the door.

It doesn't budge.

Yeah, I've been there, man. I'm right here with you, but really, I'm just watching. I'm convinced that it's all an act and Father Albert's the star of this prank. Father Albert, come on—do you really think that's going to work? He keeps trying the door and then he starts ramming the door with his shoulder. He wants to break through the door. But he doesn't need to do all that.

The door. It'll open the moment I try turning the doorknob.

Father Albert stops and straightens his collar. Says to me, "My apologies, Hunter. Let us both pray and the activity will pass. The spirit only has so much energy at its expense. It shall soon tire."

I shake my head. "Let me try the door."

I walk over and it's like some planned stunt, I turn the doorknob like it wasn't ever a problem.

The door opens and, yeah, Father Albert looks at me different, a loaded look, because of course he's going to blame me. I'm at fault. And then he tells me that things need to speed up. He says that he'll be here tomorrow. And I'm all about pretending that I don't need any of this urgent care but that's not going to work. Of course it isn't going to work. So Father Albert says one last prayer and leaves, wishing me luck.

Right before he steps outside, he whispers to me, "Stay strong. You are in a battle for your soul."

I watch him leave.

The house is quiet after he's gone.

I whisper, "All for show."

It was all for show.

Back upstairs in my room, I feel more like myself.

I stand at my bed, looking straight ahead. Time seems to pass.

I busy myself with the thoughts that should come, but instead, I'm left standing, waiting for anything, anything at all, to pop up. It's like you know that you're supposed to be doing something but you forgot what. That's the way this feels. It feels like I was thinking about something but I misplaced that thought, or it was taken from me. I stand there, looking for it. Eventually it makes me tired. I find myself in bed, sheets up to my chin. I close my eyes, waiting for sleep to arrive. I can hear movement nearby, the air changing to the left of the bed. A knot forms in my throat. I feel like my heart is going to burst from my chest. Then I remember what it was that I was trying to think of, which really helps me settle down. There are more thoughts, but they keep their distance. I'm pretty calm, waiting.

I'll be asleep in no time. It's not like before, when I kept waking up. Now I just want to sleep through the entire day. Maybe I will.

H will be waiting.

This time I'm nobody. I'm nobody named. I'll probably yawn, shiver, and scream in my sleep... but something about seeing everything from your eyes makes it better. It keeps me going. I'd be lying if I didn't mention that the danger, the sheer worry that should be here, is misplaced and made into something that seems like another reason to have fun. Like watching horror movies back when I was a kid: I didn't want to keep watching, because everyone knew that it'd only get crazier and scarier, but I'd keep watching. Even if I needed to cover my eyes, I kept watching.

That's how I feel about this dream.

My dreams have become far more interesting than my days.

It starts like the others, which tells me that this one will be different. I just don't know how. Not yet.

You stay in one place, near the bedroom door, watching as I turn on all the lights in the house. I look like an idiot, all nervous, thinking random thoughts. I keep thinking that I'm going to be able to ignore you, thinking about how there's nothing in the attic, nothing going on that isn't just a symptom of the haunting.

Nothing is "just" a symptom though.

I am beginning to understand that.

You are everywhere I couldn't have imagined. It's like I'm part of a reality television show for demons or something. I watch what you saw, and I half expect to be graded like I just finished singing or dancing. How did I do?

It's only just begun.

I should be afraid but I was really afraid then—does that make up for now? I'm watching intently, and this feels kind of like how you watch your home movies later in life and critique how bad you were: Man, what was I thinking? Always better in the future, always better in the future.

So we're watching as I walk up to the attic. I'm so damn slow.

No, this isn't in slow motion, is it? Man, why am I hesitating? Just go!

If only I knew back then that you were right behind me... following me everywhere...

Most of the time, it seems, you are close enough that I can never be completely comfortable. Wait, I'm comfortable? It's amazing to think that I can get used to that. After long, it's a normal situation.

I'll have to admit that this dream really does feel different. Yeah, and I like that, sure, but I can't help but feel like, this time, you're the one that's having all the fun. You kind of force me into that corner, making noise and making me feel like I'm going in the right direction. It's a little bit like a video game, seeing how the smallest details can get a response.

And it's because you can hear my thoughts that I can see how every little thing affected me.

The dark mass I see was you.

When I turn around, we're looking right at me. It's not like I didn't know that when it happened. I knew that. But, like, it's different now.

It's all different, seeing it from the other side. It makes me feel stupid for thinking I could just ignore everything. It was really stupid to think that I could just be like, "Yeah, I'm going to pretend that this is all just usual stuff."

It really is true, what they say:

You never know what you're messing with until it's too late.

The fear on my face, it's kind of funny.

I'm laughing in my sleep because you were finding it funny back then, and now I'm kind of finding it funny too.

It's actually kind of mean, especially when that fear starts rising to the point where I'm shaking, visibly shaking, but in the context of this dream, I can see why it would be so funny. I was acting like it didn't matter, but I was carrying all the different ideas and things I had seen and heard about from media, from school, from society. But really, I couldn't have guessed how this would fall into place.

I'm standing in the hallway, shaking.

I kind of don't want to see what happens next.

But I know what happens next.

You watch me from inside my bedroom.

I hear the words "You're messing with me" and remember what I was thinking when I said that. Strange to see how things change.

This time, I hear you say, "Let's play a game," my voice hanging there like it's voice-over or director's commentary. Then the dream kind of shakes a little.

Maybe you're laughing. Or maybe that's me, laughing in my sleep.

It really does feel like forever ago. I can watch this like it's not even me. It's because I can separate both experiences, the dream from what actually happened, that I can make sense of what's happening.

This was the night you took my laptop.

This was the night when I realized that it's just that simple, ignoring what can be anywhere, at all times.

And this dream, it's the one where maybe you're trying to mess with me some more. Maybe you're trying to show me how much of an idiot I've been. But I am able to see from your side, and because I can, I feel like I can get past all that stuff, the human fear and paranoia.

There I am, walking into the dining room, looking under the table. Now that's a real fail.

We follow me into the family room, staring at me as I stare at the TV. Then it's back around to the foyer. I, like, hyperventilate for a second.

Wow, what am I doing?

Are those tears?

All for a missing laptop?

There's something wrong about that, isn't there?

Is that what you were trying to tell me?

Yeah?

It's like I can almost understand what you're trying to tell me, but you won't just tell me. You're holding back. You want me to walk through the rest of the dream, huh? We're the ones pressing all the buttons.

I go back upstairs.

You get me to go into one of the guest bedrooms when you walk into the closet and shake the door.

I don't remember that.

All the rumbling, it's just you.

All the scratching, it's just you.

I go through all the drawers. Kind of weird to think that a laptop would just show up there. But then again, what do I know?

I remember this part.

I walk back into my room. I pretend to not care and I use my phone as a computer, meaning I go online with my phone. I look completely wrecked. I look like I've lost it all. This is the part that even I didn't see, back when it was happening. I ignored the tears running down my face. I ignored the panic. Look at how I keep checking the time on my phone like a maniac. I keep going back and forth between different apps. I can't sit still. I don't remember it this way.

You watch and find it funny.

You think it's funny, don't you?

Why are you here?

The laptop was where I found it the entire time. You moved it like you moved everything else. But in the dream, you moved it for a different reason. You are trying to get my attention. I did my best to ignore you.

You just tell me where it is.

I remembered that—how I just knew all of a sudden. And now I know why: you saw how it was fucking me up and you figured enough was enough.

That's it, right, what you're trying to tell me?

Then we watch me watching the video, the video that plays by itself and then crashes the browser.

I start shivering in my sleep.

You are watching me from over my shoulder. You are watching me right from the start. You are watching me until the very end, when I leave for the party. You are right there, giving me a sort of second look at my actions.

I was confused.

I'm not confused now.

I know more than I've ever known, more than maybe Father Albert or anyone else. I know about you. And in the context of this dream, you tell me that it was a joke. You ask me if it was funny. We're two producers behind the scenes of the reality television show version of my life. We're talking like it was all staged but we kept our parts secret from each other.

We talk it up like this isn't anything surprising.

We talk...

And you know what?

It is kind of funny.

I did most of the scaring myself. You didn't have to do anything. That's the funny part. You weren't even really doing anything. I'm laughing. I'm laughing and I can hear it.

Have you ever laughed in your sleep?

You took the laptop, yeah, but that was the joke part. I guess we aren't used to each other's sense of humor. It's cool.

I don't actually want this dream to end. Even though it's really strange and it makes me out to be an idiot, I want to see more.

But then I start hearing the sound of cars outside.

I know that they're back, and I'm—no, *we're*—going to have to deal with them. And she's with them too. Becca's back to play girlfriend after basically ditching me over the last few days.

I wake up in bed feeling more like I was just visiting a different place. I look out the window, watching them talk to each other, and I just feel like shit. Really feel like shit. I want to go back. To sleep. To that place. To where we were. I want to know more. I want to see more.

But yeah, of course I don't get to.

Because the doorbell rings.

No, I don't know what day it is. I kind of remember a time when I think I was saying something like time feels elastic. But maybe that wasn't me. Maybe it was. Or maybe it was H. Whatever it is, I still don't know what day it is. The first thing Becca says when I open the door is "Jesus, Hunter," and then she kind of takes it back, realizing that she's around holy people. "Oh, sorry."

Father Albert says, "Greetings, Hunter."

The other guy, the one with him, is introduced as Father Andrew.

I kind of nod or something, not really sure. I don't really seem to care. I just want to get this all over with.

I let them in, following them into the dining room. They sit down at the table. I sit across from them, noticing that Becca stays with the two priests.

There's a whole lot of distance between us, huh?

H kind of seems to agree, letting me know that she's afraid of me, the way I look.

What do I look like?

Maybe I look a little different—that's part of it, right?

"What are you looking at?" I catch myself snapping at Father Andrew.

He stares at me, and I know that he's trying to get me angry. He wants to get me angry.

Becca tells me—no, she's actually telling Father Albert: "He really hasn't been himself lately. . ."

So? I'm actually more myself than ever before. Not that she would understand me.

Father Andrew asks Becca, "Where are his parents?"

Becca frowns. "They're busy people, um..."

But it's like both priests put the pieces together without any trouble. I'm thinking, like, "Am I some cliché or something?" Really? It's that easy to figure out how fucked my family is?

This anger, it shows only when they're around.

Father Albert starts the conversation. "Hunter, it appears as though we've greatly misinterpreted our initial assessment. I've returned with Father Andrew so that we might better understand the severity of the situation."

Yeah, like that makes sense.

Father Andrew says it in plainer words: "We want to measure the depth of the spirit's influence."

"Whatever." I kind of say it louder than I should.

Becca looks at me like I'm disgusting. I glare at her. She looks away. What the hell was that? I tell her, "What? Huh? What's your damn problem?" She sniffles, and I'm like, "Who's really the victim here?"

Father Andrew is fearless.

Hey, H, what are you going to do to this guy?

What are *you* going to do? He's holding me down. Do something. Mess with them. Make this funny.

But then Father Andrew says, "It's breaking you down."

"Huh?"

He starts asking me questions that I cannot help but answer honestly. It's like I'm not even talking, the answers are slipping out of my mouth.

First question is "Do you see the spirit in your dreams?"

And the first answer is "Yes."

Second question is "Have you lost sense of time?"

And the second answer is "Yes."

Third question is "Do you experience moments of chatter, where your mind talks back to you?"

And the third answer is "Yes."

I answer yes to everything.

And then Father Andrew looks at Father Albert and says, "Advanced. It is near."

Becca kind of shudders, makes this noise, like she actually cares, and then asks the two priests: "What, um, what happened? What's happening?"

Father Albert wraps his hands around hers. "Breathe, dear. Hunter will be fine. Father Andrew only means to say that our unclean spirit is proving to be more aggressive than expected."

Becca sighs.

Father Albert smiles. "We are perfectly fine for it is Hunter that resists. As long as Hunter resists—"

Father Andrew interrupts. "As long as Hunter resists the spirit, he will remain himself. The spirit will begin to proliferate itself through his unconscious dreams. It will begin to create a sense of cognitive dissonance, where there is chatter of all sorts." Father Andrew walks around the table, never breaking eye contact with me. I'm frozen in place. I don't know what to think. I listen on—hearing it all and yet hearing nothing.

"Typical late-stage symptoms include body mutilation, cognitive dissonance, loss or jumbling of senses... one of the most common symptoms, after the spirit has made contact—and it has made contact with Hunter—has to do with the transformation of personality and behavior. Hunter is inside this poor body"—Father Andrew points at me from across the room—"but he is fading, more distant with every consecutive day."

Becca sniffles. "No..."

Father Andrew shakes his head. "As long as Hunter resists inviting the spirit, it will be akin to a powerful flu. He will not be himself. He has already begun to show the physical signs of atrophy: pale skin, bruising. Soon he will sleep through most of the days.

This is due to the body and mind being exhausted by the battle with the spirit's advances."

Becca asks, "Will he make it to the exorcism?"

I'm laughing but they don't seem to hear me.

Father Albert tells her, "Dear, he will make it."

Father Andrew seems to agree. He breaks eye contact with me and I start coughing like crazy. He tells her, "Hunter is very much alive. But he mustn't entertain the spirit."

When Father Andrew says that, it's like they all turn on me, getting judgmental. Father Albert leans forward and I can hear it in his voice: "Hunter, have you been entertaining the spirit?"

I don't even know what that means.

Becca is like, "Oh no," but I know it's fucking fake. Yeah, right. She cares. She cares only because I'm her boyfriend of, like, three years. That's a lot of years. She cares only because whatever happens to me, it also happens to her, socially. People will know and associate her with me.

It's not exciting now, is it?

I wear a weird look that they seem to think isn't my own face, my own grin.

"A sinister grin," Father Andrew observes, biting his lower lip.

Father Albert sighs. "My, my, my..."

Becca says, "What?"

Father Albert stands up. "Dear, I think we should let Father Andrew speak to Hunter in private."

Becca doesn't put up much of a fight. Duh. No surprise there. Whoopie.

Father Andrew walks over to me, standing at my side. He puts a cross on the table in front of me.

What is going on, H?

But then I kind of feel it from deep within, knowing that it'll be okay. This will all be okay. So random, it comes to mind and then I say it: "Damn, I haven't been drunk in forever."

Father Andrew tilts his head to one side. "That's normal."

I'm like, "What?"

Just stay calm.

Father Andrew kneels down so that he is face-to-face with me. He moves the cross closer to me. "Hunter, stay with me. It's normal—say whatever comes to mind."

I start grinding my teeth. I can feel the pain in my jaw.

Father Andrew moves the cross an inch forward. "Say what's on your mind, Hunter. Say what's on your mind."

He's trying to get H to speak.

"Say what's on your mind!"

He's trying to get a look at H. He's trying to get a lead on H.

H is resisting. H is on my left side, Father Andrew on my right. H is doing his best. It's like H is telling me to say things that make no sense, just to fight off what's happening. I'm asking H what's happening.

What's happening, H?

I say, "She doesn't really care!"

Father Andrew isn't really listening. "Say what's on your mind!"

He wants to hear H.

What's happening, H?

I say, "Who really cares about me?"

"Say what's on your mind!"

H, what's happening?

I say, "I won't be remembered!"

"Say what's on your mind, Hunter!"

H...

I say, "She didn't really like me!"

"Say what's on your mind, Hunter. Say what's really on your mind!"

Father Andrew brings the cross to my forehead and presses it there. It burns, but I'm not going to budge. H, what's happening? But I hold on, like I'm being torn in two.

Hold on, we'll be okay later.

Hold on.

It will be over soon.

H?

"I command you to show yourself!"

I say nothing.

Father Andrew shouts at the top of his lungs, "Show yourself!"

I find it all so ridiculous all of a sudden.

The tension, the pain, the sudden fever sweats... it all washes clean and I sit there, normal and maybe even a little numb, watching this funny little thing. It's like they really believe it'll work. If this is anything like the exorcism, maybe none of it works. I think about that, watching as Father Andrew says prayers, trying to, like, bring out H from my body or something.

Like H isn't standing on my left, helping me through this.

Father Andrew is clueless.

I'm thinking, like, "If the exorcism is like this, does anyone actually ever get rid of the demon?" And H is sort of playing with me, sending me those ideas, those thoughts, those signals, which makes me think that maybe I'm onto something. Maybe it's all bullshit. Maybe demons stick around, hanging around the people they haunted. Maybe that's the way it really is.

But then again, I don't see why that's a problem. It just means you're never alone, right?

Father Andrew stops, wiping his forehead with a handkerchief.

"You may step in."

Father Albert and Becca walk back in, concerned looks on their faces.

Father Andrew says, "Despite what you've just heard, it's nothing compared to what would have actually happened if the spirit had advanced itself into gripping on to Hunter."

Becca doesn't understand.

I'm kind of wondering myself. But I'm the subject here, the victim—I notice that they aren't really talking to me. The conversation is happening around me, and that's basically how every conversation is. People talk and, really, it doesn't matter much if I say anything or not. It's all up to whether I have anything to say or anything I want to say to them.

Father Albert explains to Becca that Father Andrew tested to see whether the unclean spirit had physically attached itself.

"Like..." It's on the tip of Becca's tongue.

"Possession," Father Andrew says, and nods.

Father Albert smiles. "Hunter will be fine. The unclean spirit remains close, but unattached."

Father Andrew says, "Therefore unable to manipulate Hunter. At this point, the spirit can only tease and do its best to gain attention."

Yeah, just talk about me like I'm not really here.

Becca asks, "About the exorcism, will both of you, like, be part of it?"

Father Andrew leaves my side, stepping back toward the side of the table where the "normal" people are. The two priests exchange looks.

Father Albert speaks up: "I will explain it to you, dear. We will explain the entire process shortly before it transpires."

Father Andrew adds, "We will both be in attendance, yes."

Then they all kind of talk for a while. I can't hear them. They leave me sitting here like I'm asleep, like I'm not really alive. They leave me here like I'm an outcast or something.

H, what are they saying?

I'm able to hear the phrase "his parents."

Becca talks for me, as if I asked her to do that. I try to stand up, and the fact that both priests run over to me all concerned makes me feel like I can't stand up, or that I'm not supposed to stand up, so I fall back into my chair.

It's Father Albert's hands on my shoulders that make me twitch.

"Careful, son."

Father Andrew adding, "You shouldn't overexert yourself."

Didn't they just say that I'm fine?

Becca is all worried. I look at her. She looks right at me. She looks at me like I'm a sad sack.

Hello, Becca. How are you?

Nothing like that is said though. This all happens in one big wave. They talk it out, and then it's all better again. Becca's mood changes and she's happy because, hey, they'll get rid of H in a few days!

The priests leave, bidding me some kind of fake "good day."

Father Albert as fake as ever.

Father Andrew at least says something that sticks.

He says, "It's trying to break you down. It wants to become you. Keep fighting, Hunter. It won't be long now. Keep fighting."

They leave. I'm still in the chair.

Becca's the only one left. She seems really nervous.

I can't help but think of this in the context of the dream I just had.

H, you want to?

It could be the same thing, but this time H scares her and I watch.

But what she says—"Hunter, I... I can't be around you right now"—it's supposed to be heartbreaking. She expects me to say something, waiting around, but then I kind of just shrug and stare at her.

It's like, *Hey, what do you expect? I'm haunted. You liked it up until a few days ago: popular by proxy, boyfriend the talk of the entire school.*

Becca breaks into tears. "Hunter..."

Don't say anything. Don't break the mood you have going here.

Becca wipes the tears away, smearing a bit of her eyeliner. "Hunter, I don't know what to say. " Then she's gone, leaving the room.

I hear the front door shut.

Like flicking a switch, I feel better.

I say, "Well, that was intense."

H seems to think so too.

School. Tomorrow. Seems impossible.

But then, maybe it won't be.

Besides, like Father Albert said, I'm going to be fine, right?

Ready or not, here I come.

PEOPLE LOOK AT ME DIFFERENTLY. I'M ALL ABOUT THAT difference. I think I've made that statement before. I can't remember. Some things are cloudy while others are clear like water. I like water. It cleanses the soul, whatever that means. I'm kind of just rambling until I get to first period.

People are looking at me and it's hard to not look back. They look, but now it's not with those sparkling eyes, it's not with that way where they'll walk up to you, wanting to talk to you.

No one is talking to me.

Everyone's a whole lot like...

How to describe it...

I'm getting this "stay back" vibe. Kind of like how people treat anyone who is contagious. But I'm not contagious.

They just know what I'm capable of.

Well, I mean, they know what H is capable of.

Walking toward my locker, I catch a few people literally stepping back like I'm going to attack them or something. I laugh and say, "Guess you were at my party, huh?"

It doesn't hurt me.

Not after Nikki.

Not after it became obvious that this is all it is. It's the same, but different. Like seeing things from H's perspective:

It's the same but I'm just getting a different take.

It adds depth. It shows me how people can act one way but really be something else. I mean, I do it too. I used to be better at it. You know that. I've stopped trying, I guess.

They just want the attention.

Hell, I want the attention too.

I mean, I wanted their attention. Past tense. Don't want it anymore.

Father Andrew says that H wants my attention. I can see that. I meet him in my dreams and they become far more interesting than any of this.

This school day is even more of a blur than usual.

It's like I'm really asleep, and during those dreams, I'm really awake.

What was it that Father Andrew said?

Cognitive dissonance, confusion, loss of time...

Yeah, I can see that. But maybe it's just because everything else is the same. I look around and I don't find anything here. I find only the same things. Those same things want stuff from me. Everyone wants something from me. Like I owe them something.

I walk these halls and I don't have to push through a crowd. Everyone steps out of the way. I'm untouchable.

I should feel embarrassed, but somehow, I'm protected from their gossip, their whispers, by the fact that I know how fickle they are.

Classes run together and I get really bored.

In second period, the substitute teacher doesn't know what to do so he goes up and down the aisles, asking students to talk about what college they're going to. People get all excited about that, yeah. A few are set for the Ivy Leagues. Most are going to State. When the teacher gets to me, there's a brutal hush, and I'm kind of like, *Really?* And the substitute teacher just skips over me. I didn't get to say, "I'm going to State!"

Oh, bummer.

I really, really wanted to say that.

In Mr. Yan's class, he's lecturing but, as usual, I'm not really able to pay attention. It's just facts mixed in with his own rambling, stuff that he likes, his interpretation, stuff that'll be on the final exam. What will be on the final exam? Everyone in the class takes notes. I'm staring blankly at him. I start to notice that he ignores me. It's like he completely closes his eyes when he looks to the right of the room, where I sit.

At lunch, I sit where I always sit, but they aren't there, the people I barely know. The table is empty.

Well, look at that...

As it gets on in the day, I really see how people are, how "fair-weather" they really can be. I mean, I wouldn't stick around either. That's kind of expected. I don't think we were ever more than people we sort of knew.

But then I see that asshole being an asshole as usual. He really isn't going to wander over, is he? If he does, it's just to spite me. Because he's an asshole.

Brad stops, and I can tell that he doesn't want to, but maybe he has an actual thought and maybe that thought was "Dude might fuck me up," so he walks over and sits down across from me.

He says, "Bro, um."

Doesn't really want to look me in the eye, but does anyway.

Then he says, "Oh, man, you look like hell, dude."

He looks down at the table in front of me. I'm not eating anything, no. I don't have much of an appetite anymore. Brad, on the other hand, really rips into that sandwich of his. He's nervous. When people are nervous, sometimes they eat.

There's a conversation that I'm not really involved in. It has to do with what Becca's been doing.

Sure, I'll chime in. "What is Becca"—I have to breathe in, catch my breath; being around people exhausts me—"doing?"

Brad's like, "Bro, you don't know? Fuck, man, she's spreadin' word that it's real serious. We all fucking saw it at your party. Dude, you look like shit. Everyone's talking! You caught a bad one. Real bad. Like, bro, it's eating you up."

I stare at him, just long enough to make him feel awkward.

"Bro?"

Yeah, that worked. I say, "Oh."

"Yeah, yeah, yeah..." Brad chugs an energy drink.

"You don't need any more energy. Bro." It sounds cold.

I think it's funny. I don't know why, I just do.

It kind of messes with Brad. "Yeah, well... um, are you okay, man?"

I do my best to smile and realize that the entire time we've been talking, I have had my hands folded in front of me, back straight, eyes wide, barely blinking, staring, really just glaring at him.

That's intense, right?

I know, I know.

But I get to have fun too.

If they can use me, I can use them.

Brad won't get a word out of me. This is as good as it's going to get.

I mean, I treat him like shit. I know. But I can't help it. I kind of just go with it. The words, and that sense of inaction—just happens. It's like I'm getting revenge but I can't remember why.

Brad's an asshole.

That's what I'm thinking, but there's part of me that's like, "But he's still your friend."

But in bold letters, like it's a future tattoo of mine, I think, "What makes a true friend?"

And that's why, basically, I keep rolling with it. I treat him like shit and he deals with it. He sticks around, probably because leaving halfway through lunch would be too obvious.

Brad changes the subject, putting something on the table. "It'll be cool, bud. Real soon. Just be tough, and then we'll get so damn drunk during the after party!"

I look down at the card.

Don't make me spell it out. Don't do it.

Becca. It's always Becca.

But he does. He makes me say it. That asshole.

"You get the invitation, man?"

"No, but you'd think I'd get one. It's my exorcism."

I look around and it's like they weren't there until just now. Invitations, the whole school. I spot a few in people's hands.

I look back at Brad, who finishes the rest of his energy drink. Then Jon-Jon sits down next to me, slapping me on the shoulder. It's like, *What the hell are you doing here?* Jon-Jon doesn't hang in the cafeteria.

Look on Brad's face matches how this isn't normal.

Look on other people's faces, same.

Jon-Jon looks at me like I'm made of money. "How are you faring, on a scale of one to ten, ten being I'm a demon now?"

Fuck you. I don't say anything.

Brad says, "He's going. Not going well. But going."

Jon-Jon nods, a wink. "Need anything? Anything at all?"

I don't need anything from you.

Needs to be noted that I am still sitting up straight, hands folded. It's funny to me, the way I look, the way it makes other people feel weird.

But Jon-Jon's about business. He's about money. He showed up because he just wants to protect me, his investment. I want him to get caught. I want him to get arrested. I feel like I could—all this gambling and dealing is no good.

He could be done in one single tell.

But then they start talking about my exorcism again, and I can't stand it.

Jon-Jon sees the card on the table. "Got mine this morning too." He runs his hand through my hair, like I'm some little kid. "You'll be fine, buddy. You'll be drinking and smoking with the best of 'em. And think—when you shake this demon shit, you'll be the talk of the town. Not just the school. The whole town."

Brad lights up. "Yeah, buddy, now that's what I'm talking about. Fight that shit demon. Fight it and then make bank off it!"

Jon-Jon kind of looks at Brad's hyper response and just says, "Exactly."

Trying to be all cool, huh, Jon-Jon? Trying so damn hard to keep with it.

He leaves as quickly as he showed up, saying that he's got clients looking for him. Brad's like, "I'll be over in a bit."

And I know he said that because he's looking for a way to leave the table. Sure enough, when he's done scarfing his food, he tells me, "Going to head over to JJ's." He stands up, picks up the garbage, bags it, and asks me in a way that's not really asking at all, "You wanna go?"

Maybe I say no.

Maybe I don't.

Can't really tell. He leaves in a sprint, basically.

And I stay right here.

Keep in mind that I'm the same—straight posture, hands folded. Staring. I bet I look insane, and I find it so damn funny.

Around sixth period, I spot Becca handing out those invitation cards.

I have time to reconsider but, yeah, why not? I walk over. She gets all nervous when she sees me approach.

"Hey... Hunter, are you keeping with it?"

I'm acting all action-movie tough guy. "Ran out of sick days so I brought the demon with me."

She pretends to laugh. She's getting scared; I can see that eyelid twitch thing that she does when she gets really nervous.

"He's moonlighting," I tell her.

"Who's what?" It's a gut reaction, but she gets it before I say anything. Too late though.

I tell her, "H."

Nervous laughter and then: "Hunter, you have to stay strong. Please, stay strong!"

She reaches for my hands. I pull them away.

Now's the time to ask: "Where's my invitation?"

Becca stutters, "W-what invitation?"

"My invitation," I say, "where is it?"

"Why would you need—"

I interrupt, stepping closer and closer, until we're inches apart. "It's my exorcism. Where's my invitation?"

"Yeah, yeah, but see..." Oh, look at Becca's eye twitching.

And let's just get right down to it. I'll save her the trouble.

"You figured since I'm going to be the 'star' of it, I didn't need one."

Becca agrees. "Because you don't get invitations to your own, like, thing, whatever it is. You're part of it, you are it, babe..." And then she tries to grab my hands again. "Are you okay? I'm so worried about you, Hunter."

I push away from her, acting all moody. Really playing up the whole thing to be more dramatic and emo than it really is.

I wander off because doing that would be the funniest.

Becca's all like the concerned girlfriend that, because of the situation, seems to look like she isn't actually the problem. Funny, so damn funny, how the situation changes things. Like Becca isn't obsessive. Just know that she counted every single damn invitation. She not only got them made up, but she also created raffles and other things to get more people to show up to the exorcism.

It's Becca. She does stuff like this.

I can't stand it. It really does make me angry.

Walking to last period, I see Blaire and Blaire sees me. She stops, looks right at me, and then leaves—just turns the other way, the way she came. I want to call out to her. Be like, *Blaire, it's me...*

But that doesn't happen and instead, the day keeps going. It ends exactly the same way every other school day ends.

I drive home.

I find it all so funny, seeing everyone exposed like this.

I mean, I'm not doing this to hurt them. I'm just doing this because I think it's more than a little due. They owe me. But maybe they don't.

But I got a laugh out of it.

That's all that matters, right?

On the drive home, I get to thinking about those invitations. I start fixating on those invitations. Like always, if I think about something long enough, it clicks. It becomes something real.

Turn one corner and I'm laughing about what happened today. How I really messed with people.

Turn another corner and I'm grinding my teeth, trying to tear the steering wheel off just thinking about what those invitations mean.

Left at the light—I think about Brad and feel a little sorry for him. Maybe I really was a little mean.

Left at the next light—I think about Becca and how she sees me as property, sees me as something expected, like I'm really not a person to her, just the part of her life that reads "boyfriend."

At the red light, I'm fuming, thinking about Becca.

It's my fault for staying with her, yeah.

It's my fault for a lot of things. But then there's this idea of change. People change over time. What makes me the most mad...

I really can't figure out what it is that does it, just sends me over the edge. I speed down the neighboring streets, screeching tires as I make a sharp turn up the driveway and put the car in park.

I storm up the stairs.

I think Mom or Dad is home. Someone stirs from the kitchen.

No, it isn't H. He's already upstairs in my room.

I go right up to my room.

A voice from downstairs: "What's going on?"

Dad.

This means I'll have to lock the door. What he usually does is what he ends up doing today. He follows me up the stairs, stops at the door, talks to me with his face pressed against it. "How's it going?"

Don't say anything. I don't have to say anything.

"Everything okay, Hunter?"

Everyone is asking me that like it's supposed to help. It's not helping. It's making me lose my mind. So annoying.

"Hunter."

Man, I wish he'd go. I have nothing to say to him.

Get the hell away.

I hear a crash from downstairs. Broken plates.

I hear my dad mutter, "The hell was that?"

I'm like, "Thanks, H."

Damn, I didn't realize that I was clenching my phone so tight. I broke the case. The plastic is cracked all the way down one side. I throw the case away and toss the phone on the pillow. I lie down next to it.

A video plays on the laptop.

"Yeah, that one's pretty awesome."

But it's not enough to get me off the topic of Becca. Nothing helps. I scroll through news stories on my phone. I delete text messages, most of them old ones from Becca, waiting for what it is I was trying to think of to arrive. I wait and I wait, thinking about how we have nothing in common.

Forget the phone. I close my eyes.

No idea what time it is. Don't really care.

The reason she makes me so angry is that while everyone changes, talks about change, and is going on and on about themselves, Becca remains exactly the same. Comfortable. Predictable. She is there to hold me back. She is there to make me feel like I'm small. She's become everything that bores me.

So everyone's talking in the past tense? Well, then it's starting to really feel like I can't see her. I look everywhere but the only way I spot her is if I'm looking back.

The laptop shuts off.

"Thanks."

Before I finally slip away into sleep, it registers as true.

What I must do.

For me, there's more to this than looking back at things in doubt and confusion, like they'll just go away with time. I'm not seeing how time really changes anything if you're not willing to change with it. You know what I mean? Sometimes, you just have to trust the one that gets *you*. And I mean really gets you. Sometimes you just have to trust your own instincts.

I mean, right?

The dream opens a lot like the end of most movies—darkness and a sound track. The sound track is mostly my thoughts. I hear breathing in the background. Yeah, that's me. I'm fast asleep but still not running through this fast enough. I want to go back to the good parts but I can't find it. So it's the end of the movie and I've forgotten what it is I'm watching.

What am I watching?

I guess I'm watching you.

I'm watching you standing there, a group forming around you. Wait, if that's you, then where am I?

It takes a second for it all to kind of click.

It clicks when I see her standing next to you.

It sounds like I'm talking but those aren't the right words. It's really not what I'm supposed to say. I'm getting it all wrong. What's going on?

People are watching like they belong in the scene. They are extras, faces forming a crowd. They are talking in whispers, and Becca and you are chanting the same short sentences. They're angry, what I'm saying.

What she's saying, it's a mixture of "I'm sorrys." But she isn't really sorry. She's just saying that. And you aren't falling for it, are you? No, you're not.

You tell her that it's been a long time coming, this moment, this day.

Becca's saying, "This is, like, so unlike you."

And that's kind of the point.

It's what gets me excited.

That isn't me. But it could be. It really could be, if I wanted it to be me. And she's trying to tell you what you're supposed to say. She's talking to you in that way that she always talks to me. It's annoying, right?

She's saying that it's your fault that I'm acting this way. "It's the demon, Hunter." Becca's in tears.

We're making a scene, and everyone's watching. Normally I'd care about what they're thinking, but something about the dream seems rehearsed, like you're showing me how it'll fall into place.

I'm standing where you'd be standing. And no one seems to notice that I'm standing right here—*you're* standing right here—the entire time.

Even when there's no activity, you're standing near and within reach of other people's breaths. You can breathe for them, I know you can. You can breathe just like me. In this case, you are, and I'm sensing that there really isn't a whole lot of difference between the two of us.

Like, you've got to trust your instincts, you know? You need to say what comes to mind.

This is the scene that this entire thing has been leading up to. I know that, and even so, it's like I can't actually say the words.

We're finished.

I can't say them.

I can't say them to her, and definitely not to her face.

But here, in this dream... that person standing there is supposed to be me. He's talking like he's sure about the future. He's talking like he's never been more confident of a decision before. He's talking to Becca like she's the reason he's never changed. He's talking like I should have been talking.

It starts long before the words "We're finished."

It starts when Becca walks up and says that everything's planned. My reaction, our reaction, it's basically like, "What's planned?"

And then we find out that Becca's planned the entire day: she's spoken with Halverson and gotten permission to leave school early so that I can go get some fresh air, maybe get checked again by a second source. Becca has planned it all out like I'm a kid. She does this. She always does this and it drives me crazy.

Then when it's time to finally say no, Becca acts like I've gone and done it. She acts like I really have gone crazy.

I'm not crazy. I'm not, right? Right.

It seems more like she's the one who's out of her fucking mind, saying all these things, doing stuff for me when I'm my own person. Whatever that means.

Then it's like—I don't let my mom pamper me, why do I let Becca do this stuff? It's true. You're starting to make more sense than anyone else. Everyone else is saying impossible things, like they aren't saying anything at all. But you're saying every single thing for me.

It's a real big help, thanks.

You're really coming out of your shell. People say that, right—"coming out of your shell"? You look just like me and you do a mean impersonation. Becca doesn't realize that it's you that's telling her to go get a life. Do something else for once. How it's insane that she can think that it's okay to do this to a person. How it's what's really insane—the fact that this has lasted more than a few years.

She's repeating herself now. Apologies and then it's "How can I make it up to you?" and "Sorry about the invitation thing," and also "We don't have to go."

Of course we don't have to go. I don't have to go anywhere I don't want to. I don't have to ask you to prom, and I don't have to do what you say.

This is all toxic.

If people hold you back, keeping you from being, well, you, shouldn't you fix the problem? Shouldn't you, I don't know, maybe find people who make you a better person? Find people who you can actually relate to?

I don't know, it seems kind of stupid to think that you can just be friends with anyone. Not everyone's the same. Not everyone gets along with each other.

Just like these dreams, no two are the same. They're all different, and yeah, I'm different too.

So then another thing to be said is that we have nothing in common. You tell her that, for me, and it's what breaks her down. It's the one that gets her crying. But I know it's an act. You know that too, I'm sure. It's all an act. She does that to get other people's attention. Becca does it to hopefully make it look like I'm the bad person here.

I'm the one who's "breaking her heart."

But she's really crying because she knows that it's ending now and there goes her investment. There goes three and a half years of keeping this guy on a short leash. Three and a half years down the drain.

It's a short scene, telling me what I need to do.

It really does seem easy. But I don't know if I can do it alone. I need someone at my side. Someone I can trust. I need to know that I'll be doing the right thing.

This has gone on for too long, I know.

She's going to be broken up about it because it means she'll have to start from scratch. She'll try to fix things, but I can't just get lazy and let it go, just stop halfway, you know? I can't do that. I'm in the situation I am because I never tried to meet people. I just kept whoever was there around. I let other people keep the friendship afloat. I let that all happen on its own.

It's why I'm this way.

And I have to know that it'll change.

It's getting so damn old. Everything's bogus. Everything's a bust. We're finished.

I can say it.

We're finished.

You're saying it the way I need to say it.

We're finished.

I guess I just need a little support. Friends on my side, but Brad and Blaire and Jon-Jon and everyone else, they're there to watch, not to help. We've never had anything in common except that we needed someone to hang around. It's all kind of a lie, if you really think about it. But this dream, it's the truth. It's telling me what I need to do. It's telling me what I need to hear. It's showing me what I need to see.

And don't think I don't realize that it's you.

You're the one that's making everything change. You're helping me out, and that's awesome. But I need help now more than ever.

I can hear myself saying it in my sleep, "Will you help me?"

Will you help?

Of course you will.

And then the next moment I'm calm and smiling. A smile on my face while I dream up that moment when I tell Becca to her face, "We're finished." I dream it over and over again, a dozen times, until I wake up.

It's because you're helping me that any of this is happening.

I probably didn't even need to ask.

But I know you were waiting.

It's the offer you've been waiting for.

Once I say it, it's like everything clicks into place. There's no more doubt, and I'm really sure that I'm going to be a different person someday. We all change over time. I'm confident that this is necessary.

I can't fill my life with fair-weather friends.

I need to know that I'm doing the right thing.

You make sure that I never lose confidence. You say all the things I'm supposed to say.

And that's when I know that you and I really get along.

It's like you're thinking what I'm thinking, and I'm thinking what you're thinking. It kind of goes in a circle, and now I sense that when I'm not sure, you'll be there to pick up the slack.

Like a true friend, you know?

No, I don't think I'm crazy.

I think we're getting along just fine.

WHAT HAPPENS IN A DREAM HAPPENS IN REAL LIFE. IT makes sense now. I woke up this morning with marks on my arms, just to make sure that I'd remember. Yeah, it's a dream, so what? Yeah, I didn't go through with it, so what happens now? That's a good question.

I look at the marks like they're tattoos. But yeah, they're more to help me remember that it'll happen today. They help me remember to be confident. They help remind me that I've got your help.

"Thanks," I say on the drive to school.

This happens and that happens, but it's just another day at school until we get to that part of the day. It's actually not that weird, what's been happening to me. Not anymore.

It's kind of magical, like I'm just watching it again for the second time. The second time, it's very different. This time I see it with my own eyes. I have a horrible headache but it's like I'm using the pain as motivation. It's like you're the one moving the body while I keep busy with the conversation.

Sure enough she walks up to me around fourth period, just before lunch, and she tells me, "I got us the day off!"

Say it like this: *"What?"* Almost like I'm stuttering, in shock, but really I'm already aware of what's happening.

I'm holding on to a deadly secret.

We're holding on to the secret. She won't know what hit her.

"Wow, you're looking better today," Becca says.

I'm grinning wide for obvious reasons.

I nod and say, "It's a beautiful day."

Becca agrees. "Like, you have no idea. I actually got Halverson to let us out early, on the fact that you're not feeling well. I've planned our entire day. Food, some sun, fun, and all that."

"Is that so?"

"Yup!" Becca being Becca.

You have no idea what I'm about to say.

"Oh, and I want you to see another priest too. You're not looking good, Hunter. Better today, true, but I'm worrying about you constantly and I just can't let that happen."

Of course you can't let that happen.

People are starting to form a crowd. It's because of what H is doing. H is making it so that they can't help but stop and watch. Becca notices this and gives this one person a really mean look.

Then I realize this is it. This is the moment. Do it now or never do it at all. But the latter isn't even a choice. It's like you're telling me that it'll be okay.

First line is "Listen..."

But of course Becca isn't listening. She's looking around at the people circling us, all confused.

Now you know how I've felt most times. I used to be confused but that's changed. I know now what I need to do to get things going on the right track.

Next line is "We have to talk."

That'll get her attention.

Yeah, it does. Now it's a real scene.

Becca, do you know?

"What are you, like, talking about?" she asks.

You do, you know what this is about.

Maybe she's even surprised that it's taken this long for us to actually have an argument.

Then you kind of take over from here. You say the next line: "This isn't working out."

And the next line too: "You and I have nothing in common."

I'm still the one who's saying everything, but you're helping me line up the words, the lines, in a way that makes this feel as dramatic as possible for Becca and everyone else watching.

But we couldn't be any further from this day. Moment's a blur but we're having a good buzz.

"I'm tired of being treated like a child."

That's a good one. That line makes everyone around Becca and me gasp.

She puts up her side of the fight, meaning it's the tears, and her saying sorry and all of that stuff.

I can see that it could be easy to break down too. It could be easy to trade her tears with my own. But instead of crying, I end up laughing at the thought. We're graduating so soon—why does she even care?

It's kind of funny, if you think about it.

Becca doesn't find it funny. Everyone else thinks this is serious.

Becca and Hunter are breaking up! Fresh gossip for the grapevine. More people crowd around us.

The next line is actually a long list of things I can't stand about her. It's like you're telling me to just let it all out: *You'll feel better later. Let it all out. Tell her how she's ruined the relationship. Tell her how it really wasn't much of a relationship to begin with. Tell her that it all goes down the drain the same way. Tell her that you don't actually know what that means, but then save that line by saying that it's a metaphor for everything that doesn't make sense about the relationship. Tell her that she never saw you as anything more than something who helps her get her way. Tell her about that one time you almost cheated on her. Don't mention what actually happened between you and Nikki, but use it as an example of how miserable she makes you feel.*

Go on and on until it makes sense that she's in tears.

She apologizes and says, "We've been through so much. I've invested too much in us to just let it fall apart now!"

That's enough to take it home with the one line that's left:

"We're finished."

Now it's a dramatic end where I'm looking around at everyone who's watching. I don't care about what they think. I don't care that they're looking at me like I've gone insane. I don't care at all.

I don't care that Becca is trying to hug me, trying to save it. She'll understand it better later. But she'll never understand me.

No one here really gets why I'm breaking up with her.

Later, when I'm at lunch, Brad will act like it was a surprise. He'll say things like, "Damn, bro, all those years just wasted." Never mind that he was the one who told me to break up with her way back when. Never mind that. He just forgot. It was probably just something to say at the time.

There it goes, forgotten. But Becca won't forget this. I won't either.

I look around at the faces, not knowing any of them. I pick out Blaire in the crowd. I wave to her, all happy that I finally did it. I broke up with her!

But Blaire looks at me like I'm someone else.

I'm waiting for you to tell me why.

I'm waiting for you to say something like I know you can.

But you wait until I leave school for the day. You wait until I'm unexpectedly driving back down that dirt road, getting out of the car, leaving it running. You wait until I'm running through that field, ignoring all the people there skipping school, drinking, and giving me looks when they see me show up, like I just popped up out of nowhere. You wait until I see the black crown, the darkened tunnel, and you wait until I run it again, this time without any hesitation. I just run down that tunnel, not at all worried that it might not have an end. You wait until I'm breaking a sweat, and with the sweat, I lose everything that might have been close to being an explanation.

I don't need an explanation.

I don't need to know why.

But as I run, you wait until I realize that I'm nowhere closer to the end than I was at the beginning.

You change the sound of my voice, making it more monotone.

More than that, you get me to turn and look, and I see that I'm only a few steps from the entrance.

Then, only then, do I hear you speak.

You say, "There's an end to the tunnel and I'm going to show you." I'm the one who's speaking.

Somehow that makes complete sense.

It makes sense now when before it didn't. I'm not looking for symptoms and I'm not thinking about how you're nearby.

It's because you're right here.

I hold up my hands, look at my palms.

You are here.

Right here where I'm standing.

I don't think about what everyone's been saying, their worried looks and all of them talking about me like I'm losing. I don't think I've lost anything. I think I've found it.

I've figured it out.

I've found the end of Falter Kingdom.

You're showing me, telling me it's not that far at all. So when I start running again, you're the one that's running for me.

"Just keep running," you say.

I run for maybe a minute and then I stop. I take out my phone and shine it in front of me. I see it. I see all the things that you've taken from my bedroom and from the house. At the end of the tunnel, there's another bedroom, made from things you stole.

I'm saying, "This is where you come from?"

But that's wrong, because what you're telling me right after is that "this is where I go to be by myself."

Then why are my things here?

But see, I get it. I do.

You really don't have to tell me.

I say, "Yeah, it's kind of a stupid name. That's why I didn't end up using it."

And then you say, "I understand."

You really do. H—it's not actually that cool of a name. Not that you need it, that name. Mine will do just fine.

You say it: "Hunter."

Then I say, "You get used to it over time."

We start working on a way where we can both talk and not lose the point of what we're trying to say a moment later. It's not going to work, I don't think, if we refer to each other as "we," right?

It will not work.

That's what I thought. I think it's better if we just keep things the same. Yet different. Yeah, well, it really does feel like everything's changing and I'm really happy. I've never felt this happy before, like I can do... anything.

You can do anything.

I know, I know—it feels just like that, you know?

I know precisely what you mean.

That's what's so awesome, I think. I feel, like, encouraged to not hold back anymore.

There is no reason to hold back.

Definitely. Definitely. Not when I feel this good.

There will be problems.

I know. I know there'll be problems, but when aren't there any problems? I think that's kind of why I stuck around her for so long. She was the problem, yeah, but I got used to the problem, and because I did, there was nothing else that really came up. It was always just one big predictable problem.

She needed you more than you needed her.

Yeah, that's true. And it's also like with everyone else... I met people and those people who I met became the people I stayed around. I mean, that's what everyone does. But I did it in a way where it could have been anyone, really. It could be someone else, someone totally random, and I'd end up around them if they were there.

But not anymore.

I kept it all the same anyway... Yeah, not anymore. Things are starting to feel different. I mean, like, one thing that should be bothering me is am I awake or asleep? Does it matter?

It does not.

I guess it doesn't. And then I should probably be worried about what people are saying.

Yet you won't.

No, I won't—I'm like, "Say what you want. I am trusting my instincts." I get along. This is working. Getting along just fine. I think people don't understand. They don't understand what's going on with me. They could never understand because it isn't actually happening to them.

It is only happening to us.

Yeah, exactly! It's like, it's like... we met in our own way. I know we said not to use the plural "we," but I guess in this case it works?

It will do just fine.

Cool—and, um, what was I saying? Right! You and I met just like Blaire and I met, and Becca and I met, and Brad—wait, not Brad. But it's true. Sure, we're different, but nobody's the same. We're different but actually I think we get along well. Who cares if what I tell people doesn't make sense? They don't get what we're talking about. But we get along real well.

I think we have more in common than one would expect.

I agree. The strange thing is really just how people see this as so different, so, like, fucked up.

They do not understand.

Like, you make all those crashing noises, and open doors, and do all that stuff because... why do you do that stuff?

I get bored. I get lonely. I want attention too.

Yeah, I can see that. I can definitely see that. But people see it as haunting behavior. They see it as symptoms. They see it as problems that need to be fixed. Everything's a problem to them, ugh. I just don't want to be around people who don't even try to understand what's happening to me, you know?

I understand.

Well, yeah, of course you do. But that's also why people are going to have such a hard time with this.

Many will fail to fathom it.

Fathom, yeah. That's a good word. I like words that start with the letter "f"—"father," "fixate," "further"...

"Falter."

Yeah, that's a good one. Then there's the go-to staple: "fuck."

Humans love to fuck.

That makes me laugh, man, that really does. And it's true. It's basically written into our DNA or something. Do you ever have those kinds of needs?

No. I experience what I experience, but for the most part, what is felt is what humans define as loneliness. I get lonely, which is precisely why I do the things I do.

Well, you're hanging with me now. You're right here with me. I consider you a friend. No one would have really helped me out the way you did. There's no way I would have been able to break things off with her if you weren't there, even going all out and saying the right things so that I wasn't so nervous.

I am not going anywhere.

Yeah, yeah, exactly. You can stick around. I want you to. I consider you a real friend. And we get along. We're getting along, right?

You invited me. I am not going anywhere.

That's awesome. Yeah, I can count on you. I mean, think of it this way: As long as I get what's going on, nothing else matters, right? Right?

Correct.

Yeah, they'll look at me weird. They'll think they need to save me; they'll talk about how I'm losing. But I never said I was fighting. I'm not fighting any battles, and I don't think they'll understand how I know even before I could ever know what's going to happen. Like, I know what's going to happen, like, whole days before it's going to happen. People call that a symptom. I think it's really a gift. You're letting me know before it happens.

There are plenty of surprises ahead.

Yeah, it would be boring if there weren't. That's what I was going on and on about earlier. Things are definitely different and they can't be different if everything's the same.

Nothing will ever be the same again.

Nope. Things are getting exciting. I mean, people will say it's weird, how I talk to myself... but that's what they see. They hear us talking but it's the same voice. It's like, "Who is saying what?" It doesn't matter. Hunter.

H.

I said something.

Then I spoke.

I should be scared.

You should be scared.

Why am I not scared?

Because you're smarter than most.

Right, and that's cool of you to say, but what just happened there happened without even having to say anything. But we could have said it. If we did, it would be, like, to other people, complete insanity. They'll say that I'm speaking in tongues. They usually say that about a person when he's all possessed. Oh! And that's another thing. This is possession, right?

You are possessed?

I'm not sure. I guess this is it. I was reading about it earlier. You saw.

I did.

And well, they say that when it's, like, no longer a sense of being watched and now a sense of being one, or no longer, um—what were the words?—able to think clear thoughts without there being...

Interjections.

Yeah, interjections, then it's more likely that the subject is possessed. That's what they call people in the videos: "subjects."

The subject in question is: What of bonding isn't possession?

You mean...

Bonding is a form of possession.

People wanting to be around other people, and because they want to be around those people, they sometimes start talking like them, start acting like them, and they even start dressing like them.

Other people look to be possessed.

That... actually makes a lot of sense. I mean, yeah. Yeah... that does make a lot of sense. It's sort of the same. But then it's also very different. But no two things are the same, yeah. And then I'm kind of focused now on what's happening next. I, well...

You go to school.

I don't want to go to school. Can't believe Halverson hasn't just, like, suspended me again for, you know, "looking like shit." That's what everyone's saying, even if they aren't actually saying it. And it kind of is true; I just can't stand being around people right now. I get exhausted. Dizzy. Just thinking about all the stuff I have to do, how I have to, you know, really try, it's hard to stomach. It's really hard to handle.

I'll go to school.

You can go, but I'm not.

I'll go.

Fine, that's fine. Just be ready for all that usual stuff.

I'll be fine.

But yeah, you'll be, you know, taking me with you.

No.

I don't get it—what do you mean?

Wait in the tunnel.

But you're going to be there, as me.

When I am you, you are not.

I thought we were both using the name Hunter.

Hunter is Hunter. Sometimes Hunter isn't Hunter.

So I'll stay at Falter?

Stay. You will know everything, precisely when it happens.

That's wild. I mean, you know how I feel about it. It's... strange, I mean, yeah. Okay, I'm rambling. But it's strange, right?

It is difficult at first.

I'll get used to it?

Soon there will be no difference.

What if I go along with you?

Then it will be much like what has occurred previously.

If I don't...

You wait where there is no need to worry. I am not the same.

Yeah, that's true. I... trust you. Everyone else thinks I'm crazy for trusting you, but I mean, you got to go with your instincts, right?

Correct.

Okay. Okay. I'll stay. I'm not going back to school. I don't even want to see their faces. I just want to, like, stay in bed and chill.

Stay in bed. Watch it on video.

Yeah, I'll watch it on video.

Do you trust me?

I trust you.

Friends?

Yeah, man, we're friends. It's pretty obvious that we are. Not that anyone else will ever get it.

I WALK TO SCHOOL SO THAT I MAY GET USED TO THIS body, these legs, this face, the sun. I walk to school and I wait where the locker reads "34." This is your locker. This is my locker. There are plenty of students. There are plenty of opportunities. I walked to school, and because I did, there is an odor, a stench that barely registers to those here. But they smell it.

I am going to wait until that bell rings. The bell will ring, and I will begin with your day.

I am in your head.

I am plenty, and no, I am not exhausted.

I am your friend, you will see. This will be proof.

You watch as it happens.

The video feed shall be plenty.

It shall be plenty for you.

It shall be plenty of proof that I seek nothing if not the solution to the loneliness that I have felt for as long as I have learned the nature of loneliness.

Your first period is subdued. You sit in the back, I assume, given what you've left me. Yet I am concerned for there is a lot missing—

details, such as names of acquaintances and the name of the instructor staring me down.

You see, I am not sitting. I am not sitting because I am not sure if you sit in the back or the front.

The instructor beckons: "Please, Mr. Warden."

I know you'll enjoy this, so I say, "Do you want to know how you'll die?"

"Excuse me?"

The humor that it causes, it's wonderful, isn't it? Such humor, such fear in their faces.

Not to be worried.

The instructor will select not to acknowledge what has been said. The instructor will entertain the idea of Mr. Warden being sent to the principal's office. First period, and I have already caused some calamity.

How intriguing.

The principal lives in a routine that has shut his mind off from the more curious concepts in life.

What a waste, I must say.

What a supreme waste of life. Halverson is his name, and he returns home to the same dinners, the same wines, the same few books before retiring for the night in his cushy yet unfeeling bed. There he is, your principal.

"Frankly," he begins, but as you already know, nothing else is needed.

"Frankly" this.

"Frankly" that.

You are given a warning. "Frankly" Halverson is quite concerned. He listens to my replies. He notices a change.

My voice is your voice. Soon we will speak the same. Friend, you see it as much as I have seen it. Much like you have said, there is worry, misplaced worry. They see the pale skin, the marks that I have made, the bad breath, the bloodshot eyes. The thinning hair and missing eyelashes.

Indeed, you have seen better days.

A lot of energy placed in a body such as this can achieve only so much. Soon we will find escape.

I find escape from the principal's office. Given a warning, and it's off to third period. Must I be responsible for missing the second period if Halverson kept you with his "frankly" talk for a whole hour? Regardless, I walk as best as I've been able to surmise from watching you and I return to class. During this class, I remain silent like the other students, studying from a book I have no interest in reading.

What is this subject?

I am beginning to understand why you fear the monotony of school. I am also learning quickly of how little others understand about what you are going through. They treat me like an affliction. They treat me as a curse. They treat me as a behemoth.

I encourage you to look it up. "Behemoth."

I am not a behemoth.

"Demon" is as close to getting right what I am. But so many seek the visual, what I look like, but I can only show you based on what I'm becoming. I look so much like you because of the events that have transpired where I have been able to influence and help.

The day wears on with this same undercurrent of confusion from others. They whisper words involving your demise. They whisper gossip about the breakup. They judge you based on how you look. They judge you based on the way I walk.

During lunch, I sit with Brad, who sits to the side, unwilling to say much of anything to me. I speak to him to get some practice. There is much to learn from speaking using this voice.

I inquire, "Brad, how is it that you haven't gotten laid yet?"

Yet you aren't supposed to know this. It catches him off guard.

There it is, once again, confusion and fear. You might be worried but I wouldn't be concerned. Let us have some fun then.

"Bro, what the hell you talking about?"

Brad attempts to cover up the embarrassment that bubbles up from beneath his practiced demeanor.

"You are still a virgin," I speak in an authoritative voice. I speak much like any of the instructors might. However, I assume it comes off much different from what I had wanted.

This will take some time. It will require your help too. As mutual friends, I assume we will both learn to operate the social ins and outs with relative ease.

Brad is uncomfortable.

Others are uncomfortable.

Perhaps this is a good moment to leave.

I do. I leave the table, let that bit of information hang bold and true, for it is worth remembering that even if it was I that made them feel so awkward and perhaps afraid, they still assume that it is you they are speaking to.

I believe it would be great to try a drink.

I haven't had what this is called.

I find him where anyone finds him, Jon-Jon, whose real name is Jonathan Johnson, one of the most mediocre of names possible. I saunter up—another word worth acquiring, for I enjoy that word. Saunter.

Jon-Jon is adept at hiding behind a smoke screen, a practiced role of his as a businessman. Yet upon seeing your presence, seemingly out of nowhere—I had walked in such a manner that he couldn't have noticed until I was directly in front of him—he says, "Hunter, well, you're... you're looking a little rough."

Immediately he runs through a number of ideas, turning you into a gambler's paradise.

I tell him, "Hunter will not die. He will live longer than you."

The dramatic shift from reserved to noticeably concerned is far more enjoyable when the person's worked tirelessly to be someone he is not.

Jon-Jon makes an offer, for there is little else for him to say: "You want a drink? Maybe a smoke?"

Must it all be vice?

Yet I am here to try one, and I accept a drink. The taste is familiar. I will not be able to taste this with fresh senses. You have tasted and abused this drink to help navigate the social circles. And it tastes of something else. It has no clear taste whatsoever. I taste mostly the aftermath, long after the effects of alcohol hit this body. I drink as much as you would.

I drink and discover that the body changes, becomes more difficult to navigate, after drinking enough.

I walk with narrower focus to what's next.

Fifth period and sixth, yet this body needs time to repair. It needs to rest. I sit in what is deemed study hall. The students move away from where you are sitting. You are "freaking them out."

I notice a young woman, Blaire, the only one staring back when I am caught making eye contact. She knows you, and not as what you were but what you are becoming. She wants to approach, but I sense that she feels as though she hasn't been welcome. I sit there, staring, and she sits, staring back, for the entire period. Upon leaving the school campus, I watch so many treat you as a contingency, something that shouldn't be. A lost cause.

For the one named Blaire, she is the sole exception.

Everyone else, they assume that the exorcism may arrive too late. I let the body rest before walking home. Your home is like you left it.

Now leave the kingdom.

They will be waiting for you.

Your parents.

I watched the entire thing, and man, it does seem different after it is all said and done. Seeing it from a distance, I really get this strange feeling, like they want me to be messed up, the one who got it all wrong, so that they feel better about themselves. I mean, right?

That would be correct.

It's all fixated around you, and I don't know why that is.

I am deemed an affliction.

Like something I shouldn't be around. The priests told me to fight any and all contact with you.

I remember. I was there.

They don't see you for what you really are, I don't think.

They do not. They see things for the horror that has been defined over time.

You know, I've been thinking... is it why Father Albert calls you an unclean spirit?

Perhaps.

Yeah, I think that's probably why. Demon seems too much like all the other demons in the movies and stuff.

They assume that the activity is made to terrorize. I have only done what I have done because it worked.

Definitely. It definitely worked. Okay, so I don't want this to happen.

It will happen. It is what's in front of you.

Like, she just won't go away! Now she got my parents involved?! They're both home. I've never seen it where they are both home in the middle of the day. Not like this. Now this, this is insane. She just won't leave me be.

I am here. You will be fine.

You'll do all the talking?

If I must. Yet did you not state that you would no longer take the easy and convenient way out of decisions?

Yeah. Yeah, I did say that. It's just... okay. Fine. Time to get this over with.

Of course, they're not going to let me step inside before my dad's right there, making sure I won't get away.

"Son, we have to talk."

It sounds like I'm about to be in, like, one of those TV dramas. I'm the poor son who's in a losing battle against a demon.

Mom's got her head in her hands, and it looks like she's been crying.

That bitch Becca is there, and she told them all. Of course she told them. Look at that grin on her face. You see it?

Indeed, I do.

Dad's right behind me so that I can't just run away. Run upstairs. Run back outside. Run inside so that you can speak for me. But yeah,

I know, I know, you're right there. I just don't want to have to hear this. It's so ridiculous to me.

"Son..." Dad's got a chair, got a plan, got a whole big charade.

Yeah, I'll sit, even though I already know how bad this is going to be. I'm sitting. Now it really starts.

Becca first: "Hunter, are you there?"

Of course I'm here. But I'm not going to say anything. She shouldn't be here. She should be, I don't know, somewhere else. Out of my life.

Then it's my dad saying the same thing: "Hunter?"

My mom cries. She won't stop crying.

Would you like to know how your mom's going to die?

Huh? How?

Your mom will begin coughing one day. It is a cough that fails to improve. It disappears and then returns. Your mom will begin coughing up blood. She will ignore the symptoms given that they're quite easy to ignore when working fourteen-hour days. When she gets it checked, her voice will have left her. A knot that will not leave when swallowing will send her to the doctor. The diagnosis will be cancer of the larynx. Your mom will die ten years after the first cough. You will be in your midtwenties.

I look at the tears and see how my mom really does look overworked and ragged. I take this information as something sinister but also something that'll just have to happen. It's already there, right? The cough?

The first symptoms have already begun to show.

Dad looks me in the eye. "Son, are you there, son?"

Becca too. "Hunter?"

They want you to speak.

Fine. "I'm here."

Becca, acting all concerned: "Hunter, stay with us."

And then Dad going on about being out of the loop: "Why haven't you told us, son? What makes you assume that this isn't serious?"

What is there to say? "You're never around, what do you care?"

Mom gasps, cries a little harder. Wow, what are they trying to prove?

"Like hell I don't care. This isn't you speaking. It's the demon!"

Becca nods. "You need help. And now."

I say, "Why are you, like, even here? This is *me* talking."

Becca rolls her eyes. "That was just an argument. We have been through too much to just up and end it. Come on, Hunter..."

Um, I seem to remember the scene being really, really final. I make it sound really insincere: "Come on, Becca..."

Dad's all like, "Becca was the one that had to tell us! I simply cannot believe this could happen to my son!"

It can happen to absolutely anyone. You're right. It can happen at any time.

One must simply put oneself out there.

Yeah, and they're acting like I'm dying.

You are dying.

Huh?

We are all steadily moving toward the end of the tunnel.

Well, yeah, if you put it that way.

"Son, you need to fight it. You need to think about the future. Son, do you hear me?! You need to be strong. I know you can be strong."

He's shaking me and it's making me dizzy.

Tell him to stop.

"Dad," I start, "you won't want to keep shaking me or else I'll..."

Were those your words or mine?

A little of both.

Well, it worked. Dad's taking a step back. That look on his face, he's so damn worried.

Would you like to know how your dad's going to die?

Die due to worry?

Your dad will remarry after the passing of your mother. Your dad will attempt to move on, but his attempts will ultimately fail to render anything but guilt from the fact that he had spent much of their marriage running away from intimacy. Your dad will find himself alone one night, unable to free himself from the thoughts dealing with your mom's death. He'll die much like so many have done before, a deadbeat with dull eyes staring blankly at the TV.

You just made me depressed.

I apologize.

It's okay. I mean, I guess it'll be hard for Dad, but he kind of ran away from things.

Indeed.

Dad's shouting at Mom right now. He's telling her that I'm in need of help and that this can't wait. Mom's not saying anything though. I don't know what's going on. See, they are the ones who are crazy.

Perfect example of hysterical.

That's probably it, but they're doing it to themselves.

Becca agrees with my dad. "He needs help. Like right now."

Oh, is that so? And she's the one who's going to do that? After years of being treated like a child, she's trying to get back in and stay. You know what? I'll run with it. I'll say, *Fine, then make it happen. Fix me.* I apparently need a lot of fixing.

"Then help me." Just... help me.

Dad shakes his head. "I'm trying to but you have to let us."

"I just did. Help me. Right now. *Help me.*"

What can they really do?

Mom in tears, Becca pretending to be concerned and afraid, Dad being suddenly a caring, loving father... it's all so ridiculous.

They can't do anything, you know? They are all just afraid.

"You're going to what, call a priest?"

Becca says, "We've called Father Albert who told us to call Father Andrew. We left a message."

"Left a message."

Hope they caught the sarcasm.

Becca frowns. "Hunter..." It's how she says my name that makes it sound like she's really saying something like, *Don't be stupid.*

I'm really not. It's just the situation, you know?

Would you like me to step in?

Actually, no, I think I have this.

Perhaps then you'd like to know how Becca dies.

Tell me. Does she drop dead right now?

Rebecca Mazarin will graduate with honors and pursue a second degree in literature. Mazarin will spend most of her twenties single and focused on her work. She will meet a man she will marry. Three months after their engagement, Mazarin and her fiancé will drive home from a party drunk and will be involved in a car accident. Though not fatal, Mazarin had been in the front passenger seat without a fastened seat belt. The collision will result in her falling into a coma. The fiancé and Mazarin's relatives will choose to pull the plug after failing to regain consciousness for ten months. Mazarin will have been thirty-five that year.

So you know all this how?

It is information. Information can be procured without too much trouble.

I guess. It's crazy and wild that you can know the future.

It isn't the future. It is a person's life.

Okay. Then tell me if Father Andrew's actually going to call back.

Indeed he will.

Dad starts crying too. "Son, I can't believe you didn't turn to us..."

Becca says, "He's going through a lot. He is being influenced by the demon. That's what Father Albert told me."

Mother chimes in: "What happens if we can't help him?"

Becca shrugs. "I... don't know."

Everyone looks at me.

They're afraid.

Yes. They assume you'll become a danger to them.

I'm just going to nod and smile.

Mom starts bawling again.

I say something like, "Tell her to stop crying. It won't fix anything."

But they react in a way that makes it sound like I told Mom to drop dead or something. It's like what I'm doing doesn't match what they see.

Dad sighs. "You play with fire and then you get burned."

I'm like, "You're not a poet, Dad."

Man, this is going nowhere. What's keeping me from leaving?

You. You haven't yet left.

Well, let's leave now.

Yes. Let us.

I need to get the hell out of here.

Let us go.

Where?

Let me lead and you will discover one of the few wonders I am privileged to experience.

I need to start carrying around a dictionary so I can talk better than you.

If I speak, I am using your voice. You are deemed the one that speaks. Therefore, you shouldn't need a dictionary. I am your dictionary.

You're right.

I get up and walk right out the door. It's as easy as that and I don't know why I never thought about it. They yell after me. Dad tries to grab hold of me like I'm about to do something really bad. But pushing him aside is actually easy. I guess you helped with that.

He fell down. He's probably fine. Either way…

This time we're driving. No walking a billion miles.

I mean, I don't even really need to go back home. There's nothing left for me there. I don't need to, but at the same time, home calls to me. It's something that tends to spiral around like a command: Go home, you're drunk. You know? That kind of thing.

Indeed.

So you're telling me to park two blocks away?

You do not want anyone to notice your vehicle.

Yeah, but this is actually kind of crazy, what we're doing. Even if it's someone we know; it's still out of this world.

This is what I do. Yet now I have you. It affords some new possibilities.

Can't believe I'm about to haunt Blaire.

Blaire is an interesting individual.

I've known her since grade school. We go way back. Like everyone else, she's the one that stuck around. I definitely didn't make a point to keep in touch. But even so, she's a friend, I think. She definitely cares about what's happening to me. If she's really a friend, she'll know that you're here.

Would you allow me to be the one that speaks?

Yeah, that's cool. How are we going to, you know?

It will begin by maintaining distance. Look to see whether a back door is capable of being opened. Typically I muster up the courage by simply manifesting near where I've been wanted.

You can't just go somewhere?

It does not exist without there being first a phrase, a notice of some sort.

Yeah, we can get in through the back patio door.

Listen carefully. You make a sound, then you must be quiet.

I am.

Upstairs, second door on the left.

I thought we were going to haunt the place up.

I would like to speak to Blaire first.

Okay.

I knock on the door.

Okay. The door's opening...

"Hunter, what are you doing here?"

Let me talk.

Yeah, then talk... you're not talking. She's looking at me weird!

"Hey, I needed to get away from things."

Blaire bites her lower lip. "And you chose me?"

"We're friends. Where else would I go?"

Blaire opens the door all the way, and I notice that she's in a nightgown. What time is it, anyway? It's all the same day since this really started. It's like I don't even sleep anymore.

You do, but when you are asleep I am awake. Thus, we are constantly in motion.

"I don't know. I figured Brad's or Jon-Jon's."

"You are my only real friend."

She blushes a little.

There's always been some history between us. If it weren't for Becca, we'd probably have ended up together.

It is never too late.

You're right.

Blaire walks back into her room, sitting on her bed.

Where do you want to sit?

Let's remain standing. For full effect.

Blaire starts brushing her hair. "How far along are you?"

"What do you mean?"

"You can't be alone at this point. It's probably with you right now."

"Not an issue."

"I didn't say it was. Based on how you look, yeah, the demon's definitely progressed and wearing you down."

"If that were true, then why do I feel better than ever?"

Blaire yawns. "It just seems that way."

"I simply need to know that I can come here if I need to hide."

Blaire sets her brush down. "What are you hiding from?"

"I want to know that I can count on you."

Blaire checks her phone. "Of course. You shouldn't have to ask."

"Oh, but I do."

What are you getting at?

In time, friend, in time. We must be aware of whom we can trust.

Blaire lies down, pulling the covers over her body.

She's not even a little bit afraid. Yeah, when everyone's saying I'm possessed and going to die, seeing her act like I'm normal makes all the difference. It weirds me out, actually. I guess I got used to everyone just saying I'm messed up, you know?

Indeed.

Blaire says, "You can stick around if you want. There's a guest bedroom that my parents never ever check."

"That's very kind of you to offer, but I've decided it would be best to leave. I simply wanted to stop by to see you." *To meet you.*

"I bet. You came here to haunt me, right?"

Um...

She waves at something.

She's waving at you.

Perhaps. No, she is.

"You... both can trust me. I already told you before, everyone deals with the possession differently. It's not just about taking it as far as you can; everyone deals with change their own way."

"I understand."

"No"—Blaire closes her eyes—"I know you get it. But, well, I guess I'm just a little jealous."

Another yawn.

"I just don't really know if I can start from scratch. Friends and everything. It seems like an impossible thing, you know? Making a true connection. Everyone's everywhere but you can't really count on anyone."

"You can always count on me."

"Same here, but, um, that's why I acted that way." She shuts off the lights, turns on her side, facing away from me. Then she says, "Oh, and sorry I ditched you on the homework. Hope you didn't fail."

At this point, graduation will come and go without a hitch. A C-average will do nothing to prevent the future from happening.

"Good night."

Blaire returns the greeting. "Night. Maybe I'll see you in the morning?"

Perhaps we will return later, but for now let us leave.

Yeah.

We have remained here long enough.

I want to haunt someone, and I know who that someone is.

Becca is a totally different person when she's by herself. She locks her bedroom door and keeps the music turned way high up, so that her parents hate her just a little bit more. I'm like, "Yeah, I totally feel you. I can't stand her either." Becca paces back and forth in her room and can't sit still. She's on her phone when she's not on her computer. She doesn't pick up after anything so clothes, old and new, go all over the floor. She steps on books and other things as she paces, which breaks most, but she can always get a replacement if she really cared about it. This is the person I know, the one that few do. She's selfish and spends most of her time trying to make sure that she feels popular.

This is the person that people don't see. I saw it before now. Now you see it too.

Would you like to perform the haunting or would you allow me?

I'm up for both, for whatever.

From up here, this balcony, I can see everything.

First it starts with a cold spot or something, nothing special. I tap on the window too, loud enough that she looks up and tries to figure out what it is. She doesn't so I tap again, harder this time.

It's starting to get cold in there.

Becca stops texting whoever it is she's texting and goes to her computer. She searches for causes of cold spots. Really?

Another text message. She's been texting people, talking about me, saying things like, "I really don't know, like, if he can be helped," and "No, he's not doing so well," and "You can see it in his eyes, they've changed color." Maybe some of that is true, but what's even truer than that is the fact that she's going to freak out when she notices that her room's been cleaned.

I'm still amazed that you can do all this.

If it can be visualized, it can be moved, marked, erased.

Becca looks up from the screen and then sees it. She shrieks, trembling like something out of a typical horror movie. She grabs for her phone like it's going to help her.

She dials a number.

It's her mom.

Her mom is downstairs.

How is this reasonable?

"Mom, I need help."

The mom says something and then Becca's teeth begin to rattle. It's getting real cold in there.

The mom's not going to be able to open the door. It's locked and it'll stay locked.

The mom's like, "Honey, open the door."

"I can't."

"Honey, I can't help you if you don't open the door."

Becca shouts, "I *can't!*"

I think about doing this thing where she finds out that it's me.

More tapping on the glass.

If I tap hard enough, the glass could shatter. Maybe she can catch a glimpse of me right before it happens. I think it's a good idea. So when it happens, I know that she knows, and I know that you think I should be subtle, would maybe be better if it was. But it's cool, right?

It is yours to choose.

Yeah, but now she's not as scared. She's saying my name.

Becca shivers and stands at the broken window, looking for me. I'm not there, not anymore. How about a little knocking on the door from the other side, but when Becca finally opens the door, no one is there? Yeah, that works.

By now she's really shouting my name. She's really pissed.

"Hunter!"

The mom didn't notice that she never got that call from Becca. That didn't happen; it was erased from the way this all happens.

I'm having a hard time trying to figure out what I want to do. It's like I can do anything I want, but at the same time there's only a few options.

You can do precisely what feels right. If the moment passes, you run the risk of never being able to think of the idea again. Hence the reason for opening and closing doors, cold spots, and other means. It is the bare minimum of what can be performed. Yet it is often that the different performances are lost before they can be used.

I want her to *really* be afraid. It's like revenge. This is like a revenge scenario in one of those international movies. An Asian film where the main character always ends up obsessed with revenge. That's what this is.

"Hunter!"

She's looking for me down the hall, but I'll make it so that she thinks she's really wandering downstairs, and when she gets there, the mom is gone. Everyone's gone. She's home alone. In a flash, the smell of dinner being cooked and the sound of the television on downstairs just... disappears.

Now she's really scared.

Now she's starting to wonder if she's actually haunted.

But she pushes back too.

She runs upstairs and hides in a closet. She starts dialing 911 but then realizes that doing something like that would be stupid, so she calls Father Albert.

Father Albert picks up.

"He's here," she whispers.

"Calm down, dear. Explain what you are experiencing."

"He's here." Becca has trouble slowing her heartbeat. "Hunter's here. This needs to happen now. You, like, can't wait another day."

Before anything else can be said, let's just say the battery dies.

Should have charged the phone.

She stays in the closet, not sure of what to do.

My name's a whisper now, "Hunter..." but I'm standing on the other side of the door. I've got my hand on the doorknob.

I turn it slowly, opening the door an inch. Just enough so that when she looks up, she sees one eye, peeking in. She's hysterical, screaming and crawling up against a back corner of the closet.

I stare at her for just one moment and then I walk away, making sure each step is really loud. *Thump, thump, thump,* slow, just like that.

It seems stupid to me but it scares her.

So it works.

It is often effective. It conjures up a familiar image of possession in those within earshot.

Her mom will find her. It'll be like Becca imagined it all, but it'll be so real. Because it really happened. It'll be like the dreams I had. It'll be like how things first started between us. That's how it happens. And the mom will find Becca in the closet. She will have peed her pants.

It'll be really embarrassing.

And then the broken window—her mom's going to be really angry about that. Cold spot disappears and it's back to normal.

But the fact that the room is clean will help lessen the mom's anger. Then again, Becca is hard to get along with; her parents just do whatever she wants, get her whatever she wants, because if they didn't, she'd make their lives a living hell. Like she did with mine.

No one sees the true side of Becca until they really get to know her.

That's probably true about everyone.

By the time Becca's able to do anything, I'll be long gone.

Say the name "Hunter" if you want, but we're not together, Becca, no matter what you think. Things have changed, and the sooner you can accept it, the better it will be for the both of us. Like, I know there's better for me out there. I just know it.

Becca, I'll be just fine.

Not that you really care.

I THINK THE ONLY THING THAT SCARES ME NOW IS THAT one day I won't recognize myself. You know what I mean? Maybe you don't—you're mostly the same, right? You'll do what you can to get people's attention, kind of like what anyone else does, but most of the time you're not going to have to fit into stereotypes and archetypes and all that stuff just to get by. I don't really know why I did it. I'm definitely not doing that anymore. If it means they're going to call me insane, then fine.

To be quite honest, the same applies to all. You are decreed "insane" and "possessed" for being associated with a demon. The definition of "demon" precedes anything you or I may do to reveal who we truly are.

I guess you're right.

I mean, I don't think anyone really wants to be lonely.

It's damn hard just trying to find someone with common enough interests. Like, I don't think anyone would ever want to do this with me, haunting people and stuff. But I also guess it wouldn't be possible in most cases.

People are able to haunt other people. It is yet another part of the stereotyping of the demon to suggest that only "unclean spirits" may possess and extensively influence others.

That's a good point. Never thought of that. Like, I think Becca possessed me. She really made every decision and did everything and wouldn't ever really listen to me whenever I wanted to speak. It was like she was a second mom or something. And Mom's sort of the girlfriend, which is really strange to say.

Indeed. I see the resemblance of possession: the individual unable to control himself.

Then is what's happened here, you and me, considered possession if I'm actually still myself?

I would think not, although conventional wisdom would deem the entire thing as an act of you being unwilling to understand the difference between choice and influence.

Huh?

Meaning I am influencing you to such a degree that you haven't a clue how to tell the difference between suggestion and a true personal choice.

Oh, I feel you. Yeah, like I'm the one who wants to do this, to haunt that asshole Brad. I'm the one who wants to do any of this stuff.

I am enjoying myself too.

Yeah, but, like, you aren't actually making it so that I am being led on or something. I made a choice and you're my friend. That's all there is to it.

Indeed. Might I ask about this fellow, Bradley Vola, and the reason for your distaste?

Oh, he's just always been so much like the people I can't stand. He's loud, thoughtless, and we're, like, exact opposites. I guess he stuck around just because it seemed like we were fast friends. I didn't think so, but then again I didn't think I'd still be hanging with him all the way to senior year.

Yet here we are.

Yeah, but see what I mean?

Devouring food and getting all excited about a sports game and drinking beer alone.

Quite a few people enjoy sports. I'm not saying it's cool—just that it's all he's got. And girls, he goes wild about girls, talking about them when really he's never been with one.

Brad is a lonely individual.

Yeah, but who isn't? So anyway, how are we going to go about this? I don't think he should see me. Think it'll be better to just keep it all casual and ominous and stuff.

Indeed. I will follow your lead.

Okay, cool.

Brad takes in a mouthful of chips and then rinses it down with beer. It'll wreck him later in life if he doesn't stop, but he's also the kind of guy that couldn't care less. He's got that nervous energy that keeps him active. He runs around the room whenever something happens in the game. Since there's a lot happening, there's a lot of running.

Didn't expect him to be home by himself.

But that's not really important. He's home and he's paying attention to the TV. So that's how it starts. The TV shuts off.

He's like, "The fuck?"

He uses the remote to turn it back on.

Wait a minute or so and then the TV goes back off.

This time he bangs around the remote against his palm, the coffee table, before it works again.

The third time the TV shuts off it's going to stay off. He'll be really annoyed. It's a big game. Every game for Brad is a big game when he puts all of his emotions, good and bad, into it.

Indeed. Bradley Vola invests in the sport. The opposing team represents his insecurities. The favored team represents his sense of hope that his worries will wear away, turning into good rather than bad.

Yeah, he's eating his emotions. He's basically fixating on the game like it's the only thing that matters. He's, like, got nothing to look forward to. I always knew him as being fake, wearing all that enthusiasm and energy like he'd never burn out.

But he's beyond that—totally burned out.

It's kind of pathetic, seeing this. I mean, I know from being around him enough. He pretends that he's okay even to himself. He's not even honest with himself.

People have a tendency to project themselves onto others.

Yeah. And that's back to the whole possession thing.

Indeed.

What happens to Brad when he can't watch the game? He goes around the house royally pissed. He goes into the kitchen and kind of just stands there. Then he goes on his phone and tries to find the score.

But those round-by-round stat scores aren't the same.

Phone pocketed, he runs upstairs, but there won't be light up there.

Worse, there'll be a stench.

That kind of symptom isn't used as much. Probably because it can be easily made into just some kind of, I don't know, dead animal or something.

I want Brad to really be Brad. I want to just, I don't know, make Brad just not be fake, and be vulnerable for once. I really don't care if I really freak him out, not like I did with Becca. Didn't waste any time with her. She deserved it. I felt vengeful, you know? I just wanted revenge. But the way Brad can care so much about something as small as a game, I don't know, it worries me. It kind of makes me want to stop and leave him be.

But we're already here. It's going. He's on his laptop in the dark because the lights aren't working and he's online watching a live stream of the game. Will he notice if I stand behind him?

Will he notice if I get closer?

Will he notice if there's a glare on the laptop screen and you can see me there, in the glare?

I said I wanted to keep me out of this. Just sort of keep it about the haunting, and not about the fact that I am haunting him. Sort of making it seem more like he maybe got a demon too.

But then Brad's clueless.

So that means I need to go back to cold spots and the sound of heavy footsteps walking up and down the hallway.

That gets Brad's attention. He starts listening.

The footsteps stop just before the door to his bedroom. The footsteps don't walk past, stopping short for full effect.

Brad kind of whispers, "No way..."

He forgets all about the game until he hears the sound of crowd noise coming from one of the other rooms in the house.

The crowd noise is right out of the live stream.

Brad gets excited and it's sad. "No way, bro, like shit, for real?"

Who is he talking to?

He talks to himself I guess.

Brad tweets, "First sign of symptoms or bro's a haunter."

Then he goes out into the hallway, kind of fearless, actually. Different, because most people would be weirded out. Indeed, most would interpret the activity as negative. Yeah, something that is bad. But not Brad. He's chasing the crowd noise, but it switches locations.

He ends up back downstairs, where the TV is.

Would you like to know how Brad dies?

Eh, I guess. Sort of. But I'll know anyway since you know, so go ahead and tell me.

Bradley Vola will graduate with a B-average in communications. Vola will continue with postgraduate studies, opting for physical therapy. He will spend much of his twenties in academia, attending parties and absorbing the fraternity/sorority subculture. Vola will continue as an instructor at the college, his career peaking as an associate professor. During his eighth year as a professor, Vola will meet a student and a relationship will form quickly. Vola will leave the college in order to retain ethical integrity; he will acquire a job at another state university. The switch between universities will result in his career stagnating at assistantship. Yet Vola will find peace with his once-student-turned-lover. Vola will leave the university at sixty and work as a freelance consultant from home. Vola will die of pneumonia at the age of eighty-one.

The TV is on, like there wasn't really a problem.

Brad looks disappointed. The thought here is that he imagined most of it. He really wanted the haunting.

It's kind of sad.

It's sad, right? I'm not just doing what you say people do a lot: projecting?

No. It is indeed a little perplexing.

Brad's tweet gets no favorites and definitely no retweets.

It's a bust, and I'm kind of like, all of a sudden, "Maybe give the guy a helping hand? You know, just let him think that it might be possible?"

There would be no harm in that.

Yeah, so maybe the TV shuts off again. Brad knows what that might mean. Then the TV starts switching channels, stopping on everything that isn't sports—not that he'll really notice that part.

Brad starts laughing. "Dude, this is awesome."

Just like him to be overanxious. I'm kind of like, "How is he in this situation? A house that looks like it's his, no family whatsoever?"

It's totally strange, legitimately strange.

After the TV, all the picture frames fall off the walls at once.

Gets a rise out of the guy.

Then I don't really see anything else to be done and leave him thinking he's lucky or something. But he thinks of demons as demons, like everyone else. And they all think it's so cool until contact is made. After that, it's like, "He's doomed." It's kind of hypocritical.

I'm done. You ready to leave?

Whenever you're ready.

Yeah, this is sad.

Indeed.

Sorry, Brad. No hard feelings, really. Maybe if you were more like yourself and weren't trying so hard, you'd end up not having to pretend you're friends with people. You could just actually be friends.

Like what we're doing.

Indeed.

Sorry, man. Brad, you'll be cool.

One day.

It's crazy to think that Jon-Jon lives here. It's a huge house, definitely worth... like a million dollars or more. I mean, look at this: the place is gated! If Jon-Jon lives here, either his parents are loaded or he's squatting. Maybe he's renting a room?

Either way, this is going to be good.

I've been wanting to mess with Jon-Jon since he made it clear that he cares only about business. He made money off me, off Nikki, off running the gauntlet, Falter, all of it. He makes money by pitting people against others; he makes money by selling to those same people. He basically messes with his clientele. Someone's got to mess with him, but he acts all cool and stuff so that nobody really can mess with him.

I want to mess with him.

Really, really freak him out.

You have no reason to ask for my approval. Let's begin.

This place is insane. Like, I don't even know where to begin. Jon-Jon's definitely living here. I don't know if those are his parents though. The people in the kitchen?

They are indeed his parents.

That's crazy. He's like, what, twenty-three?

Jonathan Johnson, or "Jon-Jon," is twenty-six years old.

No fucking way.

Would you like to know how he dies?

Do you even need to really ask? Bring it.

Jonathan Johnson will be arrested on assault and drug possession charges after an altercation with a woman who will be revealed to him later, post-arrest, as an off-duty officer. She will have caught notice of his activities via a vengeance burn—a competing dealer calling in a report. Johnson will serve three months in state prison before earning parole. Johnson will have difficulty returning to the life he had led prior to his arrest. Many competitors and former clients will have turned on him by the time he resumes social appearances. Johnson will attempt to break parole in order to avoid his competitors' own dead pools. On the eve of his twenty-ninth birthday, via something as fickle as using another inmate's basketball hoop without asking, Johnson will incur multiple stab wounds during work detail. His wounds will not heal.

Man, that sounds like a movie. It should be a movie.

Jonathan would like to be in a film.

I take it back. But it seems so much like how he'd want to live his life, like some kind of badass, but really he's just an opportunist. It's obvious that he's trying to be something he isn't. I can tell that he realizes what he's doing. I mean, he lives with his parents, who are raking in the cash, but he still does all the things he does for cash.

Indeed.

It seems seedy, sketchy. I really want to mess with him. What do we do to mess with a guy like Jon-Jon?

It will not require a whole lot of effort.

Jon-Jon lives in the guesthouse, all by himself. There is no need to even go inside the main house, even though I kind of want to. But he lives in the guesthouse, which is only three rooms, including the common area.

Of course, when I see him he's counting money. He's counting money even though he's already counted it more than a few times. Look at him, counting money just because he likes counting it. *What kind of guy are you?* I want to ask him.

"I watched you sleep last night. I made you stop breathing for one whole *minute*..." I whisper into his ear.

He jumps up, money going everywhere.

"Shi-shit. Hunter. Y-you—what are you doing?"

So he's scared. You're right. That was easy.

I ask him, "Why do you think you can be some gangster or something?"

He can barely look at me. Jon-Jon's looking for a weapon. He's walking away from me, and it's clear that he sees me as a monster.

I'm a monster, why?

"How about a beer?" I ask him.

"Sure," Jon-Jon stammers.

I won't be where he thinks I am when he gets to that knife.

He looks around. The knife in his hand makes it easy to notice that he's trembling.

"You scare easy."

He hears me, but he can't see me.

I think I'm getting used to this haunting stuff. It's true that it's hard for people to not notice you when they're absolutely freaked the crap out. Maybe they're just intimidated. Either way, it really gets people looking. It gets people in a state where they can't just turn you down as something they don't care about.

And then I ask him, just because it feels right, "Where's my beer?"

He keeps a whole fridge full of stuff. He's always got a cooler somewhere.

"Then a smoke? Can't a loyal bud get a smoke?"

He grows plenty under one of those lamps in that closet, the one near the entrance of the guesthouse. The door to the closet opens on its own. He turns and looks, which gives me time to steal the knife from him.

"Shit..."

I tell him, "No knives."

He's thinking, "Where the hell are you?"

He's thinking, "How is this possible?"

He's thinking, "Why isn't he dead yet?"

Because Jon-Jon figured I wouldn't last, right? He figured I'd end up like the rest, totally brain-dead. Like, just a body and no one else.

Indeed.

But how much of that is true?

It is accurate, in parts.

Which parts?

Consider this—if they banished me back to the kingdom, wouldn't you follow?

Yeah, I think so. I mean, I'd be afraid, but I wouldn't want to live without you around.

Indeed. And vice versa.

So he figured I'd be done, finished.

This is where I walk right up to him and ask, "How much of a gangster are you, on a scale of one to ten, ten being a crime lord?"

No answer. He just stands there, trying to hold it all together. He looks right at me, eyes wide, a single tear forming in his left eye.

I watch as it runs down his face, and then I answer for him: "Two. At best." I shake my head. "I'm Hunter, who are you?"

Not saying anything. He's scared stiff and shaking.

"Jon-Jon?" I shake my head again. "You're just like anyone else, but you just think you're bigger, more important." I dangle the knife he was going to use on me in front of his face. "I mean, really? You were going to attack me? Like some kind of monster?"

I drive the knife into one of the couch cushions.

"That's not meant for anybody."

And then I tell him. I tell him everything you've told me. I tell him about his future, about how he'll keep riding out that idea of being some kind of dealer, some kind of gangster, some kind of self-proclaimed badass or something. I tell him about how he's racking up the enemies.

"I'm one of them. Big surprise, I know. But I am. I've always hated you."

He's turning people against him, secretly. Only reason they're not lashing out and just ruining him is because of all the dirt and money he has on them. He gets us all warped around this idea that he might be powerful, able to really ruin us. But what's he doing? He's not doing anything.

He can't do a thing.

Jon-Jon is just an idea. Nowhere near being alive. Can't be alive if living takes some degree of care.

"You don't care," I tell him. "You won't care at all unless you're forced to, like, care to get out of what's happening here!"

Let's get out of here. I can't stand the sight of him. He's the one who looks completely insane. He's like this impossible idea that somehow exists just because so many people pretend that it's real. Like a crackpot theory that continues to go around from circle to circle because it's, I don't know, somehow believable to people with a certain kind of mind-set.

I mean, I guess.

He's just a guy, and a guy not really worth knowing. He owes me a lot, but I'm not even going to bother. Unless you want to mess with him?

I'd rather not.

Yeah. He's not worth a damn. I said no to people who made me want to be less like myself when I dumped Becca. I'm saying no a second time.

People like Jon-Jon are the real demons.

I'm just tired of being something I'm not. You know?

I know well.

Yeah. You and me, we're the same.

You know I really want to. I know you think it's not worth it and that it's just because it's her—Nikki Dillon—that I want to see. Just a glimpse though. You never do that, do you? You never just take a peek?

I don't follow.

Guess not. It's, well... anyway, you got to know that I'm interested for more than just that. I just want to see what the real Nikki is like. I've always had a crush on the girl. From a distance, she seems perfect. But then I found out that she's more like everyone else. But part of me just wants to be able to see, you know? I mean, I'm fine if you don't want to go, but maybe I need this just for closure. She was the reason I liked being haunted.

Stupid, I know.

It was before people started showing their true colors and stuff.

No reason not to, given that we're already outside her front door. But then should we be, like, more covert about it? Spy agent style or something? Should it be straight haunting? Huh?

I know, I know. It's up to me. But help me out. Be a friend. Am I scary enough to her without all the haunting and stuff?

It appears as though standing at her door for an inordinate amount of time would be enough of a fear-inducing proposal.

Ah, shit, fine. I'm ringing the doorbell. Here goes nothing.

I'm still nervous. After all that's happened, I'm still so fucking nervous. I could be shaking, I'm so nervous. I don't even know. Am I shaking?

Yes. You are shaking. Stop shaking.

I'm trying. She's not answering.

She'll answer.

But she's not really answering. I bet it's because she sees me at the door.

Ring the doorbell again.

Okay.

This looks pretty creepy, just standing here. That's kind of the point though, yeah? I guess I'm sort of hoping she's different when she's not surrounded by people. Like Brad and everyone else—kind of hoping it's like, "Hey, you're actually not a coldhearted bitch."

Ring the doorbell.

I just did.

Keep ringing it. Do not stop.

Oh, I get it. Eh, might as well go that way. This is creepy as hell. The parents are probably going to call the cops.

The parents will do no such thing.

That's reassuring.

But not as much as when she opens the door and acts like everything's okay. It's like, *What are you driving at?* I hear the locking mechanism slide open, and there she is, standing there like she would at school. And it's like, *Hey, it's been a while.*

She doesn't look at me like I'm a disaster, doesn't look at me like something went wrong.

Nikki sort of eyes me up and down and says, "Hunter." And then she looks past me and says, "I guess you'll want to step inside."

Not going to say no to that. Nikki walks over to where she was sitting before, next to her parents, who look at me and act like I wasn't actually ringing the doorbell like crazy, like I'm not that kid who has the demon, like I'm just someone from school stopping by to say hello.

So I say, "Hello." Guess that's as good as anything else to say.

Nikki motions over to an empty spot on the couch and I sit down. She offers me a drink and then fetches a glass of water that I don't actually drink.

Nothing about this seems weird though.

Like, everyone sitting here—they are already so far away from caring it's kind of like they're all still alone. There're the parents, yeah, but Nikki's that way too She looks tired. She looks bored. She looks... I really don't know.

So I ask her, "How's it going?"

She kind of nods. "Same."

The parents both ask me, "How do you know Nikki?"

Well... But instead I say, "We go to Meadows. We have a class together."

But then Nikki says, "No, we don't."

Her mom smiles. "That's nice."

Her dad says, "It's important to keep friends close. It's crazy out there. Lots of demons just looking to run you down..."

Are you weirded out by what's happening?

It is mildly disconcerting.

Yeah, this is creeping me out. Shouldn't they be all like, *Get the hell out?* They should be looking at me like I'm insane. That's what I've expected it to be. But now... Well, one thing's for sure: Nikki's definitely different outside of school. It's like the life's been taken out of her.

What's going on? I can't help but get the feeling that—

You feel it too, don't you? Of course you do. So what do we do?

I guess I shouldn't have to ask. It's kind of obvious. Got to get out of here. I guess they all knew.

I don't know. I'm just...

I'm nervous, okay? I'm nervous.

They're acting like nothing's wrong. They had a plan all along.

Nikki looks at the glass of water in my hand. "Would you like another drink?" And that's a signal or something. You're as aware as me. It's going to happen. But where, where will they enter? How will they get me? Why do they make me the insane one, when really I'm maybe just what they don't understand?

Look around. See anything?

Nikki just left the room. It's going to happen now, isn't it?

Indeed. It will.

Can we do anything about this?

There are a number of options—many of them resulting in capture. The lone choice is to invoke activity. Yet in doing so, it will result in quite the display of possession. It will not hold you in favor. It will accentuate their understanding of your situation.

Yeah. So we're cornered.

The whole thing felt wrong, you know, showing up here.

But it's kind of like I had no choice. I was going to show up here anyway. I needed to know. It's kind of like "I told you so." I know that's the case. I know you told me not to come here. It's my fault. I'm weak, I'm human. I'm not actually weak, just saying. I really shouldn't have bothered. Yeah, there they are. There's Becca.

She knew. Not long but she knew.

They followed me.

Yes. In a moment, the priests will enter the room.

Becca won't even look at me. Nikki steps back into the room. Her parents remain seated, watching television.

Nikki says to Becca, "Hey."

"Yeah."

"You're doing this, huh?"

"Yeah."

"Bummer kind of day."

Becca shrugs. "Bummer kind of week."

Nikki looks over at the TV. "Bummer kind of life."

Becca looks out one of the windows. "Okay, they're here."

"Won't need anything else, right?"

Becca sighs. "No."

Nikki nods. "Good, then leave. My part in this is so finished."

Becca mutters, "Bitch."

Nikki hears it but doesn't care. Becca isn't in the same league. Nikki did this because Becca found out about what happened between us. Becca blames Nikki, not me. Becca's made this into some kind of demon hunt or something, and I'm the one hunted.

I'm the one captured.

The priests sneak up on me. I was too busy watching them talk.

Dad's there too.

People narrow their eyes, make faces when they look at me. It's like, *Here I am, the demonically possessed. Ruined. In need of being cured. Because I'm supposed to be spared or, like, sacrificed or something.* They've caught me, and I could have easily listened and I wouldn't have been caught, would have been able to go back to Falter or something to figure things out.

But here I am, caught.

Led to a van.

Tied down as Father Albert sits next to me, saying prayers.

Father Andrew holds me down.

Dad drives.

Becca in the front passenger seat.

Mom nowhere to be seen.

Your mother had to work.

Yeah, what else is new?

Becca looks back at me, looks through me like I insulted her. And she says, "I can't believe you'd do something like that."

Maybe she's talking about how I haunted her, but really she's talking about what happened with Nikki. Nikki didn't tell her anything. Becca assumes it was a whole lot more than it really was. But I'm not going to say anything. I don't need to say anything. Becca won't leave.

I'm beginning to think that I'll be the one who has to leave. You know, leave the entire situation. It might be necessary.

Indeed.

Nikki... why did I even bother?

Would you like to know how Nikki dies?

Yeah, sure. Why not?

Nicole Dillon will drop out of college during her junior year in order to marry a man, a doctor twelve years her senior. The marriage will last two years before ending in divorce. Without any income, and having signed a prenuptial agreement before marriage, Dillon will move back in with her parents. For five years, she will work retail. A year in, Dillon will try oxycodone for the first time. Dillon will decide to relocate in order to attempt a career in acting. She will experience a moderate degree of success, appearing in countless commercials, and will catch a break upon recording a voice for a cartoon character. Dillon will begin to settle into the life she assumed she desired. Yet Dillon will be unable to shake the demons born from substance abuse. Her health will decline sharply a few months after turning thirty-one. Unable to perform, she will live in fear. Meanwhile, Dillon will struggle to maintain her habit. She will attempt to find help from alternative medicine, going so far as searching for a demon to possess her. Dillon will lock herself in a five-star hotel room one summer afternoon. Spending her life savings for a five-night stay, Dillon will overdose by the third. Her body will be found an hour after checkout on the fifth day. A Do Not Disturb sign will have been her lone defense against the outside world.

It kind of makes sense that Nikki got the longest death spell, or whatever you want to call it. I'll go with that. But yeah...

I'd say that it's sad, how her life will fall in line only to kind of fall to ashes, but I have to believe that she made it that way. It's all based on choices, trusting your instincts, you know? And it's kind of the same as anyone else—they're so afraid of and fascinated by "demons" that they forget that we can create a darker and more disturbing demon just by running away from our problems. Hmm...

Yeah. It's really like that for most people.

We're all going to die.

But we don't have to die alone.

Father Albert and Becca hold hands in prayer, while Father Andrew explains to Dad how I had been terrorizing others. "It's an indication of severity," Father Albert says. But that doesn't really say anything.

They've strapped me down to my bed.

Dad still can't get past the fact that my room has been stripped clean. Father Andrew doesn't have any real answers. And I'm not going to say anything. You won't either, because by now, I'm beginning to see that there is no "plural" version. We are the same. And I mean that in the best possible way.

Never have to be alone again, unless I want to.

Dad shakes his head. "I don't understand how even half of this is possible!"

Father Andrew explains, "Your son is in the latter stages of possession. There are three stages: infestation, oppression, and possession. Your son's condition has quickly risen from oppression to possession."

Father Albert and Becca chant prayers.

Dad asks, "Have you seen anything like this?"

Father Andrew nods. "Not exactly, but something similar, yes. I have witnessed full demonic possession. Typically, the human host falls into a coma and the demon assumes the role."

Dad says, "He... he was in school days ago, healthy as usual. He's going to graduate soon. I... oh my god."

"But what's incredibly puzzling about your son's case has to do with the fact that the body itself should be in tatters. In all accounts, your son should not be of the living."

"Jesus." Dad buries his face in his hands.

"I've never witnessed this before. However, if I do say so myself, it is more encouraging than tragic. Perhaps your son is still trapped in this body."

"I hope. I hope so."

Father Andrew gestures toward the far side of the room, where the other two remain standing, praying and chanting. "Please, join them. We need as many prayers as possible."

Dad joins them.

You join me.

Be strong.

Wait, what are you implying? I'm sensing that you're hesitating...

Father Andrew, he knows not what he's summoning. He needs to stop. Be strong.

He...

Hold on to the clearest image you can see. What do you see?

I see a field... at dawn. A car parked by itself. Someone... sitting on the hood of the car, looking at something in the distance, can't see what.

Hold on to that image. It will help.

Okay.

Do not let go of the image.

Father Andrew approaches the bed.

Keep your eyes closed. Do not open them.

Father Andrew places a hand on my forehead. It stings, scalding to the touch.

Be vigilant. Be strong.

Father Andrew blesses the bed, my body, holding a rosary in his right hand. He opens up his copy of the Bible but doesn't read from its pages. Instead, Father Andrew recites prose of his own, what I guess he wrote for this exorcism. It goes on for whole paragraphs, recited in weird intonations, like he's traded in his voice for someone else's.

Be strong.

But there won't be any party. No one is in attendance. No one cares about me anymore. No one will be toasting to my newfound "health." If anything, I'll be drinking to drown a new loss. I can't lose a friend, and they can't make me.

Be strong. Be vigilant.

Father Andrew begins with the guttural commands.

"The power of Christ compels you!"

Becca and Dad and Father Albert in the corner praying.

Be strong.

I can feel the skin on my face beginning to boil.

"The power of Christ compels you!"

The prayers continue. They don't stop.

I feel the room around me turning, stretching thin.

"The power of Christ compels you!"

The room gets warmer, the cold starting to leave. The warm cuts through my skin, making it feel like my skin has grown thin. I think I'm bleeding, but I can't be sure.

Be strong. Be vigilant. Hold on to the image.

I am. I am holding on.

You mustn't speak.

My mouth is stitched closed. I can't say anything.

"The power of Christ compels you!"

I can feel my body start to separate at the joints.

Be strong. Be vigilant.

I know that it's imagined. It's an inner force that tries to take back as much of this body as possible. But it makes me think about Becca. Like I can see her for who she really is, and I maybe start to think that I was wrong to break up with her. Maybe I was wrong to haunt her. Maybe it was all wrong... She actually does care for me and just tries really hard to make the best decision for me.

Hold on to the image. Be strong. Push all inflicted emotions away.

I am.

"The power of Christ compels you!"

It makes me think about Mom and Dad.

They live separate lives and maybe that's okay. I'm their son. I'm still their son, no matter what. Even if they aren't really there, they still put a roof over my head. They still get me the things that I need. I never needed a job, you know, because I got some kind of allowance. It's embarrassing, but maybe they really work all the time to pay for the things they actually give me. Maybe I was wrong...

Keep to the image. Hold on to it. Be strong. Push all inflicted emotions away.

I am...

"The power of Christ compels you!"

It makes me think about Brad and Jon-Jon and Nikki.

Maybe I'm the one who's been fake and too hard on Brad. He's just a guy who really wants to get along with the people around him. Maybe I was wrong... maybe he really does care and just has a weird way of showing it. Maybe he's just depressed, really depressed. Maybe...

And Jon-Jon's just a fickle person; he's worse off than most. Maybe he acts all like a gangster because he doesn't know what else to do. Maybe I was wrong to think that he's horrible...

Like Nikki, they're just as confused and lost in their relationships. They're, like, confused about how to meet people and they are more confused about how it seems more impossible the older they get. And they're young. We're all young. But already it feels like meeting and making real, true friends is as crazy as thinking we can figure people out with one look.

Maybe I'm getting it all wrong...

Push all inflicted emotions away. Hold on. Be strong.

...

"The power of Christ compels you!"

It makes me think about Blaire.

How she was always there, standing to the side, watching. She's always been there, ever since we were kids confused by how we couldn't just play kickball with the other during recess. They didn't let us, so we sat on the side, watching. Not a part of things. Just people on the side, not really there, the real attention on the kids in the game... What happens to the people who never get looked at? I can barely see Blaire, but she's been around longer than almost everyone else I know. She's been there more than my mom and dad. Maybe I wasn't looking in the right direction...

Maybe I was too busy watching people playing kickball, the people who I wanted to be friends with because they were popular. People who I had nothing in common with and nothing at all to really offer. Just kids, people, thinking that being around them would make me a better person.

I've been wrong...

Be strong. Push all inflicted emotions away. The image, remain there, on the hood of the car.

...

"The power of Christ compels you!"

Be strong. Push all inflicted emotions away.

It makes me think about the first dream, when we first met at the kitchen table.

You looked just like me.

You spoke just like me.

You thought just like me.

But you weren't me. At least not until later.

You remained around, like anyone else. But we got along. In videos we watched and tricks we played, we became fast friends. It's the one reason I have that makes me certain that I'm better for being your friend. It's like we're close enough friends now that we're living the same life. It's all the same, shared, joined, and it's not weird, awkward, or anything like that. We're just like anybody else. But we're good friends. Really good friends.

Indeed, friend.

"Leave!"

I want to hold on to the image, but it's too bold. I can feel my body shaking, spasming, and the spit in my mouth is boiling hot, foaming. I'm a wreck and I don't know how to fight back.

What is happening to me?

It tastes sour, the spit and bile that comes up from my throat.

It's like I want to say something but I don't know what.

And I'm having trouble hearing you. It's like I'm back to wondering if you're really there...

Are you there?

"Leave him be!"

I... I... something's pulling my grip loose.

There are tears dripping from my eyes. They go into my mouth and I taste copper. It's then that I get that it's blood—blood from my eyes.

Skin tearing, wounds bleeding, all across my body.

I...

...

"Leave! By the power of Christ, leave His son!"

I...

Hold on! Be strong!

...

...

"Be gone!"

...

...

...

They have inflicted a grave pain upon this body. Wilted, much like having been run over by a vehicle, the priest exhales, wipes sweat from his brow. The support network spouting prayers continues, though they have far surpassed fear and trepidation. It is now that they fail to understand what is going on, the gravity of performing an exorcism on a being that is one spirit.

We were one in the same. The priest's prayers and commands have torn us, loosening a grip on the actual.

I must use what energy I have left to silence the prayers, silence the commands.

I draw from every energy source, rendering the room, the house, the entire block a cascade of complete darkness.

Never have to be alone. A friend is always there, waiting to help.

The body must be healed. The body has withered, the body is in poor shape.

The one thing you say before disappearing in the dark of the room is what they are all able to hear so clear and plain:

"Hunter's gone."

And then you are.

Into the kingdom you roam. But you needn't worry. I will find you. When I find you, I will make sure that we shall never falter. Be strong, my friend. In the kingdom, you are incapable of the being's truest needs. Be strong, for the kingdom may break you.

I won't be long. I'm right here with you.

WITH ITS LAST OUNCE OF ENERGY, THE BODY WALKS
with buckling knees and a trail of blood, collapsing in the backyard
of Blaire's residence.

Blaire is an interesting individual.

Years of history, a true friend.

"I can count on you." It is repeated so that Blaire might fathom
what has happened. The body being what it is, she is able to take it
indoors, letting it rest on the guest bed, where there is a discussion,
quick, frank, and mutual.

"I trust you. Do you trust me?"

Blaire understands.

Blaire, in tears, understands what has happened.

She nods. "Can you save him?"

"I must have your trust." The body needs to rest. The body needs
a hiding spot. The body must not be found by the priests and those
who have only inflicted near-fatal wounds to its form.

"You can trust me," Blaire says. "You can always trust me."

Perhaps that is all that is needed, and yet, there must be more.

"Hold my hand."

Blaire glances down at the yellowed skin, the brittle bones, but there isn't a single fleck of fear. Hand held, Blaire looks into my eyes, and the image, the conditions, the location, the need, everything is given to Blaire.

It could only happen if the trust was real.

Blaire invited me in.

Blaire made no assumptions about the nature of the invitation.

Single blink, Blaire understands.

"You have to help him," Blaire says, and shivers.

With hand held, there is a physical, corporeal link.

"Good night." It is said not to end things but rather to begin again.

With hand held, Blaire looking into both eyes, she is given the truth to the legend. The kingdom has no name. It maps to wherever there is empty space to fill. The kingdom is far yet close, near enough to explore, yet impossible to master. The kingdom is everywhere when human eyes are closed, shut out from the realm that makes pain possible.

The legend of Falter Kingdom, which had been given the name by the various graduating classes that have frequented the site before moving on to forget, exists as a touchstone for the many who travel too far.

Be it human.

Be it "demon."

It is just a place with some history.

Anything with enough foreboding and energy will be a place where the conditions of corporeal things fail to apply.

But at the same time, it depends on the viewer.

It depends on whether there's enough trust. With enough trust, the veil of skepticism can be pulled and the full reveal is given, much like it is given to Blaire before leaving.

Blaire holds on to the hand, holds on to the body, long after I go searching. The search lasts a split second, and yet it might feel as much as fifty years to the human subject if the level of trust is low.

Body hidden, I must go. It won't last long.

I will find you. And later a new body will find us.

Blaire understands, as much as one who has held a demon before is able to understand. I understood this upon my first sighting of her.

Blaire does not want to let go.

She speaks: "Don't leave me."

She was haunted, but during the haunting, the demon had lost interest. The demon had left, and in such a departure, a human is left forever lonely, missing a key part of herself, perhaps never to be recovered.

She remains amiss, so I let her stay. It isn't so much as an offer as it is a plea. She has seen it—the kingdom, like the world of the living, is full of promise. Demons make mistakes too. Demons are needed as much as a human. To be wanted is to look for what was lost.

She found you. She found us.

As long as Blaire holds on, all will be okay.

Blaire does not die. It is my promise to you. She does not die.

She walks on, footsteps later to be heard by you.

See you soon.

EVERYONE'S TALKING IN THE PAST TENSE, LIKE I'M beyond being saved. But I look at the wounds, and I feel my heartbeat, and I know that I've already been saved once. This is probably not good enough for my bio. What I've written will not end up being the sort of remembrance I wanted for the yearbook, but then again, I'm fine with that. I understand that after you end up on the other side, you see this tunnel.

The kingdom is full of those looking for a way to make a connection. They dare each other to make a point, prove a point. They come to Falter Kingdom to be afraid.

But they don't go here alone.

I'm not alone. Not anymore.

My body is nearing its end. It can't take much more.

Eventually, I will look for a new host. It's how many spirits continue. I'd say we go as long as we can, but some spirits walk the kingdom and are able to find what they need for as long as they can. And that distance, it can be pretty great.

But I don't have anywhere else to go.

So I stay here in the tunnel. I sit on the bed and I use the things that I've stockpiled over time.

I often look up at the opening of the tunnel, expecting to see something.

But I don't.

I watch a lot of videos. The ASMR videos are some of my favorites now. No need to watch the unboxing vids; I've long since been unpacked. Possession porn, that's for the people who don't understand.

This body, which can barely walk, it gets only about halfway up the tunnel. I walk up there every once in a while. I'd say I walk up there once a day, but time doesn't seem to pass.

It does, but I don't feel it.

Everything feels like one moment.

And really, that one moment feels like forever.

I'm supposed to wait here. I'm waiting for someone.

I have to say, I saw a lot in the kingdom. It was a lot of the same. Everything kind of falls into place the same way. People or not people, it's energy; they are spirits, personalities, looking for homes, looking for friends, looking for families.

I would be scared, lonely, but it doesn't happen that way, not when my best friend is with me.

Hunter.

I never think about what happened before being saved. That's all in the past, and because this run is so long, the past might be a previous life.

But most days the body is my biggest problem. I know that it can't stand this.

I wonder if Blaire will show.

I notice that I'm running out of food. But the food will last longer than this body.

The thoughts grind away at my skull.

My immune system has hit a breaking point.

I develop a cough. It doesn't go away.

I feel every bit of pain, but because it's physical, I can set it in front of me, like it's some kind object. I can create that distance, the ability to understand it.

But it still hurts like crazy.

I begin developing my death.

How I die.

I know how I'll die, but something keeps me from finishing the whole story. So I keep going. It goes much like this, what has been recorded in memory, in words, but at one point, it splinters off and that's where I stop.

I get up from the bed and fall down.

I get up from the bed and fall back down.

This is a process, like anything else.

But when I can, when I get back up to my feet, I make use of it. Of the fact that I'm standing up.

I don't think about my past even though I know that my parents, my classmates, my friends often think of me. They think of me as finished. They have their own ending to how I die.

Every once in a while, I walk up as far as I can, getting as close to the entrance of the tunnel, and I listen to the wind blowing through the trees. It gets to be so much like a routine that I start counting down the number of times I have left before the body finally fails.

Maybe that's how it ends.

I'm not going to find another host.

But on the second to last time I walk the tunnel, I stand there in the dark, enjoying the sound of the leaves rustling. I hear the rustling until something else, more sounds—at first identical to the leaves— separate and turn into footsteps.

I count the number of heartbeats it takes before the footsteps stop at the entrance to the tunnel.

I see a familiar shape. Blaire.

No one goes here alone.

I wait, seeing if she will. Will she run the gauntlet?

If it's like she promised, I'll be there to run with her, like what happened when I did.

And when she leaps forward, in the first couple of steps, I feel my heart swell, beating rapidly. I shouldn't have doubted it for a second.

Nobody should ever be alone.

WHEN MAKING CONTACT FOR THE FIRST TIME, SHE WILL choose a scene from a sci-fi movie. She will run, shooting at an alien horde, until we meet in an interrogation room. First thing I will tell her is "I saw you running."

Next thing I will tell her is "I ran after you."

The scene will unfold and it will because there's trust between each other. She could make that choice—wake up from the dream, get rid of me—but the exorcism will be pushed aside.

There will be two more things said:

"There's an end to the tunnel."

And then, when she wonders, "What is your name?" she will pick out the name that was clear from the very beginning.

I will say it. "H."

And she will fill in the missing letters.

It's like the letters were always there.

Just waiting for her to say them.

ABOUT THE AUTHOR

Michael J. Seidlinger is the author of a number of novels including *The Fun We've Had* and *The Strangest*. He serves as director of publicity at Dzanc Books, book reviews editor at Electric Literature, and publisher in chief of Civil Coping Mechanisms, an indie press specializing in innovative fiction, nonfiction, and poetry. He lives in Brooklyn, New York, where he never sleeps and is forever searching for the next best cup of coffee. You can find him online at michaeljseidlinger.com, on Facebook, and on Twitter (@mjseidlinger).

EPILOGUE

There's a field, not long from now. It might be flush with green grass, marked with flowers and other vegetation; it could be barren, gutted of any green. It's not important where or what this is, only that this is where we've ended up.

There is a car. It could be yours. The sky is about to burn bright, the bright yellow sun of a brand-new day.

Near dawn, you're sitting on the hood of that car.

This is the future. Your future. You are here.

This is the ending, but because Blaire's doesn't end, neither does yours.

You will close this book. You will finish the story, filling in the rest with what you see out there, in the distance. Look. What do you see?

You'll look out into the distance, enjoying the dawn of a new day.

You'll live that day, driving the car on to the next. There's enough there to fill another book. But not this one. This is not part of Hunter's story. It is not entirely Blaire's to own. It is yours, and this is just something for you, a message from them to you. Listen to your voice, what does it tell you?

The demons exist. If they don't find you, you create your own.

Fear is there. It never fades.

But know that you never have to be alone.

Never doubt yourself, just because everyone else doesn't understand.

There's an entire kingdom out there. Hold on to that image.

Be strong. Be vigilant. Just because you can't quite see into the distance, it doesn't mean it's not there.

Know who your real friends are.

We're all the same, eventually.